"BRIGHT."—*USA Today*
"BREEZY."—*San Francisco Chronicle*
"A HOOT."—*The Boston Globe*

More praise for Claire Cook's national bestseller *Must Love Dogs*

"Heroine Sarah Hurlihy . . . will appeal to many readers, single or attached."　　　　—*USA Today*

"Reading *Must Love Dogs* is like having lunch with your best friend—fun, breezy, and full of laughs."
　　　　　　　　　　　　—Lorna Landvik, author of
　　　　　　　　　　　　Patty Jane's House of Curl

"Claire Cook's characters aren't rich or glamorous—they're physically imperfect, emotionally insecure, and deeply familiar. *Must Love Dogs* is a sweet, funny novel about first dates and second chances."
　　　　　　　　—Tom Perrotta, author of *Little Children*

continued . . .

ALSO BY CLAIRE COOK

Multiple Choice
Ready to Fall

Must Love Dogs

A NOVEL

Claire Cook

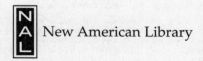

New American Library

New American Library
Published by New American Library, a division of
Penguin Group (USA) Inc., 375 Hudson Street,
New York, New York 10014, USA
Penguin Group (Canada), 90 Eglinton Avenue East, Suite 700, Toronto,
Ontario M4P 2Y3, Canada (a division of Pearson Penguin Canada Inc.)
Penguin Books Ltd., 80 Strand, London WC2R 0RL, England
Penguin Ireland, 25 St. Stephen's Green, Dublin 2,
Ireland (a division of Penguin Books Ltd.)
Penguin Group (Australia), 250 Camberwell Road, Camberwell, Victoria 3124,
Australia (a division of Pearson Australia Group Pty. Ltd.)
Penguin Books India Pvt. Ltd., 11 Community Centre, Panchsheel Park,
New Delhi - 110 017, India
Penguin Group (NZ), cnr Airborne and Rosedale Roads, Albany,
Auckland 1310, New Zealand (a division of Pearson New Zealand Ltd.)
Penguin Books (South Africa) (Pty.) Ltd., 24 Sturdee Avenue,
Rosebank, Johannesburg 2196, South Africa

Penguin Books Ltd., Registered Offices: 80 Strand, London WC2R 0RL, England

Published by New American Library, an imprint of New American Library, a
division of Penguin Group (USA) Inc. Previously published in a Viking edition.

First New American Library Printing, July 2004
First New American Library Printing (Movie Tie-in Edition), July 2005
10 9 8 7 6 5 4 3 2 1

New American Library Trade Paperback ISBN: 0-451-21721-7

The Library of Congress has cataloged the hardcover edition of this title as follows:

Cook, Claire, 1955–
    Must love dogs / Claire Cook.
        p. cm.
    ISBN 0-451-21358-0
    1. Divorced women—Fiction. 2. Irish-American families—Fiction.
    3. Dating (Social customs)—Fiction. 4. Massachusetts—Fiction. 5. Dog owners—
Fiction. 6. Personals—Fiction. I. Title.

    PS3553.O55317M87 2004
    813'.54—dc22   2004042623

Printed in the United States of America

PUBLISHER'S NOTE
This is a work of fiction. Names, characters, places, and incidents either are the prod-
uct of the author's imagination or are used fictitiously, and any resemblance to actual persons, living or dead, business establishments, events, or locales is entirely
coincidental.
    The publisher does not have any control over and does not assume any responsi-
bility for author or third-party Web sites or their content.

For Mameve Medwed

ACKNOWLEDGMENTS

It's a movie! Yahoo! Many books are optioned for film, and how lucky am I to have *Must Love Dogs* turn out to be one of the very few that actually go all the way to the big screen! I'm forever grateful to writer/director/producer Gary David Goldberg for making it happen. He's so funny and talented and hardworking and tenacious, and I like to think my comedic timing has improved just from being his fax pal. And, of course, I thank my lucky stars every day for his good taste in reading material.

The journey from page to screen was an amazing and joyful experience for me. I had a great time watching everyone's vision of my book develop. It's such a collaborative medium, and it was fascinating to see how each person adds a layer, from the writer to the director to the actors to the producers to the cinematographer to the set designer to the editor to the *dogs*. I'm thrilled and honored by their creation, and also very thankful for the many new readers the movie will bring to my novels.

Everyone connected to the film has been incredibly kind to my family and me, but I'd especially like to thank Gary's assistant, Heather Green, and associate producer, Julie Ragland, for taking such good care of us. Thanks, too, to Diana Meehan, Suzanne and Jennifer Todd, Brad Hall, Ron Smith, Bonnie Sikowitz, K. C. Colwell, John Bailey, Sam Weisman, Mike Moyer, Hope Parrish, Gail Ryan, Jane Galli, Florence-Isabelle Megginson, Paul St. John, Paul Rylander, Michelle Souza, Kathryn Peters, Mark Harden, Cindy Wasson, Claudette Barius, Eric Sears, Nick Nesbitt, Polly Cohen, and Alan Horn. And how about those actors— Gary pulled together such an amazing cast. Diane Lane, John Cusack, Christopher Plummer, Dermot Mulroney, Elizabeth Perkins, and Stockard Channing were all so kind, and even autographed my director's chair for me. Ali Hillis and Jamie Denbo went right out to buy my book and Brad Henke headed for my Web site, and the very sweet Julie Gonzalo even drove me around so I wouldn't end up in Oregon on the way to San Pedro.

Must Love Dogs is getting as many lives as a cat, and none of these incarnations would have been possible without my most wonderful agent in the world, Lisa Bankoff, and her assistant, Tina Dubois, who's on her way to becoming a terrific agent herself. Many thanks also to ICM's Josie Freedman for adding to the excitement with a Working Title option for *Multiple Choice*, and to Josie and her assistant, Michael McCarthy, for taking such good care of me in LA.

Thanks so much to the fabulous Ellen Edwards, my editor at NAL, for her enthusiasm and support with this edition, and always. And a heartfelt thanks to NAL's Craig Burke, Mark Chait, Leslie Gelbman, Richard Hasselberger, Serena Jones, Betty Lawson, Norman Lidof-

sky, Ken May, Rick Pascocello, Liz Perl, Anthony Ra-
mondo, Leslie Schwartz, Ann Wachur, Kara Welsh,
Trish Weyenberg, Philip Wilentz, Brian Wilson, and
Claire Zion.

On the hardcover side, thanks so much to my bril-
liant editor, Pam Dorman, and to everyone at Viking,
including Mike Brennan, Paul Buckley, Phil Budnick,
Leigh Butler, Rakia Clark, Carolyn Coleburn, Clare
Ferraro, Jason Gobble, Dick Heffernan, Susan Hood,
Dave Kliegman, Karl Krueger, Tim McCall, Amity
Murray, Katya Shannon, Judi Powers, Roseanne Serra,
Nancy Sheppard, Julie Shiroishi, Glenn Timony, and
Lucia Watson.

A huge thanks to friends, family, readers, booksellers, and dog lovers everywhere for cheering me on
and spreading the word.

And to Jake, Garet, and Kaden, thanks for everything.

1

I decided to listen to my family and get back out there. "There's life after divorce, Sarah," my father proclaimed, not that he'd ever been divorced.

"The longer you wait, the harder it'll be" was my sister Carol's little gem, as if she had some way of knowing whether or not that was true.

After months of ignoring them, responding to a personal ad in the newspaper seemed the most detached way to give in. I wouldn't have to sit in a restaurant with a friend of a friend of one of my brothers, probably Michael's, but maybe Johnny's or Billy Jr.'s, pretending to enjoy a meal I was too nervous to taste. I needn't endure even a phone conversation with someone my sister Christine had talked into calling me. My prospect and I would quietly connect on paper or we wouldn't.

HONEST, HOPELESSLY ROMANTIC, old-fashioned gentleman seeks lady friend who enjoys elegant dining, dancing and the slow bloom of affection. WM, n/s, young

*50s, widower, loves dogs, children and long meandering
bicycle rides.*

The ad jumped out at me the first time I looked.
There wasn't much competition. Rather than risk a ge-
ographic jump to one of the Boston newspapers, I'd
decided it was safer and less of an effort to confine my
search to the single page of classifieds in the local
weekly. Seven towns halfway between Boston and
Cape Cod were clumped together in one edition. Four
columns of "Women Seeking Men." A quarter of a column of "Men Seeking Women," two entries of
"Women Seeking Women," and what was left of that
column was "Men Seeking Men."

I certainly had no intention of adding to the dis-
heartening surplus of heterosexual women placing
ads, so I turned my attention to the second category. It
was comprised of more than its share of control freaks,
like this guy—*Seeking attractive woman between 5'4" and
5'6", 120–135 lbs., soft-spoken, no bad habits, financially
secure, for possible relationship.* I could picture this
dreamboat making his potential relationships step on
the scale and show their bank statements before he
penciled them in for a look-see.

And then *this* one. Quaint, charming, almost familiar somehow. When I got to *the slow bloom of affection,* it just did me in. Made me remember how
lonely I was.

I circled the ad in red pen, then tore it out of the
paper in a jagged rectangle. I carried it over to my
computer and typed a response quickly, before I could
change my mind:

Dear Sir:

You sound too good to be true, but perhaps we could have a cup of coffee together anyway—at a public place. I am a WF, divorced, young 40, who loves dogs and children, but doesn't happen to have either.

—*Cautiously Optimistic*

I mailed my letter to a Box 308P at the *County Connections* offices, which would, in turn, forward it. I enclosed a small check to secure my own box number for responses. Less than a week later I had my answer:

Dear Madam,

Might I have the privilege of buying you coffee at Morning Glories in Marshbury at 10 AM this coming Saturday? I'll be carrying a single yellow rose.

—*Awaiting Your Response*

The invitation was typed on thick ivory paper with an actual typewriter, the letters *O* and *E* forming solid dots of black ink, just like the old manual of my childhood. I wrote back simply, *Time and place convenient. Looking forward to it.*

I didn't mention my almost-date to anyone, barely even allowed myself to think about its possibilities. There was simply no sense in getting my hopes up, no need to position myself for a fall.

I woke up a few times Friday night, but it wasn't too bad. It's not as if I stayed up all night tossing and turning. And I tried on just a couple of different outfits on Saturday morning, finally settling on a yellow sweater and a long skirt with an old-fashioned floral print. I fluffed my hair, threw on some mascara and brushed my teeth a second time before heading out the door.

Morning Glories is just short of trendy, a delightfully overgrown hodgepodge of sun-streaked greenery, white lattice and round button tables with mismatched iron chairs. The coffee is strong and the baked goods homemade and delicious. You could sit at a table for hours without getting dirty looks from the people who work there.

The long Saturday-morning take-out line backed up to the door, and it took me a minute to maneuver my way over to the tables. I scanned quickly, my senses on overload, trying to pick out the rose draped across the table, to remember the opening line I had rehearsed on the drive over.

"Sarah, my darlin' girl. What a lovely surprise. Come here and give your dear old daddy a hug."

"Dad? What are *you* doing here?"

"Well, that's a fine how-do-you-do. And from one of my very favorite daughters at that."

"Where'd you get the rose, Dad?"

"Picked it this morning from your dear mother's rose garden. God rest her soul."

"Uh, who's it for?"

"A lady friend, honey. It's the natural course of this life that your dad would have lady friends now, Sarry. I feel your sainted mother whispering her approval to me every day."

"So, um, you're planning to meet this lady friend here, Dad?"

"That I am, God willing."

Somewhere in the dusty corners of my brain, synapses were connecting. "Oh my God. Dad. *I'm* your date. I answered your personal ad. I answered my own father's personal ad." I mean, of all the personal ads in all the world I had to pick this one?

My father looked at me blankly, then lifted his shaggy white eyebrows in surprise. His eyes moved skyward as he cocked his head to one side. He turned his palms up in resignation. "Well, now, there's one for the supermarket papers. Honey, it's okay, no need to turn white like you've seen a ghost. Here. This only proves I brought you up to know the diamond from the riffraff."

Faking a quick recovery is a Hurlihy family tradition, so I squelched the image of a single yellow rose in a hand other than my father's. I took a slow breath, assessing the damage to my heart. "Not only that, Dad, but maybe you and I can do a Jerry Springer show together. How 'bout 'Fathers Who Date Daughters'? I mean, this is big, Dad. The Oedipal implications alone—"

"Oedipal, smedipal. Don't be getting all college on me now, Sarry girl." My father peered out from under his eyebrows. "And lovely as you are, you're even lovelier when you're a smidgen less flip."

I swallowed back the tears that seemed to be my only choice besides flip, and sat down in the chair across from my father. Our waitress came by and I managed to order a coffee. "Wait a minute. You're not a young fifty, Dad. You're sixty-six. And when was the last time you rode a bike? You don't own a bike. And you hate dogs."

"Honey, don't be so literal. Think of it as poetry, as who I am in the bottom of my soul. And, Sarah, I'm glad you've started dating again. Kevin was not on his best day good enough for you, sweetie."

"I answered my own father's personal ad. That's not dating. That's sick."

My father watched as a pretty waitress leaned across the table next to ours. His eyes stayed on her as he patted my hand and said, "You'll do better next time, honey. Just keep up the hard work." I watched as my father raked a clump of thick white hair away from his watery brown eyes. The guy could find a lesson in . . . Jesus, a date with his *daughter.*

"Oh, Dad, I forgot all about you. You got the wrong date, too. You must be lonely without Mom, huh?"

The waitress stood up, caught my father's eye and smiled. She walked away, and he turned his gaze back to me. "I think about her every day, all day. And will for the rest of my natural life. But don't worry about me. I have a four o'clock."

"What do you mean, a four o'clock? Four o'clock Mass?"

"No, darlin'. A wee glass of wine at four o'clock with another lovely lady. Who couldn't possibly hold a candle to you, my sweet."

I supposed that having a date with a close blood relative was far less traumatic if it was only one of the day's two dates. I debated whether to file that tidbit away for future reference, or to plunge into deep and immediate denial that the incident had ever happened. I lifted my coffee mug to my lips. My father smiled encouragingly.

Perhaps the lack of control was in my wrist. Maybe I merely forgot to swallow. But as my father reached across the table with a pile of paper napkins to mop the burning coffee from my chin, I thought it even more likely that I had simply never learned to be a grown-up.

2

I stayed in bed until Monday morning, venturing out only for quick trips to the bathroom or refrigerator. At some point on Sunday night or so, returning to the safety zone of my bed with the last remaining yogurt, I noticed a stale odor as I crossed the threshold of my bedroom. Not quite a sickroom smell, more the smell of days piling up. And a woman aging as her life slips by.

The phone rang, which on Sunday night usually means one of my brothers or sisters. I looked at it. It kept ringing. Halfway through the fourth electronic jingle, my machine picked up. *Hello, you have reached Sarah Hurlihy. Leave a message if you want to.*

"Sarah, pick up. It's me. Christine. Come on, Sarah. I already talked to Dad."

I grabbed the phone and burrowed under the covers with it. "Oh, God. What'd he tell you?"

"Just that you're dating again. That's great, Sarah. It's about time."

"Come on. What else did he say?"

There was no sound from Christine, who is seventeen months younger than I am and happily married with two perfect children. Nothing. I waited her out. Hysterical laughter, deep and infectious and really pissing me off, finally arrived.

"Who else knows, Christine?"

"No one."

"Oh, come on, Christine. Carol has to know."

"Why does Carol have to know? Couldn't I, just for once, know something before she does?"

"Not in a million years." It drove Christine absolutely crazy that all family information filtered through Carol first. As far as I could tell, Carol's position in the family was the only thing Christine had ever wanted that she couldn't get.

"Gee, thanks, Sarah."

"Come on, Christine. Who knows?"

"Okay. Everyone. Except Johnny because he's still in Toronto on business. Come on, tell me the whole story. You know Dad never gets the details right."

So I gave up and confessed it all to Christine, knowing it would be passed along to my other siblings and immortalized as family history. It would be told, at Thanksgiving dinner or on the beach, tweaked this way and that, nudged and kneaded, and retold into infinity. Christine interrupted when I got to the part about Mom. "That old goat," she said, "his blarney level is so high that he actually believes Mom is pimping for him from heaven. No guilt, ever, now or even when she was alive. The one thing you can count on with Dad is that he'll see things the way he wants to see them."

Christine paused. I could hear her sipping something, and I imagined her with her feet arranged artfully on an ottoman, relaxed now that her kids were in bed. "So, anyway, Sarah. Tell me the truth. On a scale of one to ten, how would you rate Dad as a date?"

I climbed out from under the covers just long enough to hang up the phone on her laughter.

If I didn't have a job, I might have stayed in bed until I rotted. Instead, I got up, showered and pulled a shin-length denim jumper over a long-sleeved avocado turtleneck. I stared at myself in the mirror on the back of my bedroom door. I hated to admit it, but the muted greens and yellows I'd been wearing were all wrong for me. From earliest childhood, and decades before having your colors done was fashionable, my mother had dressed me as a "winter." Reds, whites and blues, mostly, to complement my pale skin, dark hair and brown eyes. I thought I looked like an American flag, and resented that Christine, with her hazel eyes and light brown hair, got all the moss greens and bark browns and sunflower golds, like a flag from a more exotic country.

I realized that my mother was right. Sadly, I was only eight months away from being forty-one years old, and I still couldn't dress myself. That's why Christine had kids and a husband and I didn't. I peeled the jumper off, switched to a crisp white cotton blouse and yanked the jumper back on. My skin was no longer yellow. Amazing. Not that it mattered. In fact, not only was there no one to notice, but now I was late for work.

Twelve minutes later, I screeched into the parking lot of Bayberry Preschool. I had seconds to spare, but I could just hear my boss if I passed her in the hallway on the way to my classroom: "It's helpful, Sarah," Kate Stone would say, "when the teachers arrive *before* the students."

June, my twenty-two-year-old assistant, was meditating in the middle of the rug. And I'd been the one to choose her out of a large field of applicants. But, I mean, who thinks to ask, *Do you spend inordinate amounts of time meditating when you should be scrubbing Play-Doh off tabletops?*

I flipped on the lights and June stretched gracefully, sending a wave of blond hair shimmering down her back. That was the other thing about June, she was far too pretty. I must have been feeling temporarily secure to have let that slip by. "Good morning, June," I said briskly.

"Morning, Sarah. Wow, I heard you had like quite the incestuous date this weekend."

"Who told *you?*"

"Uh, let's see. Um, your father had dinner with my mother's best friend's neighbor Saturday night." I tried to calculate how many people had been involved in this particular branch of the grapevine for the information to circle around and travel back to me.

Parents began escorting their children into the class-room, saving me from thoughts of relocation or even suicide. Jack Kaplan had a new haircut to praise. Amanda McAlpine wouldn't release a choke hold on her father's neck and needed to be peeled away from him. After the weekend break in routine, Mondays are tough on preschoolers. Our system was for June to welcome the children while I grabbed the parents, particularly the drop-and-run types. *Anything we should know?* I would ask.

I'd learned this lesson a couple of years ago when Millie Meehan unceremoniously dumped off little Max, who seemed subdued that day. He perked up a bit at recess, laughing and running around, until he suddenly stopped and said simply, "Ouch." He clutched his groin area, and stood still, wide-eyed. I picked him up and went inside to call Millie, who'd forgotten to tell us he'd had hernia surgery *the day before.* "I could have sworn I mentioned it," she said. "Are you sure you didn't forget?"

Jenny Browning didn't look quite right somehow. Her mother, Bev Henley, was wearing an expensive suit and trying to keep Jenny from wrinkling it as she hugged her good-bye. "Pick me up and hug me good," Jenny said with authority. Bev picked her up, held her several safe inches away and kissed her on the forehead. Deftly, Bev spun her around and pushed her toward me. Jenny vomited. The sharp, sudden smell was tinged with peanut butter, and I felt the damp warmth invade the front of my blouse and trickle between my breasts. Bev looked as if she'd run if she could, but wordlessly took her daughter back, placing her on the ground beside her and walking her to the sink.

June cleaned Jenny up and sent mother and daughter home. I opened the door to the adjoining classroom and, holding my nose while gesturing to my chest, let them know that I was running home for a quick change. Trying not to gag, I told June I'd be back in forty-five minutes tops. She looked at me sympathetically and said, "Take your time. Oh, before I forget,

I'm supposed to tell you to tell your dad that my mother's friend's neighbor had a very nice time with him."

At the afterschool staff meeting, I found a seat a safe distance away from the other teachers. I knew I should have changed my whole outfit. I'd rifled briefly through the pile of clothes on my bedroom floor, looking for a skirt that could pass for unwrinkled. I gave up, pulled on the avocado turtleneck, which didn't look any better than it had earlier in the morning. I threw the sullied white blouse into the bathroom sink, rubbed it with a damp bar of Dove, added some water and left it to soak. The denim jumper appeared unscathed so I decided to put it back on.

I'd been regretting that decision ever since. I kept trying to tell myself, as I opened the windows in my classroom, that the sour smell of vomit had simply lodged itself in my nostrils, or maybe in my memory banks.

Lorna, one of the inclusion class teachers, sat down beside me. "Pee yew, is that you?"

"Apparently so."

"Well, nice talking to you." Lorna stood up, held her nose, backed away a few steps. "Oh, by the way, you wanna do something tonight?"

"No thanks."

"Why not?"

"No money, no energy, no ambition."

"Perfect. I'll pick you up at six-thirty."

Kate Stone cleared her throat pointedly. She was the founding owner of Bayberry Preschool, and she stood now at the front of the all-purpose room, all business.

Dangly earrings poked through her thin brown hair, which was streaked with coarser strands of undisguised gray. Kate had started the school when her now-grown children were themselves preschoolers. Rumor had it that one of her daughters was a teacher but had moved across the country to escape the family business.

First, Kate clipped an enormous pad of white paper to a tubular steel display stand. She pulled a red marker from the pocket of her batik print tunic and uncapped it with her teeth. Still using only her teeth, she placed the cap on the marker's nonwriting end. "Single-word answers," she said. "What unique qualities do you bring to our team?"

This was my fourth time in as many years going through this particular exercise, so I got a couple of words ready in case I needed them—*dedication, enthusiasm*—and drifted off until about halfway through the next question. "Give me more," Kate Stone was saying, working with a blue marker now. "The question is, How do we teach? Sarah, we haven't heard from you yet. How *do* we teach?"

"Modeling. We teach through modeling."

I watched a nodding Kate Stone write my word in big blue letters and then floated away again. I stayed that way, suspended somewhere between asleep and awake, until I heard my name. "And, finally, see Sarah if you have something you'd like to teach for the Afterschool Outreach Program. Forty-dollar stipend per one-hour class, kindergarten through grade three, eight-week session, brochure information due by next Friday."

Starting an afterschool program at Bayberry was a smart move. There was a huge demand for afterschool activities in Marshbury, and families liked the idea that even though their children had graduated from Bayberry Preschool, they could still come back to play soccer or learn jewelry-making.

I'd asked to run the program not because I had any particular interest in it but because I needed the money. With Kevin's half of the house had come the entire mortgage. For two years I'd watched, detached, as my half of our savings dwindled. I knew I should think about finding a roommate, maybe one of the teachers from school, preferably someone who would never be home. Coordinating the afterschool program would save me, at least temporarily, from having to let an outsider into my house.

At some point during the extended blur surrounding the deaths of my mother and my marriage, it was decided that I would keep the house. Neither Kevin nor my father thought to discuss this with me. My father showed up one day a couple of months after Kevin left, which was a couple of months after my mother died, and handed me a bank check. I wondered if the money came from my mother's life insurance. I didn't ask.

"What's that?" I was looking at the check from a safe distance.

"It's good riddance to bad rubbish," my father said. Still holding the check, he put one hand on each of my shoulders and kissed me on the forehead. "God love ya, honey. God love ya and keep ya."

"Dad. I don't want your money."

"One day soon it will all be yours anyway. Don't make me die first to take care of my little girl. Take it, Sarry, with my blessing." My father smiled bravely, as if one foot had already gone over to the other side. I was always awed by his ability to add or subtract decades to his life as it suited him. At this moment he looked and sounded more like my grandfather than my father.

"No, really," I said. I mean, I didn't even like the house that much. Kevin and I had bought the three-bedroom, fifties-style ranch as a starter home, planning to fix it up and move on to something better. Maybe in Kevin's eyes that was exactly what had happened. He moved on to something better.

I tried again. "Dad, keep your money. Maybe I'll sell the house. Maybe I'll even move home for a while." After all, my father and I were both alone now. And there was such a nice long history of single Irish-American women taking care of their aging widowed fathers, selflessly putting their own lives on hold, crocheting doilies, inviting priests to dinner.

I glanced up to see my father gaping at me in horror. "That, my darlin' daughter, is not an option."

It was a relief finally to get out of my denim jumper. I stuffed it into the sink with my blouse, swished them both around, decided to leave them there until some day when I had more energy. It wasn't until I jumped into the shower that I remembered I'd forgotten to buy shampoo. Again. I twisted the plastic top off the Suave bottle and tried to aim it so that a needle-sized stream of water could find its way inside. Then I covered the top with two fingers and shook hard. The resulting shampoo was watered down and unsatisfying, a perfect accompaniment to the rest of my life.

Lorna was knocking at the door when I came out of

the bathroom in jeans and a T-shirt. "Well, at least you smell better," she said. Lorna smiled, a relentlessly optimistic smile, but a nice smile all the same. I liked Lorna. She was the one person at work who treated me exactly the same after Kevin left, as if it were a detail too unimportant to notice. "Sorry I'm late," she said now. "Mattress Man was having a meltdown. He's better now, all tucked in and happily clutching his remote." Mattress Man was Lorna's husband. I never quite dared ask her the reason for his nickname, but from what I could gather it had more to do with the time he spent watching TV in bed than with more amorous activities. Nevertheless, Lorna seemed to be crazy about him. "Okay, we can still catch the seven o'clock yoga class at the community center."

"Do we have to?"

"You have any better ideas?"

I hated yoga. I hated groups of women, or mostly women, trying to improve themselves inside and/or out. I hated having to smile at them, make eye contact, pretend that I was still one of them. "Lorna," I asked, "do you think we could just go buy some shampoo?"

3

I should have guessed fix-up. First of all, my father offered to pick me up for the Brennan Bake, something he'd never done before. Secondly, he mentioned that he had an extra ticket, and asked if I knew someone who might want it. When I said no, thinking I didn't have enough friends left to risk putting one through the ordeal, he said not to worry; he'd come up with something.

The Brennan Bake was held every year on the second Saturday of October from noon until sunset. The event was a scholarship fund-raiser in memory of the Brennans' youngest daughter, Lily, who died years ago in a car crash days short of graduating from high school. It took place under a green-and-white-striped tent on Rocky Beach in North Marshbury. The weather was usually crisp and warm, with the sun a shade less harsh than it would have been the month before.

Only once did the Brennan Bake have to be moved a

mile down the road to the American Legion Post because of rain, but it worked out fine, since the lobsters,
steamers, clam chowder and corn on the cob hadn't actually been cooked on-site for years. Instead, they
were delivered, along with sliced watermelon and fat
round loaves of Irish soda bread, by a catering company called Boston Clambake.

Every year my father was handed a stack of tickets
to sell, and every year he bought the whole stack and
gave them all away. "And let's have a big round of applause for Mr. Billy Hurlihy and his deep pockets," the
bandleader would say.

My father would feign modesty until the people sitting nearby made him stand. Lily's parents, Jack and
Noreen, would envelop him in a long hug, and he'd
wipe tears from his eyes when it ended. He'd offer up
a toast "to little Lily Brennan, eternal child of this
blessed community, eternal light of her dear parents'
lives. A kinder and sweeter little girl never graced
God's green earth. May her memory live forever." My
father had never even met Lily Brennan, but nobody
minded.

The bandleader would wait until the moment of silence ended and my father lifted his head from a
solemn bow. He'd take the microphone back and shuf-
fle his notes, announcing something like "Here's to
Bob and Betty Reilly, on their forty-fifth wedding an-
niversary. Bob and Betty, I want you to stand up now
if you can stand up."

It was understood in our family that if you were
living in New England, you either went to the Brennan Bake or you had a damn good excuse. I didn't, so
when my father picked me up, I was ready. Two

strangers were in the car with him. The woman in the front seat was wearing a straw hat with a flat top and round brim, with two long tails of red ribbon dangling off the back end. The ribbon matched the trim on her dress, which seemed to be a sort of sailor suit. The collar began in the front as two understated white triangles, only to turn into one big Popeye square in the back. My father introduced her as Marlene. I was relieved when she turned forward again and leaned back against the seat, hiding at least part of her outfit.

Her younger brother's name was Mark, and I guess I should have been thankful he wasn't wearing a sailor suit. I had a quick impression of close-set eyes and sprouting nostril hair. "Nicetameetya" he said in a nasally voice I hated immediately. I checked out his tight striped golf shirt, the soft little bulge of his belly. His jeans looked new, with a slight crease traveling down the front of each leg. He wore dark brown socks, shiny penny loafers and a kind of fisherman's hat. Mark slid his body a little closer to the center of the seat. I glared at him. He slid back. I scowled at my father in the rearview mirror. He winked.

"New boyfriend?" Christine asked. I kissed her on the cheek and whispered, "Fuck you," softly enough that my nieces and nephews wouldn't hear. I worked my way around the table, quick kisses for Michael, Johnny, Carol and their families. Only Billy Jr. was lucky enough to have escaped the Brennan Bake this year.

I grabbed Sean, my nephew, by the hand because I wanted to dance.

"Me, too," said my niece Maeve.

"Me, too," said my niece Sydney. We found a place on the patch of sand that served as the dance floor. The Irish Troubadours were playing a baffling medley of "When Irish Eyes Are Smiling," "The Marine Corps Hymn" and "The Caissons Go Rolling Along." We all held hands and danced in our own little circle.

Marlene and her brother stayed at their table, but my father joined us just in time for "The Unicorn." His grandchildren, half a dozen clustered around him by now, imitated him delightedly as he opened and closed his hands for the green alligators and flapped his bent arms for the long-necked geese. By the time he was scratching under his armpits while the singer sang about the chimpanzees, four or five women had joined the circle. Two wore Kelly-green T-shirts that said "Brennan Bake Babe."

Even though Carol used a calendar-making program on her computer to update the whole family every year, it was still almost impossible to keep everybody's ages straight. Ian and Trevor, Carol's middle two, were born the requisite ten months apart to qualify as Irish twins. I was pretty sure they were nine and ten now. They stood together on the edge of the dance floor, not really dancing but not really not dancing. Their just-turned-sixteen sister, Siobhan, slumped nearby in a beach chair, while their two-year-old sister, Maeve, began to dance hand-in-hand with her grandpa and her two-year-old cousin Sydney.

Sydney's brother, Sean, probably three, possibly already four, which would mean I'd forgotten his birthday, let go of my hands and moved over by Ian and Trevor. He adjusted his dancing, imitating their restrained motion. He grinned at them in unbridled ado-ration. "Hi, Sean," Ian said. "What's your favorite truck?"

"Firefuck," Sean said. Ian and Trevor giggled loudly.

I tried to get to Ian and Trevor before Christine did. "Wanna ice cream, Sean?" Trevor was asking. "What's your favorite kind of ice cream, Sean? Vanilla?"

"No. Fockit," Sean answered just as his mother and I arrived.

"What? What'd we do?" Trevor asked.

"I'll kill them for you," I assured Christine as I steered Ian and Trevor away by the backs of their necks. Christine, I was sure, would be on her way to tell Carol how badly behaved her boys were. I looked over to see Marlene and Mark getting up from the table and heading our way. "Consider yourself lec-tured," I said, "and next time pick on somebody big-ger. Maybe even that guy in the funny hat walking toward us."

I escaped to the rest rooms. The smell of salt air and water only partially masked the odor of urine and damp cement, so I didn't stay as long as I might have otherwise. I returned just as the band was starting to play a light jig. Michael's daughters, Annie and Lainie, finished lacing up their ghillies and joined the rest of the Irish step dancers, some also wearing their soft shoes, others barefoot.

I sat down beside Siobhan. "You going up?" I asked. Siobhan was the family's most talented step dancer, competing at every feis and feile within driving dis-tance for as long as anyone could remember. Carol had turned their den into a shrine, filling the shelves with her trophies and medals.

Siobhan twisted one of the three earrings in her left earlobe. "Oh, puh-lease."

We watched the dancers perform their rocks and clicks, kicks and leaps. My muscles still knew the steps, still wanted to dance them. Lainie and Annie smiled big winning smiles, and I remembered hanging on to my own smile dance after dance, despite blisters and burning thighs. I remembered dancing with Carol and Christine so clearly, clutching pennies in our fists to keep our hands neat, putting strips of duct tape on the bottom of our ghillies to make them less slippery. And waking up with a stiff neck from sleeping in hard plastic curlers the night before a feis, then combing the hair spray out of each other's banana curls in the car on the way home. Wide-tooth comb, working from the bottom up, small sections at a time. I could feel the pull on my scalp.

"I still miss it. Isn't it hard to just sit here?" I asked Siobhan.

"Yeah, right."

The dancers were replaced by a six-year-old named Bridget who began to sing. Badly. She was tentative at first, but when the audience joined in, Bridget unfortunately let loose, mouth pressed to the microphone, belting out "Too-wah-loo-wah-loo-wah" for all she was worth. Her red ringlets danced around her shoulders as her big green eyes gazed across the stage to her parents. Bridget's father began rocking side to side. Bridget responded to the reminder with an obedient sway of her own little shoulders.

I was so busy watching the bandleader try to wrestle the microphone away from Bridget that I didn't see

Mark sneak up on me. "How'boutadancewithyour-
date?"

I separated his words enough to understand them.
"No, thank you. And, by the way, I am *not* your date."

"Fuckyouthen."

"No. But thanks for asking." I turned back to Siobhan.
It was easy to avoid Mark after that. I sauntered
away from Siobhan and joined my brothers and sisters at their table. "Nice loafers on that guy," said
Michael. "Hope they don't get all scratched up from
the sand."

"Yeah, I wonder what kind of fish he catches in that
hat," said Johnny. "Sushi?" He combed brown hair out of
brown eyes with his fingers, looking like a younger version of our father. "Geez, Dad's probably starting to look
pretty good to you, Sarah." Damn, even Johnny knew.

"Come on, you guys," said Carol. "Leave her alone.
Anyway, I can tell it's the sister who's the real ocean
buff. How'd ya like to float on her boat?" Everybody
looked over at Marlene, who had taken off her hat in
order to dance cheek to cheek with our father. She was
holding it pressed to his back with one hand. The rib-
bons fluttered in the wind. The buckles on her shoes
were large brass anchors.

We were still laughing when the band began their
final song of the day. Everyone who could stood for
"God Bless America." People with names like Murphy
and O'Brien and Callahan, intertwined by marriage
with an occasional Smith or Rosen or Angelo. More
than a few wiped tears, flowing freely after several
hours of watery beer. I was dry-eyed and sober, although by the time the whole crowd sang the home-
sweet-home part, I was wishing I'd cultivated more of

a taste for bad beer. Passing out early might be the high point of my day.

When the final round of applause died down, I threw myself on the mercy of my siblings for a ride home.

4

Siobhan kept turning the key in the ignition. "Uh, I'm pretty sure it's started now," I said carefully. I waited a couple of seconds, then added, "So you can, uh, let go of the key now. Good. Now give it some gas. Um, not quite that much. Good. Now just, uh, move your foot to the brake and put it into drive. Nice."

Siobhan hiked up the right leg of her oversized jeans so her sneaker could make direct contact with the brake pedal. "God, you're so much better at this than my mother is. And my father sucks even more than she does."

"Okay, okay. Slow down a little. With the brake. No, we're fine, that's okay, next time just touch it lightly. Yeah, a little gas, just a little. That's it. Good." I tried to remember the safety ratings for Dodge Caravans. Siobhan had tried to hold out for her father's Mustang, but instead Carol and Dennis had switched Maeve's car seat over, piled the kids in and driven away from the Brennan Bake with a *beep beep a beep beep, beep beep.*

"So when did you get your learner's permit?"

"Yesterday."

"Wow. That recently."

"Yeah. Thanks for the birthday present. Gift certificates are so perfect."

"Glad you liked it," I said with relief. I was so bad at presents. Siobhan was particularly hard to buy for because her tastes changed so quickly. In the hair category alone, I could count her recent trials like the rings of a tree trunk. Shiny brown hair up by the roots faded into a summer application of Sun-In streaks an inch or so down. These overlapped an experiment with Jolen Creme Bleach and cherry Kool-Aid, which Carol had described to me in horrified detail over the phone, and which had grown down to about cheek level. Finally, the ends of Siobhan's once thick and healthy hair split and frizzed around her shoulders, permanent victims of over-the-counter overprocessing.

Siobhan drove along the winding Marshbury coastal roads. I kept myself from air-braking obviously on the curves. When she took one hand off the steering wheel to pull at an earring, I tried to will it back on. Looking straight ahead, for which I was grateful, she asked, "So, you have any boyfriends yet?"

"Hundreds. You?"

"About the same."

We drove for a while, past manicured lawns with water views. I glanced casually at the speedometer. "I'm pretty sure the speed limit's thirty-five here."

"My father goes fifty," Siobhan said as she slowed down. "So why did Kevin leave you, anyway?"

"Leave me?"

"Yeah. I mean, like, wasn't the sex any good?"

"Sex?"

"Yeah. I mean, like, my parents are still disgusting. You'd think they'd be sick of doing it by now." We stopped abruptly at a yellow light, then drove through. "And Maeve could be mine practically. That's my mother, though. Just keep having babies and then ignoring them when they're not kittens anymore."

I hoped she wasn't expecting me to say anything. I reminded myself never to teach kids older than preschool. About a mile from her house, Siobhan turned on her blinker like a pro, then pulled to the side of the road. She put the minivan into park. Leaning back, she worked a pack of cigarettes loose from her waistband, offered me one. I shook my head no.

"Well," she said. "At least you and Kevin didn't have any kids."

Of course, Siobhan couldn't really drive me home because she only had a learner's permit, and wouldn't be able to get back to her house legally without an adult in the car. This was the kind of little detail my family tended to overlook when I was involved. So, we drove to Carol and Dennis's house, and Carol came out and took over for Siobhan. And now, after what seemed like an awful lot of riding around just to get home, Carol was sitting on my couch. Her feet were on my coffee table, her shoes under it, and she was sipping a glass of the Australian Chardonnay she'd brought. "Thanks again for daring to drive with Evel Knievel. Did I tell you that Dennis calls her Karate Mouth? As in her mouth should be registered as a lethal weapon?"

"She's a good kid."

"Thanks for remembering. God, was I that bad at her age?"

"I think you just hid it better so Mom wouldn't wash your mouth out with soap. Remember when she did that to Billy after he called her queer? I never did get if that was about disrespect or alleged sexual preference."

"I'm pretty sure 'queer' was still just odd then. Mom certainly wouldn't have known if it was more than that. Anyway, Siobhan would call Social Services if we tried something like that. Or hire a lawyer."

I took a sip of my wine and asked Carol, because she knew everything, if Marlene was June's mother's best friend's neighbor.

"No, no, no," Carol answered, swirling the wine around in her glass. "Marlene is the ex-wife of Jonas Swift. Huge trust fund money. Generous patron of the Cambridge Symphony Orchestra. Rumor has it that Marlene slept her way through an entire section of the CSO."

I tried to reconcile this with my image of Marlene, hat removed to reveal a crisp gray French braid, snuggled up to Dad. "Which section?" I asked finally.

"I think it was the horn section."

I thought some more. "Maybe that explains the shoes. Her predisposition to brass."

Carol put her feet on the floor and leaned forward, elbows on her knees. "Yeah, maybe she has a trophy collection. You know, shoes with saxophone buckles. Tuba earrings. Bugle barrettes for her hair. A way to keep track of her progress, to make sure she doesn't miss any instruments."

I rolled the story around a bit. I liked it. It was much more interesting than the possibility that money didn't buy taste and Marlene was simply a horrible dresser. As I pondered whether to embellish the story or let it rest, I flicked my wineglass with a fingernail, trying to play a note. Instead I created a mini tidal wave that splashed over the edge. Since it was white wine and not red, I rubbed it discreetly into my jeans, then asked, "So, what about the brother?"

"He's the CEO of Wilson Electronics. Big bucks. Supposed to be brilliant. Currently unattached."

"I can see why. That nose hair."

A big-sister look came over Carol's face. I could feel a lecture in the air, and stiffened in anticipation. "Sarah, Sarah, Sarah. Everybody has something. Dennis had ear wax when we met. Gobs of it. But I didn't let that get in the way of the big picture. I waited an appropriate length of time, and then—"

"Bought him a box of Q-tips?"

"No, no, no. I discreetly pointed it out, pretending it was the first time I noticed. I think I told him how relieved I was to find out that he wasn't absolutely perfect."

Disgusting, I thought. Dennis had lots of other faults. He was an asshole, for starters, but there was probably no point breaking that particular bit of news to Carol. I took another sip of wine and waited for something conversational to pop into my head.

"Kevin used to sit on the toilet for hours, reading the newspaper. With the bathroom door open and his pants around his ankles."

"They all do that."

I hadn't realized that. I wondered for a minute if

Kevin and I would still be together if I had known. "It wasn't a very erotic pose. It got so that every time we made love I'd think of it. Him on the toilet. That and the sound he made gargling. Sort of like this . . ." I tilted the last bit of wine into my mouth, and tried to gargle like Kevin. Instead, I choked and laughed at the same time. A smidgen of wine exited through my nose.

"Yeah, and, meanwhile, you're such a class act, Sarah. Here, I'll go get us some more."

While Carol was refilling our glasses in the kitchen, I tried to isolate the exact thing that had made my marriage to Kevin not work out. Besides him screwing around with another woman. I don't know, it just seemed that at first so much time was taken up by when and where and how often we'd have sex. Then after that, there was all that planning for the wedding. Then looking for a house, and finding it, and decorating it, and having people over to see it.

Until one day, we looked at each other across the kitchen table, and I realized we had absolutely nothing to say. I suppose it was probably just time to have children. We'd talked about it some, but Kevin was never quite ready. I was thirty-five, then thirty-six, then thirty-seven, which seemed way past ready and getting close to too late.

But instead of children, Kevin decided to have Nicole. Nikki. Chatty as hell and ten years younger than I am. I found out, he left, and at this very minute, Kevin and Nikki were probably having my children. I hoped never to know for sure, even though I was certain the information would find me immediately. Someone would probably call to say when they'd had sex without birth control.

God hates glib. I could almost hear my mother say it, although I'd lost the precise sound of her voice shortly after she died. That and the sophisticated crunch she made when she chewed cornflakes, a sound I tried my whole childhood to imitate. *God hates ugly* and *God hates a smarty-pants* were also part of our family lexicon. Quoting God in this way was not at all about religion, but about bringing in enough clout to give the speaker irrefutable authority on a subject.

God hates glib. We all said it to each other, yet we were proud of our glibness. We polished it until it shone; it was our family shield. When Carol's first boyfriend's best friend phoned her to break up for him, which was only fitting since he'd also been the surrogate who asked her to go steady, she hunched over the telephone table at the bottom of the stairs. We loitered in the hallway behind her, smelling tragedy. Carol hung up, rearranged her face when she saw us. "That was Davy Jones," she said. "They're thinking it might be time for a girl Monkee." We waited to see if she'd crack. "I told him I'd consider the offer," she finished before running up the stairs.

As if summoned by her decades-old line, Carol walked back into my living room, a replenished wineglass in each hand, Dad's personal ad tucked under her chin. "Carol, what are you doing snooping around my stuff?"

"Hey, it was right on your refrigerator, underneath one of those tacky favorite teacher magnets."

"Sorry. I guess I was so traumatized I forgot about it." I waited while Carol read it through a couple of times.

"This is great. No wonder you went out with him."

"I didn't," I started to say before I saw Carol's big grin. I gave her the dirty look I'd been giving her since we were kids.

Carol didn't even bother to return the look. "Okay, Sarah, what's the next plan?"

"What do you mean?" I asked. I understood the concept of planning, even vaguely remembered that it was once part of my repertoire.

"Have you answered any other ads?"

"Now there's a good idea. Maybe I can date an uncle. Forget about it, Carol. I'm done answering personal ads."

"Then we'll just have to place one of your own. And not in the local paper. We'll go right to Boston. It'll be good for you to broaden your horizons a little. Plus, if we do it that way, you'll have all the control."

I was starting to wonder if Carol was planning to date for me. Not a bad idea, actually. She could be my surrogate dater, and I'd get to stay home, read a good book, maybe *101 Places to Hide from Your Family* or *Never Too Old for the Convent*. I sat back and let her write the ad.

"The first thing we have to do is to invoke a mood. That's why Dad's ad worked so well. And we have to have a built-in test to weed out the sickos. Think, Sarah. What's the best indicator of a person's humanity?"

"I don't know, what?"

"Come on, help me out a little. Okay, don't they say dogs and children can always tell who's nice and who's just pretending to be?"

"Yeah, the loves-dogs-and-children part was what got me in Dad's ad."

"Well, you certainly can't say anything about kids, you'll scare 'em off. We want you to avoid any hint of desperation. You have to sound as if you can afford to be choosy, whether or not that's remotely true."

If I'd had more motivation I'd probably have been feeling insulted by now. Instead, while I watched Carol scribble away, I wondered if Siobhan was right about it being a good thing that Kevin and I had never had kids. If, even though I'd ended up losing my husband, I'd still managed to gain a child or two along the way, would I be less of a failure? At the very least, I'd have a good excuse to put off dating. *Mothering*, I'd say, with a hint of the martyr in my voice, *it's simply all I have time for.*

Instead, not only was I childless, but I felt like a child myself, and I missed my own mother. If she were still alive, she would have helped me find a new life by now. I even missed Kevin. No, it was more that I missed the idea of Kevin. Having a husband, even one I barely talked to, had given me a certain status, a re-spectability, a belonging. I had a place in the world. I *knew* what I'd be doing tomorrow, even if it wasn't particularly interesting. I felt anxiety rise in my chest like mercury up an old thermometer. I decided to think instead about the kind of dog I'd get if I had the energy to commit even to a four-footed someone who might need something from me.

Carol finished the ad, made two copies, and handed me one on her way out the door. "I'll call you tomor-row, and we'll discuss any possible revisions," she said.

Claire Cook

After sitting quietly for a few minutes, I finally read it:

Barely 40 DWF, absolutely childless, seeks special man. Please be intelligent, articulate and fun. Minimal time spent reading on toilet a plus. Must love dogs.

5

I have a theory that adult personality can be accurately predicted by the way a three-, four- or five-year-old handles circle time. June and I were sitting with the students on our classroom circle, a long strip of neon pink vinyl tape stuck to the carpet. Green and yellow and orange dots were arranged on top of the circle to designate individual places.

Back in September, when the children first gathered for circle time, we placed laminated name tags on the floor in front of their dots. Brittany would see her name in block letters, along with the sticker with a picture of a cow she had chosen herself. Finding her place was a complicated process of discovering her cow, "reading" her name, locating the adjacent dot and successfully bringing her body in for a landing on it.

In a good year, the name tags would be removed some time during October, and even the youngest children would be able to find their places without them. Then we would begin circle games, marching and dancing and choo-choo training around the ring of tape, only to finish the game and sit down on a new dot. There were children who were simply undone by someone else sitting on what had become their dot. Some melted into tears; others pounded the encroachers with clenched fists.

Today we began circle time with sharing—who had a new puppy, who was wearing new shoes. It was Austin Connor's turn and, as usual, he had a lot to say. He was almost five, having just missed the kindergarten cutoff, and precociously verbal with parrotlike recall. He had already told us that his parents were "taking a break from their marriage" because his father was "incorrigible." Some of the kids looked up with vague interest.

I broke in to tell the children we were now going to learn the Danish Dance of Greeting. It was one of my favorite dances, from an old Kimbo Educational cassette. First we found Denmark on a big blowup vinyl globe and passed it around the circle. The children nodded seriously. Then we found the United States on the globe and measured the distance by holding our arms wide. Far away, we all agreed.

We stood up, June pressed the play button on the tape deck and we danced: *Clap clap bow, Clap clap bow, Stamp, Stamp, Turn yourself around.* So far, so good. Then way up to tippy-toes and we set off around the circle. We stopped when the music did and took a final bow. "Look down," I said cheerily, "and sit on a new dot."

Several round faces looked at me in horror. Therapy up the road, I predicted. Anal retentiveness, eating disorders, obsessive-compulsive behavior, extreme perfectionism. Maybe a run for political office.

Austin's customary dot was the orange one closest to the door. He sat for a minute on a green dot across the way, then sighed. Standing up quickly, he made his way back to his original space, where Molly Greene was now sitting. Very politely, he said, "Excuse me, could you please move your vagina? It's on top of my dot."

Later, when the kids were out of earshot, I asked June, "How old were you when you first said that word?"

"What word?"

"The word that Austin said."

"Oh, vagina. I don't know, I guess about the same age. Why?"

"Vagina," I said to the steering wheel on my ride home. I made my voice a little bit deeper. "Vagina. Vagina, vagina." I tried "penis" to see if it was easier. Growing up at my house, the boys all had nicknames for their penises. Michael's was Duckie. He used to talk to it while he played in the bathtub, and Christine and I listened from the other side of the bathroom door. Billy's was Herman and I forget what Johnny's was. The girls figured we didn't have anything to name, I guess. And by the time we'd grown breasts, we were too old for the name game.

As soon as I got in the door, I pulled a liter bottle of seltzer from the refrigerator and took a long drink. It was one of the guilty pleasures of living alone, drinking right from the bottle and not having to worry about spreading germs to anyone. That and not having to sit down to eat a meal. Then I checked my phone messages—just one from Carol. I thought about ignoring it, but knew she'd simply call again.

"Oh, my God, listen to this," Carol said as soon as I admitted it was me on the other end: *"Radiant, soulful dynamo, drop-dead gorgeous inside/out, 5'4", brown/ brown, naturally slim DWF, 38, seeks compassionate, emotionally aware, funny, curious, creative, sensuous, ambitious, genuinely nice S/WW/DWM, 33–48."*

"Geez."

"Yeah, they're all like that. I think we're going to have to buff yours up a bit. Definitely drop the joke about the toilet seat, nobody would get it anyway, and make you sound a little more glamorous."

"Okay, whatever. Listen, I'm going to make some dinner now. So, let me know if you need any help or anything."

"Sarah, it's *your* ad. Show a little interest."

"Okay, what's WW?"

"Widowed."

"Why not just W?"

"Because that's for white."

"Fascinating. It's a whole new world. I'm going to go eat now, okay?"

"Jesus, Sarah. Okay, I'll enhance it a little, and call you back so you can phone it in."

"What? Can't you just mail it?"

"No. You record it over the phone, too. They still print the ads in the newspaper, but people can also just browse by phone. They give you a voice mail box and anyone who wants to meet you leaves a message there. That way you can screen your responses. And guess what? The first eighteen words are free."

"Great. I'm going to go eat now, Carol. Good-bye."

I have an old frying pan that I've had ever since my mother let me take it to my first apartment. It's about half the size of an average cast-iron pan, and perfectly oiled and seasoned from years of use. I opened a can of Prudence corned beef hash at both ends. Using two fingers, I shoved the whole meat and potato cylinder out one end and into the pan. I flattened it evenly into the bottom until it made the thick round shape of a smiley face. I carved out two holes for eyes and made a great big slash of a smiley mouth.

I washed out that morning's cereal bowl, shook it dry, cracked three eggs into it. Then I scooped out two of the yolks and threw them away to make the meal guilt-free. I scrambled the rest of the eggs with a fork, adding pepper and freeze-dried chives, then poured them into the open spaces.

While dinner cooked, I opened a Sam Adams Okto-berfest and drank from the bottle. I burped and didn't have to say excuse me to anyone. I jumped up to sit on the kitchen counter, and dangled my feet, bouncing my heels against the cabinets. The black soles of my shoes would probably make scuff marks on the white cabinets. Oh, well.

I sipped my beer until the eggs were set. I tried singing a few lines of "Blues in the Night" into the mouth of the bottle, even though I knew it made me look like a loser. "Sarah," I said aloud, "you are such a loser."

I picked up the only potholder Kevin didn't take with him when he left. He said he was taking the potholders because he did most of the cooking any-way. As if it would matter who used to cook when he was gone. I wrapped the potholder around the handle of the frying pan, picked up a fork with my other hand, and ate the whole thing, smiley face, smiley mouth, smiley eyes, right from the pan.

Carol called back while the pan was soaking and I was watching a rerun of *The Brady Bunch* on Nick at Night. "It's all set," she said. "I even recorded it for you. Nobody could ever tell our voices apart on the phone anyway."

Alice, the housekeeper, was about to give the Brady kids a lecture on minding their own business. I tore myself away. "Thanks for asking, Carol. You didn't talk in a really sexy voice or anything, did you? And what did the ad end up saying?"

"Oh, it was pretty much the same."

"That tells me a lot."

"Trust me, Sarah. Anything I changed was for the better. Anyway, to check the responses, you dial 1-800-555-3967. Your box number is 991184, and your password is D-A-T-E. Actually, the numbers are 3283, but I changed it to DATE so you could remember it more easily. Plus, DATE's a good omen, I think." I ignored the cutesiness, but wrote the information down obediently because Carol would only give it to me again if I didn't.

I knew I should have asked Carol more questions, made her tell me what the ad said. And I knew, absolutely knew, that I should call in, right now, to hear it for myself. On some level, several layers down, I even *wanted* to know what it said, if she sounded like me, if we'd attract any interesting men. I was also sure that if it were someone else's ad, I'd be dying to hear it.

But because it was *my* ad, it seemed somehow too risky. If I became overly interested in it, I might start to imagine a life beyond the one I'd botched. And if I hoped for a new life, I'd be crushed if one never surfaced. I remembered visiting my grandparents, my father's parents, when we were young. In the alley behind their triple-decker in Worcester, my brothers and sisters and I would play wild games of hide-and-seek, punctuated by earsplitting screams and gentler trills of laughter. My grandfather would suddenly appear, looking out over the petunias that cascaded from the window boxes on the third floor. He'd always say the same thing: "And what are you little hellions looking so happy about down there? Don't you know that happy is for the next life?"

I waited until *The Brady Bunch* was over and went to bed without bothering to brush my teeth.

"You're sick?" I said into the phone in my classroom. "Well, I mean that's too bad, I'm really sorry, but don't you know someone who can fill in for you?" I took a deep breath. "You don't know a single other soccer coach anywhere? I mean, don't you people have a network?" Last week I'd had to fill in for the jewelry-making teacher, a student from Mass Art I'd managed to track down through Carol. She'd claimed to be sick in the kind of raspy whisper that made me think she was lying, that she really had a project due or a hot date. I'd taught the class myself, and we'd painted pasta, mostly penne and ziti, with poster paint and strung it to make necklaces and bracelets—an admittedly low-end project compared to the Sculpey beads they'd made the week before.

Shit, who was I going to find to teach soccer in three hours? I dialed my brother Michael's work number. "Hi, it's Sarah. Can you do me a huge favor?"

"Fine thanks, and you?"

"Sorry, Michael. Listen, you know the afterschool program I'm running? Well, I'm desperate for a soccer coach for this afternoon and—"

"Annie and Lainie have a game at three. I'm coaching."

"Damn. Could you use a few more players?"

"Yeah, that would go over big. The other team would have us thrown out of the league for bringing in ringers."

"Do you know anyone I could ask?"

"Not really. Why don't you just coach it yourself?"

I tried to imagine the soccer equivalent of pasta necklaces, but came up blank. "Michael, I know absolutely nothing about soccer. What will I do with them?"

"Do you have balls and drill cones?"

"Yeah, the school bought them for the program."

"Well, give the kids one of each and tell them to make up their own drills."

"What's yours?"

"Chocolate chip. Wanna lick?"

I didn't know exactly how the ice cream cone drill got started, but it spread like wildfire. Now, all fourteen children were running around with their soccer balls balanced on top of the mouths of their orange drill cones. They were having a great time, and while it didn't technically have much to do with soccer, I thought I'd let it go for a while to kill some time. I tried to think of a line about gross motor development and balance in case one of the parents showed up early.

When the kids began to actually lick the soccer balls instead of just pretending, I knew it was time to redirect. "Hang on to your soccer balls and let's make the cones into a big orange snake," I yelled. A couple of the third-graders rolled their eyes but, still, they all helped me make a wiggly row of cones across the field. I lined the kids up and, sending the eye-rollers first to demonstrate, let them take turns kicking their balls through, weaving them around and around the long line of cones.

I was feeling pretty proud of myself when Kate Stone emerged from the strip of woods between the school and the soccer field. "Nice job, Sarah," she said, flicking a dried pine needle from her shoulder, "but next time you have to cover for the coach, lose the ice cream cones."

Michael handed me a Heineken and walked over to lean against my kitchen counter. "How'd your soccer debut go?" he asked, then tilted his head back for a long slug of his own beer. The white tail of a dress shirt peeked out from under his black Adidas jacket.

I opened my beer, took a sip. "Thanks. And thanks for stopping by. It was fine. I think it's going to be a real pain to run this program, though."

"So quit."

"Yeah. Especially since I'm independently wealthy. . . ."

Michael was midsip. He opened his eyes wide to signal that he had something to say. I waited for him to swallow. "Are you okay, Sarah? Do you need money?"

"I'm fine. Really. Or I will be as long as I supplement one low-paying job with another."

Michael looked tired. He put his empty beer on the counter, looked at his watch. "Maybe you should think about doing something else entirely. I mean, no spouse, no kids, no strings. Basically, you can go anywhere you want, do anything you want." Michael sighed. "Jesus, I can't even imagine."

I looked around my kitchen, a week's worth of the *Boston Globe* stacked randomly on the table, the day's dishes not filling even half the sink. "Trust me. It's not as glamorous as it looks."

"Yeah, I guess. Well, I better go. Phoebe will kill me if I don't help the girls with their homework."

Michael has a point, I thought, as I waved to him while he backed out of my driveway. I could do anything. I tried to come up with an example, nothing ambitious or life-altering, just a toe-dipping kind of something to do. I flipped through my address book, dialed Lorna's number.

Mattress Man answered on the second ring. "Yup."

"Hi, this is Sarah Hurlihy from school. May I speak to Lorna, please?"

Mattress Man didn't answer. I waited, wondering if I should repeat myself. Finally, I heard Lorna's voice. "Hey, Sarah, what's up? Are you okay?"

"I'm fine. I was just wondering. Do you want to go out and do something? I mean, no rush, just one of these days?"

6

I've lived in Marshbury all of my life, and never even knew it had a trailer park. My father was way ahead of me, of course. He'd not only located the trailer park; he'd found a woman there to date. Her name was Dolly and for some reason we were all having dinner at her home.

Basically, it was a setup. Christine and Carol and their kids and I showed up at four for Sunday dinner with Dad, something several of us did once or twice a month, in varying configurations, whenever it worked out. Sometimes we brought food, sometimes we ordered out. If Dad wasn't there, we ate without him.

This time, when we showed up, he ordered us back into our cars and said, "Follow me."

He managed to pack all of himself into the black Mazda Miata he'd bought last year. He pulled on an ancient pair of brown leather driving gloves, smoothed his hair in the visor mirror, waited while Siobhan buckled up beside him. The grandchildren, even the oldest kids, kept careful track of whose turn it was to ride in Grandpa's only passenger seat. Suddenly, both car doors opened again. Siobhan and her grandfather walked around to change places, stopping midway for a hug.

"I know just what he's saying to her," Carol said to me. " 'Jesus, Mary and Joseph, will you look at this, my baby's baby's driving. God bless ya, honey. God bless ya all day and every day.' " Carol pulled on her seat belt, then turned to make sure the kids were buckled in. "We'll see who needs an extra blessing or two once Lead Foot with Learner's Permit gets going."

The Miata backed out of the driveway and took a left. The rest of us followed obediently. Carol started in on me right away. "Have you checked your voice mail box?" she asked, reaching behind her to grab an airborne doll before Ian could catch Trevor's pass. Without taking her eyes off the road, Carol handed the doll back to a screaming Maeve, who had a two-year-old's amazing lung capacity and flair for drama.

I gave Maeve a sympathetic look, and tried to ignore Carol's question. "So, where's Dennis?" I asked as if I cared.

"He and Joe are playing golf, then grabbing something to eat. Payback for Christine's and my shopping expedition last week. Well, have you?"

"What?"

"Okay, Sarah, do it now." Carol handed me her cell phone.

"I don't have the number with me."

Carol reached into her pocketbook and handed me a neatly printed index card. There was no hope. I dialed

1-800-555-3967 as slowly as I could. An electronic voice instructed me to please dial my password. I changed Carol's D-A-T-E in my mind to a more dignified 3283, and dialed it reluctantly. *To hear your responses, please press one*, the voice said. Although dialing a single number slowly is difficult, I did my best.

You have eighteen messages. To hear them, press one. To save them, press two, to delete them, press three. I looked quickly at Carol. Her eyes were still on the road. I pressed three.

"Nothing yet," I said pleasantly.

"I knew it. You are amazingly self-destructive, and I can't even imagine where you'd be without me." We were stopped at a set of lights on the west side of town. Siobhan was revving the engine of the Miata. Carol reached into her pocketbook again and handed me a cassette tape. "Play it," she said, gesturing to the tape deck in front of us.

"What about the kids?"

"Okay, wait. We must be almost there. Where the hell is Dad taking us anyway?" The Miata took off with a small squeal of rubber the instant the light turned green. We followed, taking a sudden left into the parking lot behind a strip mall and then over a speed bump and down a dirt road. A sign read WHISPERING PINES PARK. Our three-car procession stopped beside it. Carol and I looked at each other. The good news was I thought she might have forgotten about my personal ad.

Our father, after planting a quick kiss on Siobhan's forehead, had lumbered ahead to the door of a mint-green-and-white trailer. Carol helped Maeve out of her car seat, while Ian and Trevor and I looked around carefully. A dozen or so trailers, each with a carport on one side and a couple of scrub pines on the other, flanked a rutted circular road. Several short red signs read SPEED LIMIT 15 and SLOW DOWN.

Christine and her two kids got out of their car. "Shoeboxes," said Sydney with her flawless pronunciation. "Shoeboffas," Sean repeated. Christine shushed them and hurried to join us.

"These are trailers," Carol was saying. "Lots of people live in them in other parts of the country." The kids nodded wordlessly. We all looked up to see the door open. A tiny full-figured woman wearing a tight pink suit opened the door. Standing on her tiptoes, she put her hands on our father's cheeks and kissed him full on the mouth. They lingered and I looked down at my watch and timed it with the second hand.

"Twelve seconds," I whispered. "And I started late." Ian and Trevor giggled loudly. Carol gave me her knock-it-off look.

"Come in," the woman said. "Daddy's told me all about you." We filed cautiously toward the door, adults herding the children ahead. "Come right on in and give Dolly a hug." Obediently, we took careful turns hugging Dolly on the way inside. I tried hard not to stare, but I was fascinated by her looks. Beneath a pouf of pinky-blond hair and a delicate neckline, she looked like a female Jimmy Dean sausage whose casing had an extra tie at the center.

Christine broke the silence. "What a lovely home you have, Dolly." I bit the inside of my cheek and avoided eye contact with Christine and Carol. Siobhan looked bored. She reached up to check the positions of her earrings.

There was so much furniture in the trailer that it seemed to have displaced the air. Heavy, dark items, including a china cabinet and an armoire, all crammed in end to end as if waiting to move back into a house. A large organ, its top either belatedly or prematurely holding the sheet music for "God Rest Ye Merry, Gentlemen," faced a sofa from a distance usually reserved for coffee tables. The sofa became the organ's bench. A dining room table abutted the sofa's backside, and was elaborately set for Sunday dinner.

We grouped around the doorway to the kitchen and peered inside. A crocheted potholder with a Halloween motif hung from each handle of the wood-grained Formica cabinets. The reassuring smell of roast came from the oven. "Wow," said Carol. "Great potholders. Where did you manage to find them?"

My father put his arm around Dolly's shoulders and pulled her toward him. His fingers disappeared in the pink fabric covering her upper arm. "Everything you see is handmade by Dolly. She's very creative."

"Our mother used to sew all of our clothes when we were younger," I said before I could stop myself. Christine rolled her eyes at me.

"Daddy's told me all about your mother, honey." I glared at him, but he wasn't looking. I mean, what a traitor he was to talk about our mother outside the family. We all leaned back in the narrow hallway and held in our stomachs as Dolly turned and walked past us, her fingertips grazing Dad's belt buckle as she slid by him.

We clustered outside the tiny bathroom, its sliding wooden door tucked inside the wall to expose the view within. A satiny black-and-silver shower curtain hid the tub, and an ornate gold mirror took up most of the wall space above the smallest sink I'd ever seen. Three Barbie-sized dolls, whose flouncy crocheted skirts concealed rolls of toilet paper, kept each other company atop the toilet tank. In a split second, Maeve managed to dash inside and fill her doll-free hand with one of them. Pulling it away from her, Dolly said, "If you're a good, good girl and Mommy's Daddy's a good, good boy to Dolly, I'll make you one someday, sweetie." We looked at Dad expectantly, thinking he might object to the bribe, but he seemed unfazed.

Dolly led us to a closed door. "When my third husband died, I decided the house was simply too much. Ten enormous rooms and just little Dolly to fill them." She leaned in and kissed my father energetically. By the time I noticed Ian pointing to my watch, it was too late to get an accurate count.

Maeve rescued us from the bedroom tour. "Dolly, dolly, dolly," she screamed furiously, trying to pull away from Carol's restraining hand and reenter the bathroom.

"Isn't that cute," Dolly said. "She knows my name already."

Carol and I sat in her minivan. Christine and Siobhan would kill us for leaving them with all the kids, but that was later. Maeve had curled up in her car seat. She was sucking her thumb, her own doll clutched in her other hand, recovering from Dolly's lack of sharing. Turning the key in the ignition, Carol said, "Hand me the tape." I did, and she pushed the PLAY button immediately.

To hear your messages, press one. Carol must have done just that because, after a slight pause, the taped messages began.

Friday, October 15, 6:53 P.M. *Hi. I'm really good-looking and, uh, if you want to see for yourself, call me at this number. 508-555-1221.*

Friday, October 15, 7:48 P.M. *Hello. This is in response to your ad in the newspaper. Exactly what do you mean by voluptuous? Do you mean big breasts or do you mean fat? Direct your answer to my box number, which is 99865.*

Friday, October 15, 9:52 P.M. *Woof. Woof, woof. I love dogs, too, and I have a great sense of humor. You can probably tell that already, huh? My box number is 99743.*

Friday, October 15, 11:04 A.M. *Good morning. This is Simon. I happened to see your ad in the* Globe *and it caught my eye, so to speak. I must say that your verbal presentation was quite enticing as well . . .*

I leaned forward and pushed the EJECT button. "Jesus, Carol. What a bunch of losers. What did my message *say?* Gimme the phone." I dialed the 800 number, pressed in the password to hear all eighteen free words of my ad:

Voluptuous, sensuous, alluring and fun. Barely 40 DWF seeks special man to share starlit nights. Must love dogs.

I told Carol how horrified I was by her ad, how I would never let her meddle in my life again and, by the way, how cheap did it look to have exactly eighteen words?! She told me that technically she couldn't meddle in my life because I didn't have one. The responses, she insisted, got better, and there were actually a couple of promising ones if I'd just be patient long enough to get to them. And, by the way, did I know that one of my biggest faults, along with my passivity, was my impatience, and my refusal to cooperate with things that were in my best interest, not to mention my total lack of gratitude.

By this point, we had gotten out of the car to lean up against Carol's minivan so we wouldn't disturb Maeve. We were both talking at once, creating a kind of discordant sibling rivalry with our competing voices. Faint strains of predinner organ music from inside the trailer accompanied us.

A new voice made us both jump. "Look, Dad, it's Ms. Hurlihy. Ms. Hurlihy, what are you doing yelling in Whispering Pines Park?" It was a child's voice, and a familiar one at that. I turned to see that it belonged to Austin Connor.

7

"My father said you're nicely attractive," Austin announced the next morning at circle time.

"He did?" I asked. June noticed my slip. Her expression changed slightly, a little wrinkle appearing between her eyebrows. Blushing, I redirected the conversation. "Who wants to tell us about something fun they did over the weekend?"

"We walked by your trailer three more times while you were inside with Dracula Dolly," Austin continued. "Real slow."

I was dying to ask Austin if his father had said anything else about me, but I was a professional. I waited no more than a couple of seconds to see if he volunteered anything on his own.

I hoped June saw how easily I moved on. "Can you say 'tinikling dance'?" I asked the children.

"Tinikling dance," they repeated in unison.

"Tickling dance," Jenny Browning yelled. "Tickling, tickling, tickling dance!" The children laughed hysterically at this perfect preschool joke. Molly Greene started the actual tickling. Within seconds, a tangle of giggling bodies rolled around the center of the circle. I let it go briefly while I grabbed the globe, long enough to let them expend some energy, but not so long that someone got hurt.

June and I pulled the kids off each other and directed them back to their places on the circle. I found the Philippine Islands on the vinyl globe and passed it around. We measured the distance to the Denmark of our last dance and to the United States. While the children watched spellbound, I started the tape in the tape deck and grabbed the tinikling poles from the storage closet.

Filipino music filled the classroom, the indecipherable lyrics clearly announcing party time. June and I each held one end of the two tinikling poles, six-foot lengths of real bamboo. Facing each other in a kneeling position, we tapped the poles together to the strong beat, then opened them wide and tapped them on the ground. "In, in, out, out," we chanted together. The children joined in.

I let Amanda McAlpine take my end, reminding June to be careful to keep the poles under control. I lined up the other students and, one by one, helped them dance over the shifting poles, and then sent them circling around to the end of the line.

After his second time over, Austin decided it was his turn to hold the poles. Before I could react, he leaned to take them from Amanda, just as she was lifting up on the thick bamboo. Blood spurted from Austin's nose. Amanda screamed. Austin covered his nose, then took his hand away and looked at it. While June ran to get latex gloves and tissues, he said calmly, "Good Lord, it's a gusher."

I stayed a safe distance away from Austin while we waited for the tissues. When a child is hurt, all a teacher wants to do is put her arm around his shoulders and comfort him, but in this day and age you have to be gloved before you make contact. "Pinch your nostrils together, honey," I directed, demonstrating on my own nose the way the teachers were taught every year during our Blood Spill Protocol/AIDS Awareness Inservice. Austin obeyed, squeezing his pudgy nose with stubby fingers. His eyes began to bulge. "Breathe, honey," I urged. "Breathe through your mouth." I blew air slowly out through my rounded lips. My hands were restless and I finally settled on crossing my arms and holding my elbows.

June was back in a flash, first dropping the box of tissues on the floor within Austin's reach, then quickly sliding her hands into latex gloves. "You're going to be fine, Austin. It's just a little nosebleed," she said gently, grabbing a handful of tissues and mopping at Austin's face. Rivulets of blood were already beginning to cake along his chin and neck. I made a mental note to remember to tell his father to wash his shirt in cold water. If he was staying with his father.

Austin's voice was muffled behind the wad of tissues. "You're damn tootin' it's a nosebleed. Call 911. Call an ambulance. Call a lawyer. Call . . ." Austin looked around for inspiration, his eyes peeking over the cloud of white tissue. They rested on the tinikling poles. "You should buy softer poles." He took a long breath in and started to cry.

I resisted the urge to put on my own pair of gloves

so I could give Austin a hug. Instead, I led the other children to the reading area. They huddled close while I read a worn copy of Judith Viorst's *Alexander and the Terrible, Horrible, No Good, Very Bad Day.* Jack Kaplan put his thumb in his mouth and twirled a lock of Molly Greene's silky brown hair with the fingers of his other hand. Molly was holding hands with Max Meehan, who had his other hand on my knee. Amanda was curled up against me on the other side, helping me turn the pages.

We were halfway through the book when Austin, scrubbed clean and wearing a wrinkled T-shirt from his change-of-clothes bag, joined the group. Max Meehan let him wiggle in beside me. Finally I could give him a hug. "All better?" I asked. He nodded, temporarily silent. As I continued reading, June sprayed a bleach-and-water solution on all contaminated surfaces. The sponge she used to wipe would be added to a plastic bag along with the tissues and her gloves, and all would be disposed of carefully.

I closed the book when I finished. "Some days," Austin said, "you just can't win for losin'."

Austin's dad was the last to arrive at dismissal time. "Hey, sport, what happened to you?"

"The tinikling pole hurt me, Dad."

He scooped Austin up in a bear hug, then turned to me. He had nice green eyes, long lashes.

"Austin collided with a bamboo pole we were using for a dance from the Philippines," I explained. "He got a bloody nose, but he's fine now. You should wash his shirt in cold water. Or your wife . . ."

"Thanks. If that's a choice, I think I'll pick the shirt.

My wife probably wouldn't appreciate being washed by me in any temperature water."

I laughed. I'd never really thought about how unattractive my laugh sounded, kind of high and nervous. "What I meant was—"

"Kidding. Sorry. I know what you meant. And I will. Wash it in cold water . . . as soon as I figure out which one is the washing machine." He grinned. I grinned back. He had a great smile, too, broad and boyish. One of his front teeth was twisted slightly, which added to his childlike quality, as if he were still too young for braces. "So, Ms. Hurlihy."

"Sarah."

"I know that. What's my name?"

"Mr. Connor?"

"Bob. Well, actually everyone calls me Bobby, but I've been vigilantly trying to change it to Bob since the third grade."

I laughed again, trying to make it start lower in my throat. I wished I could think of something witty to say about calling him Bob. Instead, I was thinking about what a sucker I've always been for Bobbys, ever since my first boyfriend, Bobby Healey.

Bobby Healey was so bad that the nuns hated him with thoroughly unchristian zeal. He hated them back and was crazy about me. I memorized commandments and spit them back politely for the nuns, winning rosary beads and lace mantillas for my efforts. And I silently cheered Bobby, my hero, for having the guts not to bother.

On the day I loved him most he swore at Sister Mary Catherine, a mortal sin punished by guaranteed rotting in hell. Because Saint Stephen's didn't have a cafe-

teria, we ate lunch at our desks. The dark wooden
desks were bolted securely to the darker wooden floor,
and we jammed lukewarm cartons of milk into the
inkwells. The nuns sold the milk and also penny
candy. They said the money went to the poor, but the
kids all knew it went to buy whiskey to drink with the
priests on the weekends.

Sister Mary Catherine left the room during lunch for
a minute one day. When she came back, a piece of red
licorice was missing from her desk. Bobby had stolen
it, taken a bite and given the rest to me. I was in love
so I ate it.

Thou shalt not steal was a big one, so Sister lined up
the entire class, forty-five or so fifth-graders. One by
one she made us kneel before the crucifix that graced
the wall at the front of the classroom and swear to God
that we hadn't taken the piece of licorice.

Forty-five kids knelt before Jesus and swore they
hadn't stolen a piece of penny candy. When it was my
turn, I lied bravely, not wanting to implicate Bobby.
Even if she believed my confession, Sister would know
I had a coconspirator. I was too good a girl to sin alone.
Temporarily defeated, Sister Mary Catherine took the
wooden paddle off the wall, went down the line,
whacked us one by one on our bottoms. Made us take
another turn kneeling before God. I looked at Bobby.
He shook his head no, so I didn't confess. I pictured us
in hell together one day, and his company made the
eternal flames not matter so much.

When it was Bobby's turn, he looked Sister in the
eye and said, "You are damn stupid to keep doing
this." Nobody moved, nobody dared even breathe.
The licorice was forgotten. As Sister Mary Catherine

escorted Bobby to Mother Superior's office, I wondered if I would see him again before hell. He emerged
just before dismissal, and I worshiped him with my
eyes as he strolled back to his seat. He ignored me,
however, because he'd just fallen in love with Eileen
Sullivan. Somehow I blamed his defection on the nuns,
as if I'd been a subject of discussion in Mother Superior's office. *Sarah Hurlihy*, the nuns might have said to
Bobby, *surely you can do better than that, Mr. Healey.*

Austin's father was saying something, but I'd
missed it. Austin had gone to the other side of the
room. He uncapped a dry erase marker and began
drawing on the white board. It looked like a picture of
Dolly's trailer. Maybe it was his father's trailer.

"Do you live in a trailer?" I asked the new Bobby.
Bob.

"I prefer to think of it as temporary asylum." His
hair was curly like Austin's, darker though, and
streaked with occasional coarse strands of white. His
chinos bagged at the knees and looked as if they might
have been slept in, but he wore them with a fresh-
from-the-cleaners shirt the color of raspberry sherbet.
Unbuttoned at the neck, sleeves rolled up to just below
the elbow, curly hair peeking out from his chest,
twirling around on his forearms.

I hoped I wasn't checking him out too obviously, but
I'd never really noticed just how good-looking he was.
Nice, too. And potentially single. Eventually. I stood up
a little straighter and pretended to rearrange a display
of autumn leaves thumbtacked to a bulletin board.

"So what has Austin told you?" he asked. His eyes
focused on mine as if I were about to say something interesting. I tried to rise to the occasion.

"About you? That you're incorrigible. And taking a break from your marriage."

"I think that particular phrasing came from his mother. You must hear a lot. I never thought about what kids tell their teachers." He looked down and then back into my eyes.

"In one ear and out the other," I assured him. I resisted the urge to take a step closer to see if he smelled like soap or cologne or just himself. It was so amazing the way the next part of your life might have been standing right in front of you all along.

"Yeah, right." He smiled. "By the way, how do you know the infamous, man-eating Dolly?"

"My father's dating her." I felt myself start to blush at the mention of dating. Of course, I wouldn't be comfortable actually dating Bob Connor until his son was no longer in my class. But if we started a friendship now, it could develop at a leisurely pace and blossom into romance right around the end of the school year. Much better than risking the personal ads, where you never knew who you might meet.

"Oops. Uh, brave man." He turned his head as June entered the classroom. She looked especially beautiful, dazed and sleepy-eyed. She must have found a new place to meditate. Smiling as she passed us, she walked over to Austin, knelt down beside him and picked up a marker. She began to draw little yellow flowers around the trailer. As soon as she finished each one, Austin colored the stem and leaves green.

Bob Connor and I watched them. We stood close together and our elbows were almost touching. Finally he turned to me and whispered, "Isn't she gorgeous?"

I smiled and bobbed my head like one of those motion-sensitive animals people put on the dashboards of their cars. With each bounce, little bits of self-esteem drained down my body and out through the ends of my toes. Somehow I managed to say good-bye to the parents and students, even to June and her gorgeousness.

When the classroom was empty, I sat in one of the kiddie chairs. I automatically reached down to feel how much of my hips and thighs were spilling over the sides of the seat, a little test I always did to make sure I'd notice if they started to spread at an alarming rate. It hadn't occurred to me to start checking for signs of invisibility. Maybe I was fading away, as my bones shrank and my eggs shriveled, and soon if not already men like Bob Connor, maybe all men, would only practice their eye contact on me as a warm-up for someone younger, prettier, perkier, *gorgeouser.*

The swing dance teacher had broken her foot. I didn't ask how. Certainly K-3s were developmentally too young for swing dancing anyway, but the parents loved the idea, and she'd come highly recommended by someone who worked in my sister Christine's office. As usual, Christine was feeling abandoned. "I can't believe you left me in the trailer by myself for so long," she'd said.

"You weren't by yourself," I tried. "Siobhan was there, and Dad, and the little kids. Carol just needed a moment alone with me to try to run my life."

"That's what I mean. Why does Carol always get to do everything? Why can't I help you fix your life?"

I'd distracted her by asking about a dance teacher. And until the foot, she'd been a good referral, lining up half the class facing north and the other half facing south, no talk about gender at all, even though eighteen of the twenty children were female. *Slow, slow, quick, quick,* they'd all managed some version of the step, turning to face all four walls, "Just a Gigolo" blasting from a portable CD player.

I dragged myself down the hallway to Kate Stone's office to ask for advice.

"Why, of course, you'll call each of the parents and give them a choice: a credit for the next session after the instructor has recovered, or continued participation in a new dance class."

"But I can't find another swing dance teacher. I can't even find any kind of dance teacher." I tried to tone down the whine in my voice. "I've called everywhere."

"This, Sarah, is where you apply your creative problem-solving training." Kate Stone picked up a carved wooden box from her desk, lifted the cover. "Open up, Sarah. Step out of the box and see things in a fresh way. Then seek and ye shall find." Kate Stone rolled her office chair over to the window, pulled gently on the string at the bottom of her wind chimes. We listened for a moment to the delicate tinkle of brass before she continued. "And, Sarah, if I wanted to manage the afterschool program myself, I wouldn't have hired you to do it."

8

The Brady kids were having so much trouble sharing the telephone that Mr. Brady was simply going to have to install a pay phone. I forgot I hadn't finished my Cheerios yet, and took a sip of the wine I'd poured for after dinner. The wine made the milk taste a little off. I slid the cereal down to the far end of the coffee table. I took another sip of wine. One more and the milk residue was gone. This episode wasn't quite as good as last night's sharing-the-bathroom episode. Although who was I to criticize, since every single one of the Bradys had more of a life than I did.

I picked up the cassette tape and opened and closed the case a few times. Taking it out, I read "Personal Ad Responses" centered neatly in Carol's handwriting. Most of the tape was still coiled at one end, the end we hadn't listened to. Just one, I decided. I'll listen to just one.

Seven thirty-eight P.M. October 18. *Hi, my name is John and obviously I heard your ad. It's a very fetching mes-*

sage you left. Sorry, that was supposed to be kind of a joke about dogs. You know, fetching? Never mind. What I really want to say is that you have a terrific voice. Anyway, before I forget, let me give you my number. It's, uh, 617-555-1412. That's downtown Boston, Beacon Hill. So all right. Um . . . you're voluptuous, sensuous, alluring and fun. Well, I think that could work. And I'm a huge dog lover, too . . . I mean, not just huge dogs but any size dog. Um, okay, I guess I should start with the obvious, banal stuff first. Um, I'm forty-three, and I'm completely divorced, so don't worry about that. I'm a little over six feet tall. I get accused of look- ing, uh, like Harrison Ford sometimes. Kind of blondish hair, brownish eyes and, uh, I've been wearing wire-rimmed glasses lately instead of my contacts. Let's see, what else? The best time to reach me is in the evening. I love Chinese Checkers. And pizza with everything but anchovies. I hope we can get together and talk soon and see what kinds of things besides dog-loving we might have in common.

I played John's response four more times, and by the last time, I was able to mouth the words right along with him. I picked up the cordless phone, changed my mind and put it back down. I turned back to the tele- vision. The Bradys' pay phone had just been delivered. It might not be the best episode, but at least with *The Brady Bunch* I could count on a happy ending.

"Do you remember what Johnny used to call his penis when we were kids?" I asked Carol.

"Mr. Murphy," Carol answered. She really did know everything. "Mom was so worried, don't you remem- ber? She kept asking him if there was a real Mr. Mur- phy and if he had ever done anything to Johnny. And Johnny would say, 'No, just *my* Mr. Murphy.' And when we were all crammed into the car, taking a trip somewhere, Johnny would say, 'Mr. Murphy has to go to the bathroom. Right now.' And we'd all crack up and get in trouble for making him cry."

"Was Johnny the one who sleepwalked into the kitchen one night and peed in the refrigerator?"

"No, no, no. That was Michael." Carol looked at Michael for confirmation. Michael's hazel eyes and crooked smile came from our mother's side of the family.

"No way. That was Billy. I never would have peed in the refrigerator. Not my style at all."

"Don't you mean *Duckie* never would have peed in the refrigerator?" I asked, thrilled to have some good ammunition.

Michael leaned over to whisper in his puppy's ear. "Don't listen to her, Mother Teresa. She's delusional. I have not a single childhood memory of a penis named Duckie."

It was Sunday night and we were leaning against the kitchen cabinets in our family house. "You can't keep calling her Mother Teresa, Michael. She needs a real name," Carol said, leaning over to scratch behind the Saint Bernard's ears. The six-month-old puppy collapsed on her back on the worn linoleum. Michael and Carol and I knelt beside her.

"Mother Teresa *is* a real name. And it's loaded with good karma." The puppy was taking up most of the kitchen floor now, her legs spread wide and the hind two twitching. Six hands scratched her belly. A thick stream of drool ran from one side of her mouth.

"She's going to need all the karma she can get, after that stunt with Dolly's feather boa," I said. Carol got up, tore a square of paper towel off the roll, and came back to dab at the corner of Mother Teresa's mouth. In an instant, the paper towel disappeared.

"Mother Teresa! Drop it. Drop it now." As the puppy began to choke, Michael scooped his hands under her and, bending at the knees, tried to lift her to a standing position. Carol and I moved quickly to either side of Michael. "One, two, three," urged Michael and we lifted the puppy to her feet.

She was still choking so I straddled her from behind and executed a flawless Heimlich maneuver. The angle was different but fortunately the process was pretty much the same as with preschoolers. A wad of gummy paper towel shot across the room and stuck to a lower cabinet. A quick shudder passed through the still-baggy skin of the puppy's body, and then she flopped back down to the floor and spread her legs. Michael and I knelt down again and started to scratch. Carol cleaned the paper towel glob off the cabinet.

"Say thank you to Auntie Sarah, Mother Teresa." Michael buried his head in the fur at the nape of the puppy's neck. Her eyes glazed over with love. The black dots on the white fur around her nose looked like painted-on freckles.

"That's two strikes for you, dog," I scolded. "Wasn't that unbelievable when she bit off the end of Dolly's boa? All of a sudden I looked down and she had a mouthful of pink feathers. The amazing thing was that I don't think Dolly would have even noticed if the kids hadn't started laughing and pointing."

We laughed, remembering Dolly's face. "So, Michael," Carol asked. "How come Phoebe didn't come tonight?"

Michael shrugged. "She stayed home to read a book. I don't think she cares much about getting in good with my family these days. She says we tell too many old stories and that it always makes her feel left out."

"Kevin used to say that too," I said. Carol gave me a dirty look. "I mean, not that that means anything," I added quickly. We all knew that Michael's marriage was in trouble, but while it was all right to whisper about it behind his back, it was not something we talked about openly. I wondered if all families behaved this way. I tried not to think about what they hadn't said in front of me about Kevin.

Dad pushed the kitchen door until it swung open just enough for his head to fit through the opening. He looked at Mother Teresa sternly. "You, my four-footed friend, are in deep shit." He held out a plastic bag, a flash of pink poking out of the top. Mother Teresa was on her feet in an instant. Michael grabbed her by the collar. "Michael, I'd be the happiest man alive if you could find a way to replace this with one of the original length."

Michael reached for the bag. "Okay, Dad. I'm really sorry. She's just a puppy." Mother Teresa made a lunge. I moved faster and whisked the bag to safety.

As usual, Carol had an idea. "Perfect, Sarah. You can shop for a new boa for Dolly. Take the old one with you so you get a good match, then throw it out afterward. I'll give you a list of stores to try. Maybe pick up some nice underwear for yourself while you're at it. Just in case."

My father nodded as if he thought it was a perfectly reasonable idea, but of course he was dating a woman who wore a pink feather boa to Sunday dinner. We heard a distinct crash. "Those good-looking grandchildren of mine out there might need a little supervision. I'm going to run Dolly home." He waggled his eyebrows. "Don't wait up."

We talked until the Miata was long gone, then turned out some of the lights and locked the door. We packed the kids and Mother Teresa into their respective cars to drive off to our other homes. I was about to head out, alone, when Michael walked over to my car. I rolled down my window. "Hey," I said. "You okay?"

Michael rubbed an index finger back and forth under one of his eyes. "Yeah, I'm fine, just checking up on you. You need anything?"

"No, I'm all right. But thanks."

"Are you, um, getting out or anything?" Even in the dark, he looked embarrassed. I probably did, too. "I mean, it's okay if you don't want to talk about it."

"No, it's not that. There's just not much to talk about." Behind us in Michael's car, Annie or Lainie started to flash the high beams off and on. Mother Teresa barked.

"Well, maybe you should push yourself a little." He waved at the kids, who responded by flashing the lights faster. It felt a little like being in a disco. "I know it's gotta be tough, but, Sarah, you have a chance to make a whole new life, you know? You just have to get out there and meet someone."

"Oh, yeah, right. Who would want me?"

"Come on, Sarah. Lots of guys would want to go out with you. You're smart, you're funny. You're even kinda pretty when you're not wallowing in self-pity."

My whole life, my brothers had teased me, making fun of my outfits, pointing out my pimples, belittling my boyfriends. Michael being this nice to me made me want to cry. "Okay, Michael," I said, not daring to look in his eyes. "I'll try."

I stripped down to my underwear, a graying cotton sports bra and nylon panties that had seen better days. Rifling through the mess on my closet floor, I found the open-toed silver Italian mules I'd bought and never worn. They were the only backless shoes I owned. Besides two pairs of boiled wool clogs.

I tried not to clomp on the way to the kitchen. I'd thought these shoes would make me feel as glamorous as, say, Sophia Loren or Gina Lollobrigida, but every time I tried them on with an outfit, I'd look at my feet in the mirror and laugh. After a year or so, I gave up on them.

I reached to the back of the cabinet under the kitchen sink, found the Lysol. I picked up the plastic bag from the counter, and shook out the boa until it collapsed on the floor like a dying pink flamingo. I sprayed the exposed side thoroughly, then flipped it over with the edge of the Lysol can and sprayed again. I wasn't quite sure if I was disinfecting Mother Teresa's drool or what my nieces and nephews would call Dolly's cooties.

The boa was looking a little damp and matted; the bedraggled feathers decreased its drama potential. I put it in the dryer and pushed DELICATE CYCLE then START. While I was waiting, I checked my answering machine. Nothing. Not even Carol.

A quick tumble in the dryer did wonders for the boa. I wrapped it around my shoulders. The warmth and fluff were encouraging. I held the boa by both ends and jump-roped the length of the kitchen, not an easy feat in mules. When I stopped, a few pink feathers floated in the air. I slid my hands closer together along the boa, let it fall behind my shoulders and shimmied for a bit. Added a step-kick, then a step-kick-kick. Then a long low hip circle and a couple of bumps.

Okay, this is it, I decided. I walked into my bedroom, lit a candle. Turned the lights down low with the dimmer switch by the door. The tape deck was on the bedside table. I played John's message, said the words along with him as I paraded around the room. *Hi, my name is John and obviously I heard your ad. It's a very fetching message you left. Sorry, that was supposed to be kind of a joke about dogs. You know, fetching? Never mind. What I really want to say is that you have a terrific voice.*

It had been a long time since I'd had a compliment from a man. I supposed that technically it was Carol's compliment, since she'd recorded my message, but I decided to take it anyway. I wrapped the boa around my neck a few times, sprawled on the bed with my legs arranged seductively. I looked down at my feet, still wearing the mules. Considered painting my toenails.

You have a terrific voice, I repeated. Then I picked up the phone. And I called him.

9

I figured I'd go through Michael's wife, Phoebe, to borrow Mother Teresa for a couple of hours. Less chance of word leaking out that way. Phoebe was an only child and had never developed a talent for mining sibling gossip.

I was wearing black jeans that looked good either standing or sitting, plus a cuddly red fleece jacket that had big pockets so I wouldn't have to think about what to do with my keys. My hair was having a good day, curling crisply rather than frizzily, for which I was thankful. I felt as if anything were possible. This was more than meeting up with a man. It was staking a claim on a life. Grabbing some gusto. Catching a wave. Well, maybe not catching a wave, but still.

"Did Michael talk you into this?" asked Phoebe as she struggled to hook a hot pink leash onto the puppy's matching collar. As soon as she attached it, Mother Teresa grabbed the other end in her mouth and started to walk herself out the door. "Get her! Oh my

God, this dog is driving me crazy." Now that she mentioned it, Phoebe did look slightly deranged. Her straight blond hair didn't seem to know in which direction to fall, and her pale blue eyes looked lost, too.

"No, it was my idea. Just thought you could use a little break. I'd offer to take the kids, too, but I really need a workout. Mother Teresa and I are going for a very long walk. Could be hours. I'll make it up to Annie and Lainie next time."

"That's fine. They have homework anyway. And the girls are a piece of cake compared to Her Holiness here." Mother Teresa looked up at Phoebe adoringly, then leaned her body into Phoebe's thigh. Phoebe took a few quick steps backward and braced herself against the wall.

I buckled Mother Teresa into the front seat of my Honda Civic. She seemed to like it and, keeping her eyes on the road, began to gum the seat belt contentedly. It was kind of nice to have company. The twenty-minute ride to the puppy playground was over before I knew it.

We entered a chain-linked gate with a sign that said WELCOME TO PUPPY PARADISE. I sat on a green park bench. Mother Teresa jumped up beside me. I unbuckled her leash. "Go play with the other puppies, honey." I elbowed her. "Come on, don't be shy." She put her head in my lap and looked around cautiously.

I looked around, too, for someone who resembled Harrison Ford. Maybe even wearing his Indiana Jones hat. Probably from the second episode, *Indiana Jones and the Temple of Doom*. Daredevil archaeologist hot on the trail of the legendary Ankara Stone. And a ruthless cult that has enslaved hundreds of children. I would have been a less whiny costar than Kate Capshaw. I could have kept up with all the action, wouldn't even have considered a stunt double.

A man leaning against a concrete tunnel was glancing my way. Actually, he seemed to be glancing surreptitiously at my breasts. I looked down, thinking Mother Teresa might have left a conspicuous deposit of drool. Nothing. I looked back up. Harrison Ford he was not.

It couldn't be him. This guy was actually kind of cute, but he definitely wasn't over six feet tall, more like five-nine or five-ten. Although maybe he just looked shorter from a distance. I tried to remember what else his message had said. Let's see, he *was* wearing wire-rimmed glasses, though the effect was more Michael J. Fox than Harrison Ford. He was a little pale, too, and had shiny hair it would be a stretch to call *blondish*, though maybe *tannish* would fit. I searched for some hint of Harrison—his wry grin, the confident sway of his shoulders, the way his whole body smoldered with intensity. Nothing.

I scanned the playground for more desirable possibilities. Two exceptionally gorgeous guys who had eyes only for each other. Their Jack Russell terrier frolicked nearby. A couple of mother-child-lab combos. A sweet old guy and his beagle. Jeesh.

Mother Teresa jumped down from the bench. "Good girl," I said encouragingly. She waited while I scratched behind her ears; then she lumbered off toward the concrete tunnel, stopping to sniff every couple of feet. When she was a few yards from the tunnel, a Yorkshire terrier exploded from within, a tiny yelping whirlwind of tricolored fur. Mother Teresa froze, except for her tail, which continued to wag hopefully.

The Yorkie was almost under Mother Teresa's nose when she stopped. Her barking got louder, the pitch higher. I didn't know about Mother Teresa, but the little yapper was certainly getting on my nerves.

"Clementine, sit!" the man who was not Harrison Ford ordered. Mother Teresa sat. The Yorkie kept barking. She was jumping up and down on her hind legs. Mother Teresa slid to the ground and buried her head between her front paws. The Yorkie backed off a couple of hops but kept barking.

"Nice bitch," said the man.

"Excuse me?"

"Your dog. She's a bitch, right? Show-quality, looks like."

"Oh, I thought you meant your dog." Now there's a bitch, I was thinking.

He didn't get it. "Yup, Clementine's a bitch, too. Best of breed, twice. The Eukanuba Classic, two years ago and Newport, last summer. How 'bout yours?"

I was starting to get a headache. "Is there any way you can make her stop?"

"Sure." He turned to the dog and said sternly, "Clementine, sit." Clementine kept barking. He took a step forward. She barked louder. He reached out a hand. She bit it. "Jesus! What is your fucking problem?" Shaking his hand, he turned to me and managed a smile. "Sorry. That hurt. A lot."

"Did it break the skin?" I asked.

He examined his hand. "No, I don't think so. Listen, can you watch her for a minute while I get her travel crate? That should work."

I didn't say a word, and since I hadn't committed
to anything, I figured Mother Teresa and I could just
take off if things got rough with Clementine. She had
stopped barking, but her stance was defiant. If her
owner had any brains at all, he would have hopped
in the car and taken off. Instead, he raced back with
the crate. Fortunately, Clementine jumped in, se-
duced by a doggie treat, and he whisked her off to
the car.

"John Anderson," he said, extending his hand, when
he came back. I looked for signs of blood before I
shook it. Through the cracked window of the car, we
could hear the faint sounds of Clementine barking.

"Sarah Hurlihy." I wondered if I should have used
an alias. I wondered if he was using one.

"So." He sat on the green bench and patted the
space beside him. Mother Teresa jumped up. I sat
down on the other side of her.

"So. Who told you you look like Harrison Ford?"

"The same person who told you you were voluptuous."

We looked at each other. *What a jerk,* I thought. It
wasn't as if I actually thought of myself as voluptuous,
but what gave this guy the right to an opinion? "Well,
gee, thanks," I said finally, wondering if it was too
soon to get up and leave.

"Sorry, I didn't mean it like that. Usually voluptuous
goes the other way—toward the fat end of the spec-
trum. 'Rubenesque' is even worse, a tip-off for mor-
bidly obese. 'Weight proportional to height' is another
one to look out for. Anyway, next time you should
probably just say 'attractive' or 'great body.' Just don't
say 'athletic.' That means flat-chested."

"So if you didn't like my ad, why did you answer it?"

"I didn't mean I didn't like it. Let's see. I'd have to say it was the 'seeks special man to share starlit nights' that got me. Slightly overused but a nice image all the same. And I thought 'alluring' was an excellent word choice."

"Why, thanks a bunch. You certainly sound like an expert." I was feeling a little bit like I was playing a game of tennis but couldn't tell if I was winning or losing. In fact, I was pretty sure I wanted to lose. "Well, John, the truth is that I didn't even write the ad. My sister wrote it for me. And I thought the starlit nights line was awful. I'll tell her you liked it, though."

He nodded. "So what got you in my message? Harrison Ford?"

"Yeah, sorry. What made you write that?" I mean, you could break someone's heart with that kind of promise. All those expectations with nowhere to go.

"I guess I thought it captured my adventurous spirit."

Now there was a stretch, I thought. I supposed I should feel a little bit sorry for him. I wondered if it was too late to let him down carefully. "Oh. Well, I also liked the fact that you love dogs. Although the joke about fetching was pretty bad."

"Yeah, I know. Sorry. But I do love dogs. Yours is a beauty."

"She isn't even my dog. I borrowed her from my brother." I was scratching behind Mother Teresa's left ear, and John was working on her chest. It was kind of nice, like talking through a wall of dog. I searched for something else to say. "So, how long have you had Clementine?"

"She's not mine. Thank God. I borrowed her from an old lady in my building. Her full name is Darling Clementine."

"I don't think she was quite the look you were trying to achieve." It was getting dark already. Horizontal stripes of pink and blue sky plummeted along with my mood. They were followed by a thicker band of dismal gray.

"Yeah, I know. I was supposed to get a greyhound from someone else, but it fell through."

"A greyhound would have been better. Too bad."

"I read an article about show dogs, too, to impress you. That's where I got the bitch line. I also had one about show points I didn't get to use."

"You can say it now if you want to." I mean, it wasn't as if I had anything else to do, since the real Harrison probably had plans already.

"No, that's okay. I'll save it for another time."

"You mean, save it for someone else?" He sounded so ready to move on that all of a sudden I wasn't sure I wanted him to.

He laughed, which made the corners of his eyes crinkle. "From the moment we caught sight of each other, your disappointment was all over your face."

"Sorry," I said. "It's nothing personal. I think I was just expecting Harrison." I pulled back behind Mother Teresa so he wouldn't see me blush.

"Do you wear all of your emotions like that?"

I reached up to touch my cheek, felt silly and pulled my hand away. "I don't know. I'm not sure I even feel all of my emotions anymore, let alone wear them."

"That sounds serious. Maybe this is where we exchange tales of woe."

"You go first." I heard the muffled sounds of Clementine barking again. "Is she all right?"

"Damn. She doesn't even have any water in there. I'd better get her home while she's still breathing. Listen, Sarah, maybe I could call you or something. You know, maybe we could try it again without the dogs."

I looked at him. Behind his wire-rimmed glasses, his eyes were interesting, kind of a toffee color, like the inside of a Heath bar or the coat of a lion. "Okay," I half-surprised myself by saying.

Why not? I thought as he ran toward Clementine, whose barking had grown disconcertingly faint. Maybe if we didn't fall in love we'd at least get to be friends. What was wrong with connecting with another human being, adding to my circle of friends, enlarging my too-small world?

I watched as John Anderson opened the car door and leaned inside. I knew it was a superficial observation, but I couldn't help but notice that, from this angle at least, he was kind of fetching himself.

I dropped off Mother Teresa without a hitch. Phoebe invited me to stay for dinner. Annie and Lainie set the table while Michael sliced a pork tenderloin at the kitchen counter. I would have felt better helping them, but Phoebe insisted that I chat with her in the living room.

"Siobhan is teaching Irish step at Bayberry? That's great. Can you squeeze the girls in? I'd love them to get some extra practice." Phoebe held up a finger, then turned to yell into the next room, "Michael, can you drive the girls to Bayberry after school on Thursdays?"

Michael poked his head in from the dining room. He

looked tired. "Phoebe," he began. "I can't keep leaving work early. Soccer days are tough enough." I knew it wasn't my business, but I never quite understood why Phoebe never left her job early.

"Please, honey bunny," Phoebe said in a helpless, little-girl voice that made me feel embarrassed to be in the same room with them.

"I can swing by and get them after I pick up Siobhan," I offered, if only so she'd stop talking like that. "I'll drop them off afterward, too. No big deal."

"Thanks, Sarah," Michael said. He turned around without looking at Phoebe.

We all joked and laughed through dinner, though I noticed that Michael and Phoebe directed their comments to Annie or Lainie or me, but not to each other. It made me think of Kevin, the many dining room tables we'd sat at together with family and friends, pretending everything was fine. I couldn't wait to leave.

Michael followed me out to the car after dinner. "Thanks, again, Sarah, for taking Mother Teresa. And for offering to drive the girls to step dance."

"Are you all right, Michael?"

"Yeah, I'm fine. Just a little overextended. We'll talk soon, okay?"

There was a message from John Anderson on my machine when I got home. *Hi, Sarah. It's me, John. Anderson. Just wanted to say I had a good time and that Clementine was still alive when I returned her to her owner. And you really are kind of voluptuous, in a minimalist sort of way. Anyway, while I was driving home I had some ideas for our second date, or our first dogless date, depending how you want to look at it. What would work for you? We could walk along the banks of the Charles River and maybe have a picnic? A good champagne, nice sandwiches? Would you want to go to Cambridge for the Gospel Brunch at the House of Blues? Take a ferry to one of the Boston Harbor Islands? Have you ever done that? Oh, no, I'm doing it again, talking too much. I was just thinking of some fun things to do if you want to give it another try. And, if not, that's okay, too, and, um, I hope you find what you're looking for. Well, take care, Sarah. Hope to hear from you.*

I started to call John Anderson back, I really did. I had the phone in my hand and everything. Maybe I was still grieving Harrison; maybe I just didn't have the nerve. But mostly I was thinking about all the things that could go wrong. And all the things that did go wrong all the time for people. Like Michael and Phoebe. Like Kevin and me.

10

I was almost going to be early for school when Carol called. "So, how was your date? Tell me everything."

"Why am I not surprised, Carol? How'd you know?"

"Phoebe. I called and she said you had just left and that you'd borrowed Mother Teresa. The rest was obvious."

I was beyond questioning Carol's radar. After years of lapsed Catholicism, it was the one miracle I still believed in. "I don't want to talk about it, okay, Carol? And I have to go now or I'll be late for work."

"What do you mean, you don't want to talk about it? Didn't he like you?"

"Thanks a lot. If you must know, the guy might not have been what *I* was looking for. He wasn't anything like his ad."

"So what. I'm sure no one is ever anything like their ads or they'd already be taken. Did you give him a chance?"

"Yeah, I guess. No big fireworks or anything."

"What's that got to do with anything? Lots of good relationships start off gradually. Why I knew Dennis for months before I felt anything."

Enough said, I wanted to say. "Listen, Carol, I have to go. I'm going to be late. Oh, and I'll pick up Siobhan tomorrow at three-thirty."

"Thanks. Hope you know what you're getting your-self into."

"She'll be fine, and she's such a good dancer. I mean, what could she do?"

"Would you like a list? Never mind, let's not antici-pate. I'll talk to you later. Oh, I almost forgot. Dad wants you to hurry up and buy Dolly a new feather boa. He says she's getting impatient. And that maybe you can drop it off at the trailer. Today would be good, he said."

Even though my back was turned, I could actually feel Bob Connor come to the door of my classroom with Austin. Quickly, I took a few pieces out of the wooden puzzle on the shelf in front of me, just so I could look busy putting them back in. I was glad I was wearing a fairly decent black sweater and skirt. Just in case he should happen to notice me on his way to looking at June. I kept myself focused on the puzzle, little wooden children planting a little wooden garden.

"Hey," he said from somewhere about an inch be-hind me. I jumped and the puzzle jumped with me, pieces scattering all over the floor. Bob laughed and we bent down at the same time to pick them up. I'd never known that squatting on the floor next to some-one could feel so intimate. I stood up.

"Don't worry about those. I'll get them later," I said, smoothing my skirt down carefully.

Bob finished picking up the last couple of pieces. His hair was curly and still damp from his morning shower. He straightened up and handed the puzzle to me. He smiled his twisted-tooth smile and when his hands grazed mine, I tried not to notice. "Well, I guess that'll teach me to come in and say hello to my favorite teacher."

"Oh," I said. "June's over there."

Bob laughed. He was close enough that I could smell his toothpaste. "I mean my other favorite teacher. Who, by the way, looks very nice this morning."

"Thank you. Well, I'd better get to work." I turned and walked to the other side of the classroom. From the corner of my eye, I saw Bob give Austin a hug. He waved casually across the room to June, as if he'd never even noticed her gorgeousness, and was gone.

I called the kids to circle. June and I pushed the tables and shelves back to make more room. Cho-cho-chuckie was always a hit. I'd found it years ago in a book called *International Playtime.* Basically, it was an African version of duck-duck-goose, so that's where we started.

"Duck . . . duck . . . duck . . ." I began, tapping each child gently on the head as I moved around the circle with exaggerated slowness. Molly Greene was so excited that she jumped up in anticipation just before I tapped her head. I waited patiently until she sat back down. Molly was one of those children who came to school coifed and wearing an ensemble, then became more like her true self as the day wore on. First she'd yank off the grosgrain bows that tied her elaborately braided hair. June and I would never see the actual dismantling. Instead we'd find one bow next to the fish tank, another on a pillow in the reading corner. As the morning continued, Molly would shed her pearl-buttoned cardigan and kick off her shoes. Her tights would start to stretch out and bag around the knees; then eventually the bagginess would work its way south until several inches of empty fabric flapped around in front of her toes.

"Duck . . . duck . . . duck . . ." I continued around the circle. When I came to June, I said, "Goose!" and tapped her on her silky blond hair. I wondered briefly what kind of conditioner she used. It was quite possible that Bob Connor had no romantic interest at all in June, that he'd only commented on her gorgeousness in a conversational manner, the way you'd point out a child and say, "Isn't she cute?" It was even remotely possible that Bob Connor had wandered into the classroom this morning to talk to me.

June got up slowly and gracefully, as always, just as we had rehearsed. As June chased me, I ran as slowly and gracefully as I was capable of around the circle. I got to June's place before she tagged me, and sat down quickly. The children clapped appreciatively.

In theory, when teachers model safe indoor movement, children imitate it. In reality, sometimes it works and sometimes it doesn't. Today was a good day. Everything went smoothly: June chose Max Meehan who chose Jack Kaplan who chose Molly Greene.

Before Molly could start tapping heads, I put my

hands on her shoulders. "Can you say, 'Benin'?" I asked the children.

"BAY-nin."

"In the country of Benin in the continent of Africa, there are lots of chickens. And when the children of Benin call out to these chickens, this is what they say: cho-cho-chuckie! Can you say that?"

"Chuck-chuck-chuckie!" Amazingly, every year this happened. The children changed the "cho" to "chuck" to make it rhyme with "duck." I figured the children of Benin would never know, so I didn't bother to correct them.

"Chuck . . . chuck . . . chuck . . ." Molly Greene began. She tapped Amanda McAlpine and then June and then Jenny Browning on their heads. When she came to Austin Connor she shrieked, "Chuckie!" and ran all the way around the circle. She stood in Austin's place on one foot, flapping her arms like a chicken.

Austin was still moving around the circle, in extreme slow motion. He looked like he belonged in one of the running-on-the-beach scenes in *Chariots of Fire*. As he touched first the heel and then the toe of his left foot while circling his right arm forward like the wheel of a train, he smiled at June. "Look at me, June. How'm I doing? Don't you think *I'm* the slowest?" June smiled back.

"Chuck . . ." Austin said as he touched my head. "June had dinner with my dad and me last night. We had Chinese food with extra chicken fingers just for me."

"Chuck . . ." Austin said as he touched Jack Kaplan's head. "June read me a book before bed." He stopped, his hand still resting on Jack's head. He took a deep breath. "She let me pick the book. I wanted the fourth Harry Potter but she said well then only one chapter. Except then she read me two."

"Austin . . ." I prompted.

"You can come to my house, June," said Jenny Browning. "I have a very big house."

"No, my house."

"My house!"

June's palms were turned up on her knees, her middle fingers and thumbs touching. She smiled vaguely. I raised my eyebrows, intending to send her a look to let her know that, while Bayberry Preschool didn't have an official rule prohibiting teachers from dating the not-even-divorced parents of students in their classes, this was why it was generally *not* a good idea.

Victoria's Secret always makes me feel as if I am an impostor. As if the minute I lift a padded satin hanger off the wall rack to consider its silky lace camisole a little closer, an alarm will go off somewhere. A spotlight will shine in my face and a store full of glamorous women will point to me and say, *Hah! As if.*

Today wasn't too bad. There was an older man off in one corner, talking quietly to himself as he looked at the bras. The salespeople seemed to be occupied, too, moving clothing from one of the racks to an identical rack nearby. I'm sure they had a good reason.

My plan was to buy something I needed and then casually mention feather boas while I was paying for my purchase. Telling the whole story about Dolly and my father was completely unnecessary. What did I care if someone I didn't even know thought I was buying a pink feather boa for me?

The old guy had moved to the back of the store, so I stayed toward the front. The number of choices in underwear was daunting. Satin or lace, underwire or not, colors that matched your outfit, but once you weren't wearing an outfit, what would it matter? That was it: a commitment to buying underwear here was an admission of hope.

I moved in the direction of cotton. Thirsty terry robes, nonintimidating nightshirts. Flannel pajama pants. And then I saw them—maybe long underwear, maybe pajamas, maybe loungewear; how was I to know? Gray cotton pants and a matching cardigan top with tiny snaps. Navy blue silhouettes of playful dogs, the breed not quite identifiable, romped everywhere. I couldn't wait to get home and put them on. I found tops and bottoms in a size medium, and considered comfortable versus *really* comfortable. I put the mediums back, matched up a pair in size large, and carried it to the register.

"Excuse me, but do you carry pink feather boas?"

The woman looked down at my purchase, which she was folding between sheets of tissue paper. She smiled.

"I wasn't planning to wear them together. Actually, the boa isn't even for me."

She smiled again. It was a hard smile to read. Discreetly, I moved my eyes lower, trying to figure out if she had implants. "I'm sorry, we don't. You might try Boa-Boa, across from Sears."

I was in luck. No sign of Dolly or her Ford Fiesta. I stopped in front of the Whispering Pines Park sign, left my Civic running, picked up the Boa-Boa bag and tiptoed to the front door of Dolly's trailer. A grapevine wreath studded with small plastic turkeys hung at eye level. I turned the knob on the storm door to tuck the bag inside.

"Why, Ms. Hurlihy, what brings you here?" Bob Connor, minus Austin and wearing old sweats and new sneakers, appeared to be returning from a jog. His cheeks were pink and he was breathing hard. He looked rumpled and friendly and boyishly handsome. His hair was curly on one side and sort of flattened and sticking up on the other, as if he had taken a nap before going out for a jog. I tried not to notice, but his eyes were particularly green in this light. I pictured June, looking spectacular in impossibly short shorts, jogging beside him. That helped.

I shut Dolly's boa safely between the doors. His eyes followed. "Boa-Boa?"

"Yeah, Boa-Boa."

"Shop there often?"

"It's always a pleasure to run into one of my students' parents, but, sorry, I'm in a rush right now. Take care. Say hi to Austin."

"You can say hi to him yourself if you want. He's getting dropped off in ten minutes or so. I could offer you a beer. Or learn to make coffee."

"Thanks, but it might be confusing for Austin to see his father entertaining more than one of his teachers in any given week."

"Ouch. You mean June, right?"

"Good guess."

"Actually, I was kinda hoping to talk to you about that."

"Maybe you can bring it up at the next parent-teacher conference." I smiled sweetly, incredibly proud of coming up with the first good parting line of my life. Taking extra care not to trip and ruin the whole effect, I sauntered away from Bob and toward my Civic. When I turned back for a final wave, he was grinning.

11

Siobhan was driving my Civic; Annie and Lainie were buckled up safely in the backseat. I was riding shotgun. "Nice job, Siobhan. You were great. The kids loved you. And thanks for picking up on my not wanting my boss to know we were related. I wasn't sure she'd think my hiring relatives was professional."

"What a bitch."

"She just takes her job seriously."

"I guess." Siobhan's driving had improved. She had better spatial awareness now, hugging the sides of the road on corners instead of straying over the center line if a car wasn't coming the other way. I breathed uneasily until we dropped the younger girls off, wondering if Phoebe or Michael would be mad at me for letting Siobhan drive when their kids were in the car. Fortunately, nobody came to the door and, as soon as Annie and Lainie were inside the house, Siobhan and I made a clean getaway.

We drove across town, and arrived at Carol's house

just as she was pulling into the driveway. Ian and Trevor jumped out of the minivan first. They waved and ran screaming into the house. Carol leaned in to unbuckle Maeve. I wondered how she found the energy for car seats in her forties. She balanced Maeve on one hip and smiled. Even though Carol was three years older than I am, she looked about ten years younger than I felt. "So, how'd it go?" she asked Siobhan.

Siobhan popped the trunk of my Civic, walked around to grab her shoe bag. I circled around the other way, held my arms out to Maeve, who shook her head and buried it in the crook of Carol's neck. "Okay," Siobhan finally answered.

"She's a born teacher," I said. "The kids loved her." Siobhan's face was perfectly bored.

"That's great, honey. You really are good with kids. I knew you could do it." Carol tilted her head, trying to get Siobhan to look at her. Siobhan focused all her attention on twisting the straps of the shoe bag. "So," Carol continued. "Spot any talent, Siobhan? Anybody with championship potential?"

"Rebecca Lowenstein looked pretty good."

Carol smiled. "Great name for an Irish step dancer."

Siobhan gave Carol a look of astonishing hatred. "Oh, my God, you are such a racist I can't even stand it."

Still holding Maeve, Carol started to rock back and forth in that special way all mothers seem to have. Too quietly she said, "Siobhan, don't you ever use that tone with me."

Siobhan stomped off to the house. It seemed proper to observe a moment of silence. Afterward, Carol said,

"An invitation to a bar mitzvah for a Dermot O'Toole would be funny, wouldn't it?"

"Yeah, I know how you meant it. But don't you remember being Siobhan's age? I have this image of Grandpa stopping the car to point out a man just to say he was black as the ace of spades. And Dad talking about Aunt Nora marrying an Eye-talian. I'm sure they'd been saying stuff like that for years, but one day I heard it and I was stunned. Maybe that's part of a teenager's function, to help you evolve to the next level."

Maeve squirmed in her mother's arms, began to fuss. "Don't you start," said Carol.

Lorna was sitting at my kitchen table. "Okay, there's line dancing at the Knights of Columbus hall, a wine tasting at O'Brien's, or we can use these before they expire." She handed me two gift certificates, each one good for a manicure at the Nail Trail.

"Teacher presents?" I asked with a smile.

"You got it. The only perk in this business. I think the parents buy them for us to feel less guilty that their Land Rover cost more than their child's teacher makes in a year. I even got a gift certificate for a full hour massage for my birthday from Lucy Wheelright's mom." Lorna rolled her shoulders back. "It was great. I'd get rid of Mattress Man in a second if I could have one of those every day."

Even at the bitter end, I never would have joked about Kevin that way. A lot of good it did me. I ran through Lorna's suggestions. "How 'bout the manicure?" I asked. "Can we walk in or do we need an appointment?" Later I'd try to remember where I'd stashed my own gift certificates, and find out if they'd expired. If not, I'd share them with Lorna.

"We'll find out."

I am never very comfortable letting people do things for me. At a restaurant, I always stack the plates for the waitress, clean up any stray bits of food from the table-cloth so the waiter won't have to. Now I sat at a ruffled table in front of an Asian manicurist who didn't smile. She pointed, so I obediently perched my fingers in two cut-glass bowls of soapy water. I looked at her, trying to figure out what country she was from, thinking maybe I'd get her to teach me one of her childhood games for the kids at school. I waited for her to look up. She ignored me.

I cleared my throat. "Uh, excuse me, but where are you from?"

"Plymouth."

"No, I mean what country are you from?"

She grabbed my right hand. I jumped. "United States American." She glared at the hand as if it had asked the question. "What color?" she asked.

It took me a minute to realize she meant my nails. "Oh, whatever you think," I said, thinking I'd make up for asking her stupid questions.

"Your nails, not mine." Beside me Lorna and her manicurist were laughing away together as if they'd known each other their whole lives.

"Okay, this one, please." I pointed to a nonadventurous shade of pink.

When the right hand was finished, she turned on a tiny green fan, tapped her fingernail on the counter to signal me to place my hand in front of it. I obeyed.

She finished polishing the left hand, moved the fan

to let my right hand know it was the left hand's turn. "Good nails," she said with a scowl. "Women pay lotta money get these nails. Nevva happen. Rubber gloves to clean, good lotion and come see me every week. Or twice month. You decide." She picked up my right hand, turned it over and gazed at my palm. "Not much lifeline."

My father squinted at the television. "Now there's one fine-looking woman."

"Mrs. Brady?" I waggled my fingers, admiring last night's manicure.

"No, the brunette with the curtains."

"Dad, that's Alice. She's the housekeeper."

"We all have to earn a living, Sarah. And you, my darlin' daughter, were not brought up to be a snob in any way, shape or form. Your mother never had any airs about her at all."

My father and I were sipping Campbell's tomato soup from coffee mugs in my living room. Our feet were on the coffee table and an open bag of oyster crackers rested between them. We'd each crushed a handful of crackers into our soup by rubbing our hands back and forth over the mug. Powdery crumbs dusted the tabletop.

Alice was explaining to Mrs. Brady that she wouldn't be able to sit for the Brady kids that night because she had to deliver the olive-green café curtains she'd just finished making for Sam's house. Sam was a new boyfriend, and Mr. and Mrs. Brady were encouraging the relationship. "But if you had a choice, Dad, I mean if Mrs. Brady wasn't married, wouldn't you pick her over Alice?"

"No."

"Why not?"

"I've learned a bit of what there is to learn about women over the years, Sarah, and I can tell you, without a smidgen of doubt, that the brunette is the better choice. The blonde is too high-strung. Squirrelly."

"Squirrelly? What's squirrelly?"

"What do you mean, 'What's squirrelly?' Look out your window, Sarry girl, and watch the little rodents, like rats wearing fur coats. All nervous and running here and there without ever finishing anything. That's squirrelly."

I took another look at Mrs. Brady. She seemed calm to me. She and Mr. Brady were agreeing that it would be unconscionable to stand in the way of Alice's date. The plot was thickening. Marcia and Greg were announcing that they were too old to have a baby-sitter anyway. Actually, Greg was announcing it, but Marcia was backing him up one hundred percent.

I took another sip of my soup. My father took a sip of his, too, wrapping both hands around the mug just like I did. The crackers were nice and soggy. "Sorry I don't have anything better to offer you for dinner, Dad. I wasn't expecting company."

"I wasn't expecting to be company. It was an impulse born of necessity." He removed a wrinkled white handkerchief from his pocket and wiped his mouth. I should have remembered napkins.

"What do you mean?"

"I inadvertently made two sets of dinner plans. I thought it best to cancel both before any hearts were broken. And then make myself scarce."

"Wow, you're cheating on Dolly?"

"The concept of cheating does not apply to the situation."

"Why do I think Dolly wouldn't agree with that?" Mr. and Mrs. Brady were in a fancy restaurant now, taking turns sneaking off to the pay phone to check on the kids. I still couldn't see squirrelly. "Is Dolly squirrelly, Dad?"

"Dolly is the least squirrelly woman I have ever met." He was running his fingers through his thick white hair. He looked like a big cat grooming himself after dinner.

"Is that what attracted you to her?" I mean, what would attract a handsome man like my father to a little pink woman like Dolly?

"Sarah, why one human being is attracted to another is one of the great mysteries of the world."

As soon as my father left, I picked up the phone. I'd been doing this on a regular basis, picking it up, holding on to it for a while, eventually putting it back down. Building a new life was such a great idea and one that, in theory, I believed in completely. In reality, though, I found that I could feel myself wanting a life and I could picture myself having a life, but I had a hard time making myself connect the dots between the two.

Forward motion, little steps, I coached myself, wishing I'd had the tenacity to make it all the way through one of the self-help books Carol was always handing down to me. I took a deep breath and dialed John Anderson's number. I had never even thanked him for our date, or for leaving the message on my machine later that night.

"Yellow," he said when he answered, making me question my impulse.

I forged ahead anyway. "John. Hi. It's Sarah Hurlihy. Remember me?"

"Mother Teresa's friend?"

"Yeah. Um, I just wanted to thank you for our sorta date."

"You mean, our sorta date of three weeks ago?"

"Wow, has it been that long? Gee, time flies." I couldn't imagine why I had called. "So, how've you been?"

"I'm okay. How 'bout you? I take it you didn't like any of my second date suggestions."

"No, that wasn't . . . I mean, yes, I liked all of them. Thank you very much."

"But?"

"Well, I kept meaning to call you, but I never seemed to do it. I guess everything just feels like too much work lately. Like even getting out of bed in the morning is a part-time job."

"Maybe it would be better to think of it as a hobby."

"Is that how you think of it?"

"Lately I've been trying not to think much at all. Actually, I have another hobby I was just playing around with when you called. Anagrams."

"Anagrams? Which ones are they?"

"When you mix up the letters in a word to spell something else. Usually I use people's names."

This guy was either slightly strange or kind of interesting. Maybe both. "So, give me an example."

"Okay, pick one—Madonna or Shakespeare."

It was probably a test of some sort. Maybe you could rate people based on their preferred cultural icons. "Shakespeare, of course."

"Okay, William Shakespeare comes out: 'I am a weakish speller.' "

"Cut it out. Does it really?"

"Write down the name, then cross off the letters. It works."

"This is fun. How about Madonna?"

"Madonna Louise Ciccone. The best one is 'Occasional nude income.' "

"Oh, that's great. What about me?"

"Okay, give me a minute. Sarah Hurlihy . . . hmm . . . that's a tough one. Umm . . . How about this: 'Hi! Ha ha! Slurry!' "

"That's awful."

"Okay, I can do better. 'Hi! A lush Harry'? Or 'Has hurly hair'?"

"Gee, thanks a lot."

"Hey, I didn't name you."

"That's true. And I hate my name anyway so I won't feel insulted. Sarah's too whispery, not a strong name."

"I think it's a beautiful name."

"Thanks." I'd never really liked talking on the phone that much, but it was kind of nice tonight. There was only sound. No sight or smell or touch to worry about. I could hang up at any time and be safe at home, all by myself. I curled up on the edge of my bed, waited for John to keep talking.

"What would you rather have for a name?" he asked.

"Well, when I was twelve I wanted to be Heidi. I tried to take it as a Confirmation name, but the nuns wouldn't let me because it wasn't the name of a saint."

"Heidi Hurlihy. Sometimes things happen for the best."

"And then I wanted to be Juliet. I know, not much better. How 'bout you, did you ever want another name?"

"You don't think John Anderson is unusual enough?" John's voice was soft and rich and gently teasing.

"You know," I said, forgetting to answer his question. "You have a terrific voice, too."

It's not like it's really a date, I told myself. It was just a quick cup of coffee at Starbucks on Boylston because I'd happened to mention to John Anderson that I was taking a one-day professional development course in Boston. It turned out John's office was just down the street from the conference center where the course was being held.

Everything always seemed more sophisticated in Boston. There was something stimulating about getting out of the suburbs, where you could live your entire life in sweatpants. The women I passed looked neat and crisp and were dressed mostly in black, as if stooping to wear color would be far too frivolous for their important lives.

I was early, and I sat at one of the tall stools at the counter by the window, wishing I'd remembered about the black thing when I was getting dressed that morning. My simple purple dress, which had seemed perfectly appropriate at home, now felt too bright, too cheerful, practically circusy. The seat I'd chosen had a great view, but it was the kind of stool

I never knew whether to climb all the way up on, or to just sort of angle myself back against casually. I tried both techniques and neither felt right, so I walked across to a table with two shorter, less intimidating chairs.

Nobody looked at me. Almost everyone grabbed coffee to go, and the few people who sat down immediately buried themselves in a newspaper. The woman directly in front of me wore a beautifully cut black suit with shoes that looked as if they would have cost me a month's salary. She pulled an expensive black leather agenda out of an expensive black leather bag, and examined a page carefully. I wondered what kind of job I'd have to get in order to sit at a Starbucks every morning dressed like that.

I realized that school hadn't even started yet. I wondered how the kids would do without me. I hoped the substitute would remember everything I'd told her, that she and June would follow the schedule I'd left. Consistency was so important to preschoolers. I hoped June would be able to handle it if one of the kids melted down because I wasn't there. I hoped everybody missed me.

John Anderson stood at my table, holding two cups of coffee. I hadn't even noticed him standing in line to get them. "Hi, Sarah. Don't you look nice."

"Hi, John. Thanks." I looked down at my purple dress doubtfully. I looked back up at John. He looked too—nice, too, kind of casual business with a black leather coat and a gray silk tie that reminded me of old polished silver.

"Milk and sugar?"

"Yeah. No. I mean, milk, no sugar. I'll get it."

"Please. Allow me. I'll be right back." He put his cup down on the table and walked off with mine. I sneaked another look at him. He looked pretty much like all the other guys in Starbucks. Everybody was well groomed, industrious, more or less good-looking, more or less in shape. As if they all had things to do and places to go and a gym to work out at when they were done.

So why exactly was I here with John Anderson? Was it just that he'd stumbled upon my not-too-personal ad randomly, and left an equally impersonal message in my voice mail box? Was it simply that I happened to call him back? What if he'd left messages for hundreds, maybe thousands, of women, and I was the only one to answer?

John handed me my coffee. "Thanks," I said. "I can only stay for a minute."

He made a face, looked down at himself. "What is it, the tie?"

I smiled. "No, the tie's good."

"You're sure? I've got five or six others in the car if you don't like it."

"What makes you think something's wrong with you?" I really wanted to know. Maybe then I could figure out why I always thought something was wrong with me.

"That's a good question. Maybe it's just a natural first assumption. Then again, it could be all those years of listening to my ex-wife."

"Uh-oh, here we are again. The tales of woe."

"Well, we certainly don't have time for mine this morning." He smiled and I smiled back. "My bad habits alone could take days. Weeks, even." He put his elbow on the table and leaned his chin on his fist. He sighed loudly.

"That many, huh?" I shook my head in mock sympathy. "Okay, just give me one." I took a sip of my coffee and wondered if the people standing in the take-out line thought John and I were a couple.

John looked over both shoulders, then leaned forward and whispered, "You're probably not going to believe this, but I've been accused of being more than a bit of a dork."

"No. You? Oh, my God, you didn't wear the Indiana Jones hat around the house, did you?"

"I'm afraid I did. And with white socks, no less."

I giggled. I couldn't put my finger on exactly what made it so, but John Anderson *was* kind of a dork. A nerd. He could drive a nice car, he could get his hair cut on Newbury Street, he could wear a stylishly distressed leather coat. But he was still the guy who sat next to me in advanced math class in high school and wore mechanical pencils in his shirt pocket and had a crush on me. I wouldn't have wanted anything to do with him back then, partly because if he liked me, there had to be something seriously wrong with him. But also because if he was a nerd and I went out with him, then I'd be a nerd-lover, which was pretty much the same thing as being a nerd, too.

All these years later, I imagined the rules had changed. I couldn't be sure, but John's residual nerdiness seemed more endearing than not. For the rest of the day, as I tried to stay focused on "Preschoolers and Emerging Literacy," my thoughts kept drifting over to John Anderson. I pictured him walking around in the Indiana Jones hat and the white socks. Then I pictured him walking around in the Indiana Jones hat and the white socks and nothing else.

I looked around at the other teachers, by now practically reclining on the padded chairs of the conference room, and wondered if they noticed I was smiling for no apparent reason at all.

12

Michael and Mother Teresa and I were going for a walk. Borrowing Mother Teresa that time had made Michael think to invite me: "The pooch and I come here a lot. It's one of our favorite places."

Always, since we'd grown up and moved out, I talked to Carol and Christine at least once a week. It was different with the boys. Maybe they were more involved with their wives' families, but it seemed as if Johnny was always traveling and Billy Jr., even though he was only a year older than Carol, acted as if he were from another generation. The last time he'd shown up for Sunday dinner at Dad's, he'd worn a gray, button-down sweater and talked about retirement. "I'll be dead and buried before you bring up that subject again, young man," Dad said. "My best advice to you is not to rush the seasons."

I was happy to have something to do, happier still to have a chance to hang out with Michael. We walked around to the back of Michael and Phoebe's Toyota

4Runner, and he opened the back door so Mother Teresa could jump down. THE MARSHBURY MUNICIPAL GOLF COURSE, read a sign at the edge of the parking lot. A smaller sign was tacked below: CLOSED FOR THE SEASON.

Michael put his keys in the pocket of his jeans. We were both wearing sneakers and we set off briskly down a paved road that wound along the side of a fairway. Michael stopped to unhook Mother Teresa's leash and she galloped ahead. At the edge of a pond, we stepped off the blacktop, tromping across a mixture of beach heather and scrub grass, our sneakers sinking into the sandy soil. "What was this place before it was a golf course?" I asked Michael.

He stopped, plucked a golf ball from the base of a small cedar. "Nice one," he said, putting it in his pocket, "practically new. Don't you remember? This was all a big sandpit. We used to sneak in the back way from Edgewater Road, drive right by the NO TRESPASSING signs, go drinking and skinny-dipping right there." He pointed to the charming, tastefully landscaped pond.

"Oh, my God. This was the pond with the shopping carts and car parts at the bottom? Supposedly you'd get polio if you even touched the water with your baby finger, a new kind of polio the vaccine couldn't prevent."

"You didn't believe that, did you?"

"Of course I did."

"That's just what the boys said to get you to make out with them instead of swimming."

I laughed, even though not a single boy had tried to lure me here in high school. I spotted a ball wedged in the crook of a white birch branch, stood on my tiptoes to retrieve it, handed it to Michael.

"Can't keep this one. It's a range ball." He tossed it toward the fairway. Mother Teresa ran after it.

"What's a range ball?"

"It means it belongs to the golf course. For use on the driving range. You can tell by the red stripe around it." Mother Teresa had the range ball in her mouth now. She jerked her head back, threw it up in the air. When it landed, she pounced on it repeatedly, some ancient prey-killing ritual she hadn't quite evolved beyond. The ball disappeared into her mouth again, and she trotted over to Michael, dropping it at his feet.

"Good girl," he said. He picked up the ball, put it into his pocket, patted Mother Teresa on the head. "I'll have to put it back when she's not looking," he whispered. We reached another small paved roadway with two signs. One pointed up a hill and said 9TH HOLE. The other pointed in the opposite direction and read PEBBLE BEACH 3182 MILES.

We headed up a hill that was so steep I imagined golf carts somersaulting backward down it. Michael and I stopped talking to concentrate on looking for balls. It was a special kind of awareness, scanning the area with slightly blurred vision so that a golf ball would suddenly seem to jump out from where it rested in a pile of fallen leaves or a thicket of briars. Our pockets were bulging. "This is so much fun," I said. "It's like an Easter-egg hunt. What do you do with them, save them to golf with in the spring?"

"I don't golf. So I keep them in buckets in the garage."

"Why?"

"I don't know. I just like having them, I guess. Phoebe says it's a sickness. She told me I have to either get rid of them all or go get some help." He grinned at me sadly. "Do you think they have a twelve-step program for golf ball collectors?"

"They must. Why does it matter to Phoebe?"

"I think it's just one more thing for her to dislike about me."

"Cut it out, Michael. Phoebe's crazy about you."

"Yeah, right. I don't think I've done one thing to please her in the last five years."

"Did you try bringing her here?"

"Of course I did. I thought it would be romantic. She hated it, said I was ignoring her to look for balls."

We'd reached the top of the hill. A small green took up nearly all of the available space. A tiny post-and-rail fence was the only protection from a sharp drop, though the fence looked as if it would be more apt to catch you by the shins and propel you forward than save you from a fall. The view was breathtaking—most of Marshbury, it seemed, and the ocean stretched endlessly beyond. "Is that Old Smokey?" I asked, pointing to the huge hill we'd sledded on as kids.

"Yeah. Isn't this the best? If I had to pick one place to stay forever, it'd be right here."

A couple of guys were standing around what I presumed was the ninth hole. Both wore hooded sweatshirts with the front center pocket bulging with bumpy golf balls. The look was part derelict, part J. Crew. One of the men was holding a rusty putter, or maybe it was a driver, and two golf balls rested within a couple of feet of the hole. Two open cans of Bud waited on the ground nearby.

Michael whispered, "They're part of one of the world's last remaining indigenous subcultures. Anthropologists are studying them for clues in the search for the meaning of life."

Mother Teresa, showing admirable speed for a dog her size, grabbed one of the balls in her teeth, and threw it up in the air. It landed on a can of Bud, which fell over sideways with a glugging sound.

"Jesus!" one of the guys yelled.

"That was your beer," the other one said.

"Your ball, though, hotshot."

Michael bent down to stand the beer can up again. "Shit. I'm sorry, guys."

"Rule number one," said the bigger of the two, "never apologize for anything your dog does." He turned to me and glared, leaning on the rusty golf club. "Did he spill my beer?" he asked, gesturing to Michael.

"No." I smiled nervously. It was starting to get dark.

"And it's a damn good thing he didn't!" he practically roared. Then, holding the golf club horizontally with his arms wide apart, he jumped forward over the club and then backward. He finished with a little tap dance of sorts.

"Sarah, this is Mitch," Michael said. "Mitch, my sister Sarah."

As I shook Mitch's hand, the smaller guy reached into his sweatshirt pocket, pulled out three golf balls and started to juggle with circuslike precision. "Balls," he said, taking off his baseball cap and catching them in it one by one. "You can't ever have enough of them."

Michael shook his head. "This is my sister, Sarah, Jeff. Be nice to her, you two."

As I was reaching to shake hands with Jeff, we heard the sounds of an engine straining up the hill. A golden retriever and an Airedale ran by barking, followed by Mother Teresa. Michael grabbed my hand. "Run," he yelled.

I ran.

Michael and I sat in the 4Runner, breathing hard. "I thought you were in good shape," he said.

"I was so scared I forgot to breathe." We laughed. We could hear Mother Teresa panting heavily in the backseat. "What would have happened if we got caught?"

"Seventy-dollar fine for an unleashed dog."

"That's it?"

"Seventy dollars is a lot of money."

"But we wouldn't have gotten arrested for trespassing? That wasn't the police?"

"No. The dog officer. People who come here to jog or walk sometimes call to report the unleashed dogs interfering with their exercise. Assholes." He turned his head to the backseat. "Right, Mother Teresa?"

"I don't think you should teach her words like that, Michael." I started to laugh again. "Oh, my God, that was so much fun. Thank goodness you had a flashlight. I can't believe how fast it got dark. I liked your friends, too, what little I saw of them. Do they live around here?"

"I have no idea. I don't even know their last names. Those aren't the kinds of things we talk about."

"Then what do you talk about?"

"How many balls we found, how we're hitting them, if anybody runs into any assholes. Sorry," he said to Mother Teresa. "Once Jeff, he was the juggler, thought he saw a couple of coyotes out there."

"I'm glad you have people to hang out with, Michael. Do you talk to Billy Jr. and Johnny much?"

"Only when I run into them at Dad's." Michael started the car. "Jesus, it's late. Phoebe's gonna kill me."

We drove quietly for a while and I realized that a part of me hated Phoebe for not appreciating my brother. Michael was sweet and funny and she was lucky to have him. And if she ever said one bad thing about him in front of me, I'd strangle her for him.

When Michael pulled into my driveway, I asked, "Do you think things ever get better between two people, or do they decide what they're willing to put up with?"

"Do you want the happy answer or the sad answer?"

"I don't know. Surprise me."

"Well, what I'd like to believe is that maybe you get to the point where you can see both sides of things. I mean, sometimes Phoebe has a point. I'm really not that interesting and I forget to notice things a lot." He put the 4Runner into park. "But then maybe the other way to look at it is that, other than those couple of faults, I'm a pretty nice guy to have around the house."

I leaned back against the passenger window and looked at Michael. "So what happens?"

"Well, I can't speak for Phoebe, but I know I'll hang in there. Keep trying. I can't even imagine leaving. How could you tell your kids something like that? Or anybody else, I guess. Would you ever have left Kevin? I mean if—"

"If he hadn't left me first? No, I don't think so. I just figured that was the life I picked, so I had to make the most of it. Sometimes I'm not even sure I deserve a new life now. I mean, I blew it, you know. Maybe that was my only chance."

"Where did we get these bad attitudes, do ya think?" asked Michael.

"The nuns?"

"Yeah, that works. Let's blame them." Michael locked his elbows and pushed off on the steering wheel, stretching his arms and shoulders and yawning at the same time. I yawned in response. "Seriously, Sarah. You have chances now, lots of them. Are you getting out to meet people yet? I'm just going to keep bugging you until you say yes."

"I guess so."

"What do you mean, you guess so? It's a yes or a no answer. You're either trying to meet someone or you're not."

"No, I think you can also be trying to try."

Crystal Gale was singing on the radio. Michael turned it up. "I used to think she was singing, 'Dough-nuts make my brown eyes blue.' "

"Don't they? I don't know, Michael. Sometimes I think I'm missing a few of the essential rules." We sat listening to the song, joining in with Michael's version of the chorus, until it was over. "You know that Cree-dence Clearwater song, the one about there's a bad moon on the rise?"

"Yeah, I love that song," Michael agreed.

"Well, I always thought they were singing, 'There's a bathroom on the right.' "

"It's not quite as powerful that way."

"Michael, what if I say to myself, I'm ready, I want to have a whole new wonderful relationship, and then it never happens?"

"So what? So then you're back to square one. And you're there now anyway."

13

"Yellow."

"How can I talk to a man who answers the phone that way?"

"What way?"

"With a color."

"Is that what it sounds like? I thought I sounded like I was in the middle of doing something extremely important when you called."

"What, like naming your crayons?"

"Cute. Very cute."

So what if John Anderson had a few quirks. Everyone had something. At least John didn't bray or snort when he laughed, or I hadn't noticed it yet if he did. And he was fun to talk to. I realized he was waiting for me to say something. "Well," I said. "I just wanted you to know that I'd been giving some thought to our second date, just like I promised. Sorry it took me so long."

"That's okay. I eventually tore myself away from pacing circles around the phone and actually went out a few times. I even went to a networking soiree for singles."

I felt my heart drop to about knee level. "Oh, good," I said. "Good for you." I should have called him back sooner. Instead I'd spent a couple of weeks floundering around in my indecision. Did I like him enough? Would he still like me once he got to know me? If so, what was his problem? And what was mine? Would any relationship I touched go the way of my marriage? Would I bore him to death?

"A friend dragged me there. I didn't want to go. What a bunch of whackos."

I laughed, hoping it sounded believable. I wondered if I was feeling bad because I liked John more than I realized. Or was it because he was so willing to move ahead without me? "So, um, what was it like?"

"Awful. It was at this woman's house in Cambridge. She was probably older than my mother. You know the type. Big house, money so old that you'd never even guess she had any. Tweed skirts with knee-high rubber gardening boots."

"Or a pearl necklace with lace-up oxfords."

"Yeah, that's it. Anyway, she'd sent out invitations to all the single people she knew, roughly between the ages of birth and death, and asked them to bring friends who were single but not romantic possibilities for themselves. It was like being in a twisted version of *A Christmas Carol*, seeing the Ghost of Singles Past, the Ghost of Singles Present, the Ghost of Singles Future. You know, the entire continuum of loneliness. Believe me, it wasn't a pretty sight."

I tried to face the fact that I should probably ask John if he could get me added to the list for her next party. I mean, now that John had moved on without me, what was left? "So what did everybody do?" I asked.

"Drank okay wine. Ate so-so hors d'oeuvres. Checked each other out. Then the hostess made us all sit in a circle and tell something personal about ourselves and what we were looking for. You wouldn't have believed these people."

"What did they say?" Despite my impending depression, I was interested.

"Well, the first couple of people just whined about their ex-spouses."

"Look who's talking," I said before I could stop myself.

Fortunately, John laughed. "I do whine about my ex-spouse, don't I?"

"Well, now that you mention it . . . but finish your story."

"Thanks for pointing that out. I'll work on it. Okay, let's see, the next person talked about conflicted sexuality. The one after that about conflicted geography."

"What?"

"You know, whether he'd be happier on the West Coast."

"Oh, I get it."

"And then, get this, one woman stood up and said a couple of years ago she thought her marriage was over. So she had an affair with another man and suddenly the sex in her marriage had never been so good and the sex with the other guy was pretty good, too, and it was all a bit complicated but seemed to work for her. But then the guy she was having an affair with got sick of waiting for her to leave her husband so he found someone else. But not before he told her husband about the affair. The husband left her. And so, she said, she was grieving them both and hoping to transcend the pain and move forward into a new relationship."

"Wow."

"Yeah. I left before it was my turn. Pretended to go to the bathroom and took off."

"I don't blame you." I was so busy being relieved that he hadn't stayed around to meet someone that at first I didn't realize someone was knocking at my door. "John, someone's at my door."

"Sarah, if you want to hang up, just say so."

"No, someone's really at my door. Can you stay on the line while I see who it is? Nobody ever comes over this late."

"Okay. Don't just open the door, Sarah. Check first."

I couldn't see a thing when I looked out the peephole. The knocking started up again, loud and insistent. I stood on my tiptoes and looked down. Dolly's scalp showed through her hair quite dramatically from this angle.

"Oh, Jesus, it's my father's girlfriend," I whispered into the phone.

"Do you want to call me back?"

There was probably no way to avoid answering the door. I could picture Dolly still knocking the next morning. Maybe that's what my father meant about her not being squirrelly. "No, stay on the line. I'll pretend it's an important phone call and get rid of her fast."

"That's a pretty big stretch." John's voice was tight.

"Oh, God, I'm sorry. I didn't mean it that way. Wait

one second, okay?" I opened the door and took a couple
of quick steps back. "Hi, Dolly. Did you get the boa?"

"Where is he?" Dolly was dressed in a full-length
satiny mauve down coat, the big puffy kind with
stitched rectangles holding the feathers in place. I
wondered if it would have been a jacket on a taller person. Her Ford Fiesta was idling angrily in my driveway. I hoped it meant that this would be a quick visit.

"Where is who?"

"That no-good alley cat of a father of yours. Where
is he?"

"Dad?"

"Don't be cute with me, missy. Of course I mean
'Dad.' " Later I would tell John how much Dolly
looked like Clementine, the Yorkie he had borrowed,
and how I wanted to sink down to the floor and bury
my head between my paws just like Mother Teresa
had.

"I don't have any idea where he is. Did you try him
at home?"

A muffled voice came from the phone in my hand.
"Is that him?" Dolly grabbed the phone from my hand.
"Billy Hurlihy, you no-good, two-timing son of a gun."
She paused, listening. "Well, how was I supposed to
know? She'll have to call you back when things aren't
so busy around here." Dolly pushed a button on the
cordless. Her eyes were like chunks of watery ice.

Dolly handed me my phone. "Find him. Now."

While Dolly turned off her car, I dialed my father's
number. I could almost see him, tilted back in the re-
cliner we all called Dad's, looking at the phone and not
answering. His machine picked up. Frank Sinatra

crooned about his regrets being too few to mention. The music faded and my father, sounding more like Dean Martin than Frank, said, *What's tickin', chicken? Billy Boy's not home right now, so don't bother to beat your gums off time. Just plant your message and I'll dig it later.*

The beep was long and loud. "Hi, Dad, it's Sarah. It's, um, nine seventeen Friday night and Dolly's here. At my house. And, um, she wants me to find you. So pick up the phone, Dad." My voice hit an unexpected high note. I cleared my throat and continued. "Come on, Dad, answer the phone." I forced myself to look at Dolly, who was standing across from me again. "He's a very heavy sleeper. Always has been."

"Tell me another while that one's still warm. Listen, you just inform that good-for-nothin', low-life father of yours that Dolly's staying right here until Daddy comes to pick her up." Releasing a short puff of breath through pursed lips, Dolly took off her coat and hung it over the back of my couch. She crossed her arms over her torpedo-like breasts defiantly, then nodded at me to continue.

"Uh, Dad, Dolly says she's planning to stay here until you come to get her. Dad, if you can hear me, PICK UP RIGHT NOW." I waited. This is the last girlfriend of his I will ever meet, I vowed. "Dolly," I said, "how about if I keep trying to call my father and, in the meantime, you drive over to the house. If he's not there, you can always come back. I'll make tea." I tried to smile convincingly. If I could just get her out the door again, I could lock it and turn out all the lights. Maybe go into my room and hide under the covers for the rest of my life. I mean, it's not like I'd be missing all that much.

"I have news for you, missy. Dolly does not chase men. Never has, never will. I'm going to sit right here until Daddy comes to get me. No ifs, ands or buts." Dolly walked around to the front of the couch and plopped herself down.

I was still holding the phone to my ear, even though my father's answering machine had long since beeped the end of my message. It was hard to know quite what to do next. I took a deep breath, put the receiver down and thought, *Sarah, you are a grown-up.* "Dolly, I'm sorry, but you can't stay. I mean it. This is my house and I want you to leave right now." I waited for her to say something, maybe even to stand up. "I go to bed really early and it's been a long week. Dolly?" I walked around the couch and looked her straight in the eyes.

Dolly looked straight back. "So, go to bed already. Those circles under your eyes aren't doing the rest of your looks much good at all. Daddy and I will lock up when we leave."

I dug deep. "No, I *really* mean it." Pitiful. I dug deeper. "You cannot wait for my father here." I caught myself before I softened it with an apology.

Calmly, Dolly reached for her pocketbook, which looked like a small wicker picnic basket. A scrimshaw oval on top of it read DOLLY. She flipped the latch and reached inside. I was half-expecting her to pull out a gun, maybe a small pearl-handled affair that doubled as a cigarette lighter. I could even feel my heart picking up its pace in anticipation. Instead, Dolly removed a small clear plastic pouch. I watched her shake out what looked like a rain hat, only made of white netting instead of plastic. She draped it over her hair and tied it in a perky bow under her chin. I must have been staring, because she said, "You should try one of these. It'll save your hairdo for an entire extra week." I nodded. Found myself reaching up to smooth my hair.

Meanwhile, Dolly kicked off her shoes, pulled off her knee-high nylons, wiggled her toes. Fluffed up two of the pillows from my couch, slid her puffy coat off the back and drew it over her like a blanket. "You run along now. Don't worry about me. Dolly will be just fine."

Maybe the direct approach wasn't going to work. I would pretend to be docile—not a big stretch—and come up with something when she least expected it. I tiptoed into my kitchen, grabbed the remnants of a bottle of wine from the refrigerator and the cordless phone. Tiptoed on into my room, closed and locked the door behind me.

14

"Carol," I whispered when Carol's answering machine instructed me to please leave a message. "Answer the phone if you're there. Come on, Carol, it's an emergency." I waited for a minute, then hung up softly.

I tried Christine. Four rings and then her machine picked up. "Christine . . ." I whispered. "It's me, Sarah. Pick up. Please." Great. A pattern seemed to be emerging. Why, the rest of the world actually went out on Friday nights.

Michael answered on the second ring. "Mother Teresa! Drop it! It's not a toy! Phoebe, will you get her so I can answer this? Phoebe . . . Hello."

"Michael, it's Sarah."

"Is something wrong with your voice? I can hardly hear you."

"I'm whispering. Dolly's here. In the other room."

"Who?"

"Dolly. Dad's girlfriend. She's trying to find Dad

and Dad isn't answering his phone. And now she says she won't leave my couch until he comes to get her."

"Bummer. Guess you've got your night cut out for you."

"Michael! Listen, you've got to help me. Go get Dad and bring him over here." I was sitting on the edge of my bed, talking as softly as I could.

"Jesus, Sarah. I'm exhausted."

"Come on, Michael. You're my favorite brother."

"Yeah, right. I haven't fallen for that one since I was about six and found out you were using the same line on Billy Jr. and Johnny, too." Michael paused. I waited him out. "Oh, all right. I have to take Mother Teresa out again anyway." I heard a bark in the background as Mother Teresa recognized her name. "*Shh.* Oh, God, I better go before she wakes the kids. You don't want a slightly used dog, do you, Sarah? Listen, I'll walk her and then go over to Dad's. In the meantime, why don't you just ask Dolly to leave?"

"Now why didn't I think of that . . ." I whispered sarcastically, but Michael had already hung up. I pushed the OFF button on my cordless, thought for a minute, then dialed my father's number again. When Frank Sinatra started to belt it out, I joined in with a few regrets of my own. Frank's cheery attitude was really starting to piss me off. My father, instructing me to plant my message, was getting on my nerves, too. I whispered, "Dad, Dolly is on my couch and I'm in my bedroom. She won't know if you pick up. So, Dad, PICK UP THE PHONE RIGHT NOW. Dad, I mean it. Get her out of my house. Now." I thought about telling him that Michael was on his way over, but decided not to tip him off.

And then it occurred to me: what if my father wasn't home? I thought about this for a minute. What if he'd run off with another woman? I wondered how long an unsquirrelly woman like Dolly would stay camped on my couch, and if I'd be responsible for feeding her. I kind of admired her, in a way, from a safe distance, and considered trying to pretend she was giving me a lesson in assertiveness training. I reached for the bottle of wine. I noticed that I had neglected to bring a wine-glass into my bedroom. I looked around for strays. Nothing. I pulled out the cork and took a long slug from the bottle.

Even with the wine for company, there wasn't much to do. I tried calling John back but he didn't answer. I hoped he didn't think I'd hung up on him on purpose. The television was in the other room with Dolly. The book I was reading was in the kitchen and I didn't want to risk disturbing her by leaving my bedroom to go get it. I tried thinking about my life. I knew for certain I didn't want to spend the rest of it alone in my house, where the only company I'd had in eons, besides the Bradys, was my father's crazed girlfriend.

Beyond that, things got a little foggy. I'd spent so much time scrunching my eyes shut, trying to stay numb, telling myself, *Well, this isn't so bad,* that I'd all but forgotten any other way to behave. As painful as it was to think about having to open myself up and actually *feel* again, I couldn't think of any graceful way around it. Maybe I could try to think of dating as an adventure.

I looked at the tape deck. The tape Carol had made was still in it. I let that realization flop around for a few minutes. I thought about John Anderson, wondered if he was already planning his next singles soiree, if he'd stay for the whole thing this time, how long it would be before he met someone else. I wondered how I felt about that. Should I attempt a similar approach, maybe try a few more dates myself? I took a sip of wine. Just a small one in case I had to make it last all night. Watched the tape deck for a while longer. Okay. Just one more, I decided.

Ten twenty-seven P.M. October 26, the ad began. That was almost a month ago, the guy could be married by now. *Um, my name is George. I'm forty-four years old. Five eleven with brown hair and brown eyes. A non-smoker. I'm the divorced father of two great kids. You didn't mention kids in your ad so I hope that doesn't scare you off. They're really good kids, though, and they live with me in Hanover. I'm college-educated, gainfully employed and in reasonably good shape. If you'd like to give me a call, it's area code 781-555-8236. The best time to call is after eight o'clock in the evenings when the kids are in bed.*

I looked at the clock. Ten past nine. What the hell.

Of course, my life being my life, even George from Hanover wasn't home. Some father he was. Before I thought about how desperate it would make me sound, I left a short message. *Hi. My name is Sarah. You answered my personal ad about a month ago. Well, it's Friday night and you're not home, so it could be that mine wasn't the only one you answered. But just in case you're having a lousy date right now, my number is 781-555-7773. I'll probably be up late.*

It seems that when it's Friday night and you're locked alone in your bedroom, listening to just one personal ad response is not all that different from eating potato chips. Okay, just one more, I decided. Nine-nineteen P.M. October 19. This response was even older than George from Hanover's. *Hi. My name is Maxwell. I'm forty-nine years old. I realize that's the upper end of your range, but be assured that I'm distinguished-looking and financially secure. People tell me I look a little like Ernest Hemingway, in part because I have gray hair and a beard, I would assume, but also because I am a true adventurer. Interestingly enough, my personal ad box number is one higher than yours—185. That's 991185 to your 991184. Kismet? Karma? Destiny? Fate? Call me at 508-555-3030 and let's find out.*

I wasn't surprised when Maxwell's machine picked up. How could it be otherwise? "So, Maxwell," I said. "Is your resemblance to Hemingway still running?"

I waited a long beat. "Well, you'd better hurry up and catch it!" I hung up quickly, then laughed uproariously into my pillow. The tears wouldn't stop. Either it was all just so damn funny, or I was spending too much time with the kids at school. Austin Connor had told that old joke the other day at circle time. Except he said it the traditional way—*Is your refrigerator running?* Anyway, the kids all laughed. Kids always know when to laugh. Maybe instead of trying to date, I should just baby-sit on the weekends.

Thinking about Austin made me think about his father. I felt this little kick in the center of my chest. I pictured him in a crisply laundered shirt, with his wayward curls and twisted-tooth grin. Impulsively, I called information and got his number. Looked at the clock. Nine forty-eight. Called him anyway.

When Austin's dad answered, I said, "Sorry to bother you so late, but do you happen to know if all three of Dolly's ex-husbands died and, if so, was it of natural causes?"

"Who is this?" Bob Connor sounded as if he had been sleeping. Maybe he was just otherwise occupied in bed. It had been so long since I'd heard the voice of a man in bed, it was hard to tell.

"Oh, God, I'm sorry. It's Ms. Hurlihy, I mean Sarah Hurlihy. And I'm in the middle of a crisis. Well, a small crisis. It involves one of your neighbors."

"Dolly?"

"Yeah, Dolly. You see, I can't seem to get her to leave my house, and I was thinking you might be able to tell me if she's potentially dangerous."

"You wanna back up and tell me the whole story?"

So I curled up on my unmade bed, pulling the comforter over the tangled sheets and blankets until it covered my legs, and whispered the whole story to Bob Connor. When I finished, he said, "Rumor has it that all three of Dolly's husbands are buried somewhere in the trailer park."

"That's not funny!"

"Sorry. Let me think, what can I do? How about if I come over and convince her to leave?"

"How?"

"I could tell her there's a meeting of the tenants' association or something. It's a bit late, and we don't exactly have a tenants' association, but it could work. . . . Or I could just keep you company until your father shows up."

"All right," I said, though even I knew it could be trouble. Bob Connor was the parent of a child in my class. He'd already made mincemeat of my flagging self-esteem with a casual reference to another woman.

But there was just something so . . . so . . . okay, so *hot* about him.

"Can I please tell you the June story?" Bob Connor asked. "Every time I try, you walk away." Bob and I were sitting on the couch. Dolly had relocated to my kitchen to scramble some of my eggs.

"Your personal life is your business, not mine."

"What an interesting thing to say to a man who's sitting on your couch at ten thirty on a Friday night. At your request. Although, I must say, that's quite the chaperon we have in the other room."

"I have not one iota of interest in what the two of you are doing out there. So take me off your chaperon list," Dolly yelled from the kitchen. "I am here for one reason and one reason only. To make sure that big-talking, double-crossing father of yours knows that I'm on to his shenanigans. The day that Dolly can be snowed by the likes of Billy Hurlihy is the day . . ."

We waited patiently for her to finish. Instead, she let the sentence hover in the air. Bob and I looked at each other, wondering what to say now that we knew Dolly was listening. "So, how about those Patriots," Bob said loudly. "You think they have a chance at the play-offs?"

We could smell that the eggs were done. We listened as a fork jabbed a plate repeatedly. "You hungry?" I whispered. He caught my eyes with his and nodded, and I felt that little jolt again. This was all simply too much for a woman in my weakened condition. I tried to remember sex. I traced it back through two years alone to when I was married to Kevin. And had to admit that the best sex I'd had in the last couple of years of my marriage was with the handheld shower massage turned to pulse while Kevin was out of town on business. I would edge the lip of the bathtub with candles and play soft classical music. It was always great. I knew exactly what I wanted.

"You gonna eat all those eggs, Dolly?" Bob yelled.

"If there's any left, you two just help yourself. After all, it's a free country. But don't think I'm serving you." I started to giggle. Bob picked up a pillow, held it playfully over my mouth. Managed to twist me sideways a little, then started pushing me backward on the couch. I grabbed the pillow from him, hit him over the head with it and jumped to my feet.

"I am absolutely famished, aren't you?" I was so glad I'd changed my clothes before he got there. I was wearing perfectly faded jeans with a soft blue V-necked sweater and I knew I looked good. Not June good, but good. I wondered briefly if I wanted to hear the June story or not.

He reached out a hand. "Help me up?"

I extended my hand to him, then pulled it back just before he touched it. "Right. I'm about to fall for that one. . . ."

"Whaaat?" He widened his big green eyes as he cocked his head to the side. He really had that boyish thing down. It would probably get old after a while, but at the moment it was pretty compelling.

15

Carol never knocks. She doesn't say hi or how's it going, either. She just starts talking as she walks right into my house, as if she's simply picking up where she left off last time.

"Sarah, you remembered to give Dolly the new boa, didn't you?" Carol didn't seem the least bit surprised to see Dolly in my kitchen.

The three of us looked up from our plates of scrambled eggs. Carol and Bob checked each other out. Carol gave Dolly the briefest of hugs, then held out her hand to Bob. "Hi, I'm Sarah's sister, Carol. You must be one of Dolly's sons."

"Or I could be courting your sister," Bob said. "Besides, Dolly would have had to give birth to me when she was three or four years old. If that." Dolly and I both beamed at him. He had a definite talent. Still shaking Carol's hand, he said, "Hi. Bob Connor. A pleasure to meet you."

"Did you answer Sarah's ad?" Shit. Carol seemed bound and determined to ruin this for me.

"What ad?"

I stared hard at Carol. Her psychic abilities were apparently limited. "Oh, nothing," I said in Bob's direction. "I was just trying to sell some old stuff." To Carol, I said quickly, "Bob's son is one of my students." Carol's face showed far more surprise than was necessary. She gave Bob an encouraging smile.

"You haven't seen Dad tonight, have you, Carol?" I asked casually. "Dolly's waiting here for him."

"Gee, no," she answered nonchalantly. "Well, I just stopped by to say hi. Good to see you, Dolly. Nice to meet you, Bob. We'll all have to go out together some night soon. Uh, Sarah, there's something I want to show you. It'll only take a minute, I promise." She turned and walked out of the kitchen.

"So, Dolly," I heard Bob say as I followed Carol. "I've been meaning to ask you, are you wearing that hat in case it rains and there's a leak in the roof? Or just because it looks so damn good on you. . . ."

Carol pulled me into my bedroom. She tucked her chin-length hair behind her ears and nodded her head a few times. "Okay. Michael and that foolish dog are driving around looking for Dad. Christine's at the house, calling every possibility she finds in his address book. It's a longer list than even I would have thought. So, how're you holding up at this end? Oh, by the way . . ." She pointed toward the kitchen. "Not bad."

Carol was in her glory. Ever since we were kids, she loved having a crisis she could be in charge of. "Gee, Carol, you're so good at this stuff. How 'bout if you talk Dolly into going with you?"

"No way. She's yours till we find Dad. Just sit tight and I'll be in touch."

"You don't think anything could have happened to him, do you, Carol?"

"Do you?"

We looked at each other. "Nah," we both said, remembering a lifetime of Dad's escapades. Carol left as abruptly as she'd come. When I returned to the kitchen, I found Dolly washing the dishes, and Bob drying. It was kind of cute, really.

Minutes later, a knock at the door startled us all. Dolly threw her sponge in the sink. "Just let me at him."

Bob grabbed her wrist. "It's Sarah's house, Dolly. She should answer the door."

Dolly patted his cheek with her free hand as she moved past him. "Dolly might give you some real competition for this boyfriend of yours if you don't watch out, missy." As soon as she was out of view, Bob put his dish towel over his mouth and widened his eyes in terror.

"I don't know. I think you and Dolly might make a simply adorable couple. And the older woman/ younger man thing is really in right now. If you'd like, I could leave you two alone for a while."

"Keep that up, Ms. Hurlihy, and you're the one who's going to be left alone with Dolly."

"Oh, please. Anything but that." We smiled at each other.

Somehow, John Anderson's voice was coming from the other room.

"Excuse me, is this Sarah Hurlihy's residence?" John Anderson was asking Dolly.

"It is, it is. Come right on in, honey bunch, and make yourself at home. Let Dolly take your coat." She raised her voice. "Company! Of the male persuasion!"

"John," I said when I finally managed to walk toward the door. "What are you doing here?"

"I was worried. First, someone"—he glanced quickly at Dolly and then back at me—"hung up on me. I waited and waited for you to call back. Finally, I called you. Repeatedly. The line was always busy. I wasn't sure if your phone was off the hook, and I suppose it seems silly now, Sarah, but I was worried about you." He smiled sweetly. I could tell he'd rehearsed this speech during his drive south from Boston. About an hour's drive, I figured.

"But how did you find me?"

"Drove to Marshbury. Found a phone book. When I had the address, I asked directions at a gas station."

Bob made an entrance from the kitchen. He was still holding the dish towel. "You asked directions? I thought real men never ask directions. What's it like?" Bob grinned and moved to stand as close to me as possible. I waited to see if he would pee a circle around me to stake his claim. Instead, he draped an arm across my shoulder and stuck out his other hand to John. "Hi. Bob Connor."

"Oh, I am so sorry, Sarah. I had no idea you'd have . . ." John blushed right to the tips of his ears. He reached for Bob's hand, shook it silently. Bob shook back with extra vigor, clearly enjoying himself.

I stepped out of Bob's one-armed embrace, and walked over to kiss John on the cheek. His light brown hair felt soft and silky against my forehead, slightly damp. He must have taken a quick shower before he left. He was wearing jeans and a deep olive sweater that made him look more handsome than I remembered him. In the reflection of the outside light, his eyes looked almost golden. I noticed that his lower lip was slightly, adorably chapped. "Thanks for coming, John," I said. "What a nice thing to do. Um, come in."

"No. No. As long as you're fine, I'll just be running along. I didn't think you'd have quite so much company. I'll talk to you soon, okay?"

"Really. Come in. Please."

John was holding the doorknob, half in and half out of my doorway. Dolly leaned past him, scanning the street for signs of my father. "Listen, baby cakes," she said to John as she leaned back in. "Make up your mind. You're in or you're out. We can't keep heating the whole outdoors."

Bob Connor and John Anderson sat at either end of my couch. I imagined them as the ingredients that would combine into one perfect guy, not too sweet or too spicy, too coarse or too fine, too risky or too safe. Then I imagined them both split down the middle, lengthwise, with half of John welded together with the opposite half of Bob. Too messy, I decided, not to mention hard to find clothes for.

Dolly maneuvered past the coffee table and Bob's feet and sat down between Bob and John. She untied her bonnet and took it off, pulled both ends to pleat it like a fan. Folded it in half once, then twice more, snapped it into its clear plastic case, put it away in her picnic basket purse. We followed each step as if it would lead us to conversation.

"Be right back," I said, escaping into the kitchen. I

looked around to find something to fix for us, to delay my inevitable return to the other room. I managed to unearth a cardboard box filled with individual servings of instant cocoa. The packets were a little hard. I bent them back and forth a few times until they softened.

I found four mugs, and realized that if a fifth person arrived, we'd have to share. Or use the wedding-present cups and saucers. As I blew potential crumbs out of each mug, I read: FAVORITE TEACHER, I LUV MY TEACHER, TEACH PEACE and VIRGINIA IS FOR LOVERS. I dusted off a tray I found tucked between the stove and a cabinet. Kevin and I used to call it our breakfast-in-bed tray.

"Go fish," Dolly was saying to John as I placed the tray in the center of the coffee table. I sat on the floor, across the coffee table from the couch. Bob scanned the mugs, put his cards down and picked up VIRGINIA IS FOR LOVERS. He took a sip, then pretended to read it for the first time. He opened his eyes wide in an exaggerated look of surprise. "I think it's a sign," he mouthed. He put the mug down, crossed his hands over his heart and pumped them up and down. I rolled my eyes at him, and hoped John hadn't noticed.

"Deal you in, Sarah?" John asked. I couldn't read his expression.

"Sure," I answered. Since playing go fish required only partial concentration, I found my thoughts drifting. Bob picked up his mug again and I wondered why I'd bothered to save it from the trip Kevin and I took to Virginia Beach. Four years ago? Five? It was July, hot and sticky even in coastal Marshbury, and by the time we made it through the ever-changing maze of signs and arrows to Logan Airport, we were ready to kill each other.

Kevin had chosen Virginia Beach. It was his turn. The year before, we'd gone to a small island off the coast of North Carolina. We'd driven in our rental car along U.S. 17 from the tiny Wilmington airport, past clusters of tar paper shacks and rows of tobacco. Isn't this charming? I said. I hope it gets better, he said.

Eventually, we traveled over a narrow causeway to a small paradise called Ocean Isle. We met up with my family at a secluded house at the far end of the sandy white beach. Three stories, two decks, plus a gazebo with a Jacuzzi. Everybody was there—all six brothers and sisters and their spouses, all the nieces and nephews. Mom was still alive then; she'd been sick for so long that we were all temporarily lulled into thinking she'd live forever.

Dad was on his best behavior, content to play poker and Monopoly with his children and grandchildren, to walk to the docks to finagle a deal on more pounds of shrimp than we could ever eat. Kevin was the only one who couldn't settle down. *How far is Myrtle Beach?* he asked. *Isn't there anything to do around here? Anyone want to go for a drive?* Nobody did, and Kevin never really forgave me or my family for that.

The trip to Virginia Beach was Kevin's way of showing me. How to have fun. How to do things right. How not to be with my family. We stayed in a chain hotel near the boardwalk. The public beach was loud and crowded. Kevin rented a surfboard and I tried not to get sunburned while I read, assaulted by boom boxes on all sides. We played strikingly similar games of miniature golf at Shipwreck, Around the World, Jungle Lagoon.

Finally, because Kevin wouldn't go, I traveled by myself to Assateague Island to see the wild ponies. The next day I drove to Newport News to the Mariners' Museum. Bought a miniature gondola and a Chinese sampan to show the kids at school. By the end of the week, Kevin and I had entered a new phase of our marriage. We were polite. We talked only when necessary.

"Sarah, your turn."

"Oh. Sorry." I had drifted away so completely. I wasn't even sure who had spoken. I might not have had many coping skills, but I sure knew how to detach from an uncomfortable situation. I looked at my cards. "John, do you have any sevens?"

The phone rang. Dolly and I both jumped up. She was closer to the hall table I'd placed it on, and I was kind of tired of bailing out my father at this point. So I let her go. I sat back down. Smiled reassuringly at John. Gave equal time to Bob. "So," I said.

"Go fish," John said.

Dolly yelled from just around the corner, "Telephone for Sarah Hurlihy! It's another bo-oy! Heavens to Betsy, girl, you're on a roll!"

16

"I shouldn't have called this late. I'm sorry, I thought you'd live alone. What is it, a boardinghouse?"

Oh, my God, I thought, it must be George from Hanover. Or, worse still, maybe Ernest Hemingway had caller ID. I hadn't factored that in. "Who is this?" I sat down hard on the straight-backed chair beside the little telephone table in the hallway.

"My name is George? You called me earlier? You sounded really depressed, and you said you'd be up late, so . . ."

"Sarah, honey . . ." Bob was leaning over my shoulder, aiming his voice at the telephone receiver. "Are we out of champagne, or is there another bottle in the fridge?" I elbowed him. Hard. He made a loud kissing sound.

"Who was *that*?"

"No one. Listen, things are a little crazy around here. Can I call you back tomorrow?"

Before I could hear George's answer, Mother Teresa

careened around the corner, lapped my face, then grabbed the receiver with her mouth.

"Mother Teresa! Drop it! Right now!" Michael said coming down the hallway right behind her.

"Good girl, Mother Teresa. Give it to me," I said.

"Mother Teresa," John said, coming around the corner with his arms out. "Remember me?"

By the time I got the phone back and wiped away the drool with a paper towel from the kitchen, all that was left of George from Hanover was a dial tone.

All of a sudden, my father stood in the doorway, wearing an old plaid yard jacket over a dress shirt and slacks. It looked like a quick change to me. I tried to remember what he was wearing when he was here earlier tonight. A sweatshirt and sneakers?

"Dolly, my darlin' angel, what kind of trouble have you been causin' these children?" My father was still standing in the doorway, a sign that he was pretty sure it wasn't going to fly.

Dolly had the couch to herself at this point. "Don't hand me any of that darlin' angel jazz, you two-timing gigolo." Michael, Bob, John, Mother Teresa and I were kind of lurking in the hallway behind the couch, not wanting to miss the show, but not wanting to attract Dolly's attention.

"Come on, Dolly, honey. Don't blow your pretty little top. I rode over with Michael just so you could drive me home. You must be beat to the socks and I wouldn't mind piling up a few z's myself." My father smiled his most charming smile, reached out a hand from the doorway.

"Not me. I've just been sitting here all night with nothing to do. I've had nothing *but* rest. Not much chance of you being able to say the same would be my best guess, Mr. Billy Hurlihy."

My father took a few steps toward Dolly. "Nothing like a jealous woman to make a man feel wanted."

"You stay right there."

He kept walking toward her. "Did anyone ever tell you the madder you get, the prettier you look?"

"I'm immune to your sweet talkin'. It'll never work on me again." Dolly picked up her pocketbook from the coffee table. She stood up, handed him her coat. He helped her into it, leaned down to kiss the pinky top of her head. "There is not a blessed thing you can say to convince me you weren't out runnin' around with some floozy tonight."

My father put his arm around Dolly, escorted her through my front door. Looked back over his shoulder as he closed it. Wiggled his eyebrows at us, then winked.

We were all clumped around Mother Teresa. Bob was the only one not scratching some part of her body. "Thanks, Michael. Where'd you find Dad?" I asked from my station behind Mother Teresa's right ear.

"I didn't. He just came home. I told him what was going on and we hopped in my car."

"So where was he?"

"He didn't tell me. I figured Carol would get it out of him later."

Mother Teresa noticed Bob's inattentiveness and leaned forward to nudge him with her nose. He moved back slightly, tucked his hands behind his back.

"Big dog you got there." Nobody said anything. "I'm not exactly a dog lover," he added.

"Dogs always know who loves them," John said. "What a good girl you are, Mother Teresa." He knelt down, picking up the pace on the front of her chest. "Are you planning to show her?" he asked Michael. "I've done a bit of research in that area."

"My wife would like to show her, all right. Show her the door." Michael shrugged. Tonight there was no sign of the crooked smile that reminded me so much of Mom. "Which reminds me . . . Sarah, any chance Mother Teresa could stay with you for the rest of the weekend? Phoebe and I need a break from her. Bad."

"Sure. Want me to follow you home to get her stuff?" I was having a hard time picturing Bob and John actually leaving. It might be easier to just go somewhere myself for a while.

"Uh, as a matter of fact, her stuff is in the car. I was kinda counting on you to understand. Thanks. I'll go get it."

"Need a hand?" asked John. "Does she sleep in a crate?"

Michael stared at him. "Yeah, we use a small U-Haul trailer."

John looked hurt. Michael noticed. "Sorry. No, she sleeps pretty much wherever she chooses. I'll just go get her food and dish and toys. And her other leash in case she eats this one."

Mother Teresa was chewing on a stuffed doggy toy, a pig that squealed every time she bit down. I yawned loudly. "Well, thanks a lot, everybody. I'll talk to you all later." Michael headed toward the door. Neither Bob nor John made a move.

Michael owed me and he knew it. "Okay, guys, on the count of three, we're all leaving."

"I'll call you tomorrow, Sarah." Bob blew me a kiss from the door and walked out with Michael.

John hesitated. Walked back in. I kissed him on the cheek. "Thanks for driving all the way down here, John," I said.

Bob stood in the doorway. "Cheater," he said to John. "Didn't you hear her brother say we were all leaving together?"

When Mother Teresa and I were finally alone, I filled her water bowl and put it on the kitchen floor. Made a place for her with an old blanket at the foot of my bed. Went into the bathroom, washed my face and brushed my teeth. Spent a little extra time putting on moisturizer. Wondered what George from Hanover must be thinking. Wondered if I'd call him back. It had been a long time since I'd had much to wonder about at the end of a day, and I had to admit to myself that it felt pretty good.

When I returned to my bedroom, Mother Teresa was lying on my bed, her head on one of the pillows. I stood beside her, scooped both hands under her furry body and shoved. "Don't even think about it," I said. "That's my side."

17

Mother Teresa and I slept late. We ate a big breakfast, went for a long walk on the beach. I brought a tennis ball, threw it as hard as I could along the rocky expanse of sand. Remembered Billy Jr. and Michael saying to me when we were kids, *If you don't practice, Sarah, you're always gonna throw like a girl.* I practiced, but I still threw like a girl. I never quite grasped that flick-of-the-wrist thing.

Mother Teresa didn't seem to mind. She bounded after the ball again and again, as if each time were her first. Sometimes she brought it back to me; sometimes she let me chase her for it. On the way home from the beach, we stopped at Surfside Variety for a couple of spring waters. I taught her how to drink from the bottle. She was a natural.

We'd been pretty much sitting by the phone ever since. Phoebe called around two. "Thank you so much for taking the dog, Sarah. Can you stay for dinner when you bring her back tomorrow?" *Sorry,* I wanted to say, *I'd really like to. But I've fallen madly in love and I need to spend every waking moment with . . . And, by the way, you'd better start being nice to my brother or else.*

"Thanks, Phoebe. Can I bring anything?"

"John Anderson."

"Oh, my God, you didn't say 'Yellow.' "

"It's one of a couple of habits I'm trying to break."

"I think I kind of miss it." John didn't say anything. I waited to be sure. "Um, I'm just calling to say thank you for last night. It was so nice of you to drive all the way down here. I really appreciate it."

"Not a problem. I was happy to do it."

I waited for John to start chatting. He didn't. "Have you come up with any new anagrams?" I asked.

"Not really."

"Mother Teresa is staying with me this weekend."

"I know."

"She's really fun. We went to the beach. Now we're just kind of hanging around."

"That's nice."

"Are you mad at me?" I asked pitifully.

"Well, if you want to know the truth, last night you didn't seem very date-delayed. . . ."

"It was a-a fluke, a momentary surplus. I mean, Bob Connor lives in Dolly's trailer park and the guy on the phone was someone who answered my ad ages ago and I just called him back because I couldn't get out of my room, and Michael is my brother . . ." Why was I sounding so defensive? Why did I have to explain anything to John Anderson?

"Listen, Sarah, you don't have to explain anything

to me. It might be a good idea to figure it out for yourself, though. Anyway, thanks for calling, but I have to be somewhere in about half an hour."

I hung up without answering. *It might be a good idea to figure it out for yourself, though,* I mimicked silently.

I dialed Bob Connor's number. It rang and rang. No answer, no machine to decide whether or not to leave a message. I called my father, thinking I could kill some time yelling at him for last night. *Billy Boy's not home right now. . . .* I hung up. I tried Lorna. She wasn't home either.

I checked to make sure my answering machine was still plugged in. Pushed the PLAY button even though there was no blinking light. Nothing. Went outside to check the mail. Bills. And an invitation to change my life by changing my credit card. Somehow, I thought it might take more than that.

"We're becoming one-dimensional," I said to Mother Teresa. "We can't spend the rest of our lives waiting for boys to call." She didn't seem to disagree, so we jumped back in the car and wound our way to the Southeast Expressway. "Where should we go?" I asked.

Wanna try Puppy Paradise? I imagined her replying. I confronted the fact that I was not only talking to a dog, but answering for one. Decided it was the least of my problems.

"Great idea, Mother Teresa. Let's do it."

Most of the leaves had fallen off the trees. They rustled around our ankles as we walked a lap around the fenced-in area, giving it a once-over. A large dog jumped up, placed his forepaws on the horizontal bar of the chain-link fence to get a good look at Mother Teresa. "You can do better than that," I whispered. I started to sing, just loud enough for the two of us to hear, that old song about being nothing but a hound dog. Mother Teresa gave me a look not unlike the one Carol would have given me.

"Yeah, I know, Elvis does it better," I admitted. "I'm way off-key." I opened the gate, stood back to let Mother Teresa go in first. She circled around behind me. "Oh, all right. Follow me. But you can't spend your whole life waiting for the other person to go first."

We sat on our old green bench. Slim pickings for humans today, only slightly better for dogs. At least the dogs weren't all half of a couple. The hound came up for a sniff. His owners, a man and a woman nauseatingly clad in matching Boston College sweatshirts, called him from across the length of wood chips. We sat for a few minutes, watching a little fluff-ball cocker spaniel puppy roll around delightedly. Broken bits of leaf clung to its coat.

A gorgeous Newfoundland trudged over to us, black fur glistening, tail wagging. After a few minutes of indecisiveness, Mother Teresa followed him off to the big red plastic tunnel. "Don't do anything I wouldn't do," I whispered. I laughed a little too loudly.

So this is desperate, I thought. Sitting alone, absolutely alone, on a park bench, making crude comments to a dog that doesn't even belong to you. I watched as a nice-looking guy leaned over to say something to the Newfie. I waited and, sure enough, an even nicer-looking woman came around the corner to take his hand.

*   *   *

"Is this George?"

"Who's calling, please?"

"Um, this is Sarah. You called me last night."

"Umm-hmm."

"Listen, George. I'm really sorry about last night. The truth is, I hardly ever have company. I live alone, at least I have since my divorce, but last night my father's girlfriend showed up and wouldn't leave, and then some other, uh, people. And, anyway, you must have a completely inaccurate picture of me at this point." I waited to see if he was still on the line. "George?"

"Umm-hmm."

"So, how old are your kids? I love kids."

"You know, there are a lot of crazy people out there, and I'd like to think you're not one of them, but in the meantime, let's not talk about my kids, okay?"

"All right, I'll let you wear the boa, but you have to promise me you're not going to eat it. Okay?" I wrapped Dolly's original pink feather boa twice around Mother Teresa's neck, and tucked the ends out of the way so she wouldn't be tempted. "Okay, now we have to find something for me." I located the silver mules in my closet, slipped them on. Looked for something to go with them. Settled for a long knitted scarf, light gray with white snowflakes. "I know I'm pushing the season, but the colors are good together." The scarf must have been a wool blend, because it felt scratchy where it touched my skin. I hiked the neck of my cotton T-shirt up a little higher.

I lit some candles, even though it wasn't quite dark

yet. Lay on my back on the bed, closed my eyes and reached over to start the tape. Had to reopen my eyes to find the right button. "Okay, this is it," I said to Mother Teresa. "Let's pick a winner."

Seven thirty-three A.M. October 18. Almost five weeks ago. *Good morning. My name is Lennie. I'm a little nervous on this . . . because you're only the sixth ad I've answered. The other five did not . . . there was no . . . chemistry . . . it didn't pan out . . . obviously. Consequently, if you'd like to give me a call, I'd appreciate hearing from you. I've been a little depressed lately. It would be nice to have someone to talk to. The number is 617-555-1812. Many thanks.*

I scratched Mother Teresa's current favorite place, just above her nose. "I guess I should be a better person, but I barely have enough energy for my own depression."

Ten-forty-one P.M. October 17. *Hi, there, my name is Ben. I'm in my mid-forties, totally toned, very, very fit, handsome, blue eyes, a good complexion, five-foot-seven, about a hundred and ninety pounds, give or take. I'm very captivated by dogs. I'm also into wines, into growing herbs. I make my own sprouts, too. Mostly alfalfa. I'm professional, successful, and I think you'd really like me. So, give me a call. 978-555-9658.* Mother Teresa sighed, burped loudly. "You're absolutely right," I agreed. "We are not, either of us, that desperate."

I pushed the OFF button. Clasped my hands behind my head, and flopped back down to my pillow. Mother Teresa leaned over and lapped my face, sighed again, then tucked her nose between her paws on the other pillow.

I forced myself to a seated position, picked up the

phone again. I dialed Bob's number. I imagined laughing with him about how he'd forgotten to call me. *What is it about you guys,* I might say as if I found it amusing, *that whenever you say you'll call, you never do?* Austin answered on the third ring. I hesitated. Should I ask for his dad? Most likely, he'd tell the whole class on Monday.

"Who is it, Austin?" I heard a female voice say in the background. "Hello?" the voice said into the receiver. I didn't say a word. By the second hello, I was sure it was June. I hung up quietly.

I flopped back down on the bed, synchronized my breathing with Mother Teresa's. We stayed like that for a while, one big gulp of air for me to every four of hers. Twenty-four hours ago I had so much hope, and now I was so discouraged. It certainly hadn't taken me very long to end up back at square one. Maybe it was my fault for wanting things too much. "My whole life," I said to Mother Teresa, "my family has always said don't get your hopes up or you'll jinx everything. I really hate it when they're right."

18

I almost forgot about my Monday morning before-school meeting with Kate Stone. By the time I remembered, three sips into a cup of coffee, it was too late for breakfast. My stomach rumbled as I sat in Kate Stone's office watching her nibble on minuscule pieces of a blueberry muffin she broke off one by one, between sentences. I concentrated, with great difficulty, on what she was saying.

"Let me summarize. You'll keep Irish Step Dance. Reinstate Swing Dance if the teacher gets the final doctor's okay in time. And you'll add Indoor Games Potpourri. And Never Too Young to Cook." She wiped her hands on a paper napkin, picked up a red marker, wrote "Winter Offerings" at the top of a fresh sheet of the pad she used for staff meetings. "We'll open this up at today's meeting to see if there are any takers. Otherwise, I'll leave you to your own devices to come up with instructors. Can do?"

"Can do," I said.

On the way to my classroom, I poked my head into

Lorna's room. "Do you have any food?" I asked. She opened her pocketbook, threw me a Snickers bar.

"Bless you," I said, unwrapping it and biting off at least a third of it.

"Oh, I got the message you called. Several days later, that is, when Mattress Man remembered. I think he thinks that if he doesn't give me my messages, I'll stay home or something." She smiled as if she'd just said something wonderful.

"Do you really think he does that?"

"Probably."

"Doesn't that piss you off?"

"Why?" She folded her hands together and sighed dramatically. "He loves me, he really loves me." Sally Field couldn't have said it better. She picked up her calendar from her desk. "Okay, let's pick a date right now before we get too busy with the holidays."

"I'd appreciate it, Ms. Hurlihy," said Patrice Greene, "if you'd spend some time with the children reinforcing proper respect for one's clothing." Molly's headband was among the missing, and Mrs. Greene had probably paid big bucks for it. "It's confusing for Molly to receive one message at home and a contradictory one at school."

I didn't want to get Molly in trouble by telling her mother that each morning Molly started flinging her accessories around the classroom the moment Mom was out of sight. I wanted to tell Mrs. Greene that Molly was a joyful, carefree child and hadn't she noticed she was cramping her style with all that *stuff*? I ventured a careful step into these waters: "I think she just likes to be comfortable."

Patrice Greene eyed my outfit, a pants and jacket set

that had begun the day as *unstructured,* but was by now downright wrinkly. I loved its bagginess and deep cinnamon color. "Well, wouldn't we all," she said, shrugging her shoulders with the impossibility of making someone who wore lightweight cotton in late fall grasp her standards.

"Hey, Teach, how's things?" I jumped at Bob Connor's voice, composed myself quickly, checked to see if I'd been dismissed by Mrs. Greene. I had. She was attempting to straighten out Molly's tights. They had sagged and twisted so that the crotch was centered just above her right kneecap. *Good luck,* I thought.

"Austin, your dad's here," I called, even though Austin, wearing a big grin just like his father's, was already heading in our direction. I started to walk away, hoping I looked as if I had something else to do.

"So, Sarah, I hear Dolly's cooking your Thanksgiving dinner," Bob said.

"What?"

"I helped her carry the turkey to her car last night. Big sucker. Thirty-two pounds, I think she said."

Why was I always the last to know anything? We couldn't possibly be having Thanksgiving dinner in Dolly's trailer, could we? I wondered if Bob knew, but I certainly wasn't going to give him the satisfaction of asking. "What makes you think I'm spending Thanksgiving with my family?"

"You're not?"

I hesitated. "No."

"Where are you going, then?"

I was aware of a certain tightness working its way out from my neck to my shoulders. "I can't imagine why that would be any concern of yours." June floated over to us, stopped too close to Bob, smiled that spaced-out smile of hers.

"June Bug," Bob said. "How's it going?"

"Nice job, Siobhan. I know I keep saying that, but you really are a good teacher. And the kids really do love you. And now I really will shut up." I leaned my head back against the passenger seat of my Civic. Siobhan drove just barely over the speed limit. She hadn't even pulled over to smoke a cigarette since the first time. What a great kid she was.

Siobhan looked straight ahead. Her hands were on the wheel at ten and four o'clock. "Aunt Sarah, can I move in with you?"

"Oh, Vonny." I hadn't called her Vonny since she was about four. "Honey. Siobhan. Your parents would never let you. They'd miss you too much."

"Yeah, right. I asked my mother last night."

"What'd she say?"

"The exact quote is 'There's the door.' "

"Her feelings were just hurt. She didn't really mean it." At least I hoped Carol didn't mean it. As much as I loved Siobhan, I was having a hard enough time trying to find a life without having to deal with a sixteen-year-old roommate. "You know, the holidays always make everyone more emotional. Just try to get through them and then things will calm down. Teenagers aren't supposed to get along with their parents."

"Whatever." Siobhan pulled into her driveway, put my Civic into park, and started to cry.

I put my arms around her and she leaned her head against my shoulder. "It'll be okay," I said, "but if it gets worse, call me right away."

*   *   *

When Carol called, I was sure it was to talk about Siobhan. She didn't even mention her, though, so neither did I. I was too busy trying to grasp what she was saying instead. "What? You're kidding. That's ridiculous."

"The bottom line is, Sarah, Dad's never going to change. So if we can cover for him until he can let Dolly down gently, what's the harm?"

"Why can't he get rid of her before Thanksgiving?"

"Well, he tried, but she said she'd already bought the turkey."

Oddly, I knew this to be true. "Okay, let me get it straight. We're supposed to keep Dolly busy at *our* house while Dad's having an early dinner *with another woman?*"

"What, you'd rather have Thanksgiving dinner in Dolly's trailer?"

"Carol, why are you pretending those are the only two choices? Why can't we tell Dad to grow up? Why can't we make plans of our own?" I pictured Dolly in our kitchen, touching Mom's dishes. Carol, Christine, Billy, Michael and Johnny all half of a couple, flanked by kids. Even Dolly would be part of a matched set once my father finally showed up. I was speeding into another holiday season, alone, and I wanted to get off the train. "Count me out this year, Carol. I'm going to find something else to do."

"Yeah, yeah, yeah. Like what?"

The only thing I'd done with the Sunday paper so far this week was move it from the driveway to the coffee table. I had just finished a quesadilla I'd managed to make for dinner—a major step forward in the culinary department. I took the last sip of wine and shoved the plate and glass down to the end of the coffee table so I could open the paper.

I wasn't sure exactly what I was looking for, but I started with the travel section because I found it first. The rates to Europe were good. Maybe I could leave Wednesday after school, come back Sunday night. I'd sit at a sidewalk café in Paris sipping something French, less lonely somehow because I couldn't understand what anyone was talking about.

A waiter would approach, not a career waiter, but a waiter on his way to becoming someone famous. Maybe he'd made a couple of independent films and was saving his tips to go to America for his big break. Finding me would be a great connection. The waiter was vaguely dark-eyed and handsome. His English was very good. He'd have to be younger, because if he was still hoping for his big break at my age, he would be fairly pathetic.

Who was I kidding? I didn't even have a passport. How could I possibly go to Paris in two days? I flipped the pages, ended up once again at the personals. *SJF wanted for serious relationship or as sperm donor recipient by healthy SJM. Would like family relationship but in today's world must be practical. Your sexual orientation not an issue if you're a good parent, healthy and raise the child Jewish.* Apparently, I wasn't the only one in the world who couldn't figure out what I wanted. Hmm . . . do I want a serious relationship or do I want to be a sperm donor?

I kept flipping until I came to the South of Boston community events. "Nightlife" (not much). "Museums." "Lectures and Readings." Tucked under "Special Events," I found it.

> *Volunteers wanted to serve Thanksgiving dinner to Cape Cod residents in need. First Parish Church, Route 3 to Route 28S, Falmouth. Noon to four.*

19

Flecks of snow sprinkled the windshield as I headed toward the Cape. I'd checked when I called, and First Parish was a Unitarian church. It was funny that, even though I'd lapsed years ago, I still felt Catholic the moment I stepped inside a Protestant church. There just wasn't enough standing, sitting and kneeling. I missed the fonts of holy water, the genuflecting, all those signs of the cross to make, the stained glass, the priest up on the altar pretending that sip of wine was just part of his job.

Growing up, the nuns taught us we would go to hell forever if we set foot in a Protestant church and then happened to die before we went to confession. They never even mentioned other religions. Anna Doherty asked one day if it was okay to have a friend who was a Protestant. Sister Angeline said only if you didn't go to church with them and were careful to change the subject if they tried to talk you into their religion. "What about bringing them to your church, Sister?" Anna asked.

"Something to be discouraged. They're generally not in a state of grace."

The traffic wasn't bad until right around the exit for Cranberry Crossing in Kingston. I'd just looked off to the right to check out the cedar swamp that ran along the side of the highway. Like a scene from a scary movie, gnarled and twisted trees stood knee-deep in murky water. As kids, we'd scour the swamp for monsters whenever we whizzed past on the way to Old Silver Beach or Plimoth Plantation. "Look!" my father would say. "There's one!" He'd point behind him and the car would swerve and my mother would gasp and grab the wheel.

"*Where*, Dad?" We tried so hard to see those monsters.

"You've gotta be quick," he'd say.

Then he'd floor it until my mother said, "Billy, slow down right this minute. You're going to ruin the whole day." He'd slow down. She'd say, "That's better." He'd speed up. We'd all laugh, including Mom. We knew the routine by heart.

The church hall, painted white to match the church and most of the other buildings in town, had a large, recently paved parking lot. Rather than look for a space closer to the church, I parked in a slot at the empty far end. There was no sign of snow this far south. The air felt more like fall than winter, and I threw my hat and gloves back into my Honda before I locked it.

"Are you here for dinner?" a man asked me just inside the door.

"Uh, no." I looked down, checking to see if my outfit had invited the question.

"Then you must be here to serve. Welcome. The food stations have been filled. This is the volunteer line. Put your coat over there. Then just follow it to the end and hop in."

As I searched for the end of the line, I saw that four Japanese people, three women and a man, sat at the one occupied table. The other dozen round tables, decked out in dark green tablecloths and chrysanthemum-filled vases, looked fresh and inviting. "Yes, come here every year," one of the Japanese women was saying to the tall blond woman refilling her water glass from a pitcher. "Nice custom. Good food."

The volunteer line petered out about three feet before it would have had to double back. I stood on my tiptoes, trying to see the door I'd come through. I felt as if I were standing in a receiving line at a very large wedding, waiting for the guests to arrive. A white-haired man in front of me turned around. "What would you say? Forty people here and thirty-six of them are volunteers?"

"Really? So what do we do?"

"Wait our turn, I guess."

"It'll get busier, won't it?"

"Your guess is as good as mine."

It didn't. We all waited, the buffet people stirring huge stainless-steel chafing dishes, the rest of us shuffling forward a few feet every twenty minutes or so, when a nonvolunteer actually showed up. A couple of families with young children, who ate quickly and left. A few elderly people delivered by the local taxi company, which had donated its services.

"Jennifer, darling, it smells delightful." An old woman, wearing heavy gold jewelry and lipstick that had mostly missed her lips, smiled up at me. A man wearing a Towne Taxi baseball cap supported her elbow with one hand.

"Let me know when you're ready to leave, Mrs. Wallace."

Mrs. Wallace ignored him and reached for my arm. "Jennifer, you look wonderful. Where are the boys? We must sit right down to dinner before it gets cold."

I was more concerned about cutting in line than with the fact that a strange woman was calling me Jennifer. The handful of people ahead of me were twisting to look over their shoulders at us. "Excuse me, Mrs. Wallace," I said in a voice that would carry. "But it's not my turn yet."

"Nonsense, Jennifer. Just call them. The hostess always calls the guests to dinner. Doesn't the table look lovely."

The table did look lovely. I helped Mrs. Wallace into her chair, adjusted the centerpiece, wondered if I should try to borrow some boys. I smiled at her. She smiled back encouragingly so I headed toward the buffet table. I thought about asking one of the buffet servers for some advice along with the two plates they were piling high with turkey and stuffing and mashed potatoes. Excuse me, I might say, but I'm sitting with a woman who thinks I'm Jennifer. Should I encourage this misperception or nip it in the bud?

The servers seemed more interested in the plates they were filling than the psychological condition of their recipients, so I thanked them and returned to the table. Mrs. Wallace solved the problem of the boys for me. "Don't you just love the way the children rush off as soon as they finish eating? And Timmy so loves it when they all conjugate in his bedroom."

"Mmm," I said. I had a clear image of our imaginary children practicing their verbs. *Yo tengo, tu tienes, usted tiene* . . . I watched as Mrs. Wallace, using the tines of her fork, lined up her peas around the outside edge of her plate. It looked like a green pearl necklace. I wanted to make one, too.

One by one, Mrs. Wallace began to squash her peas. I winced as each skin exploded. The insides catapulted across her plate, colliding with the mashed potatoes. So far she hadn't eaten a single bite. Once I got used to her bursting peas, I started in on my own dinner. I set a good example by bringing each forkful directly to my mouth instead of moving the food around creatively on my plate. As children, we'd made igloos with our turkey dinners. We mounded the mashed potatoes and shingled them with carefully cut pieces of turkey. We dribbled the gravy evenly over the entire dwelling, then scraped it off in the shape of doors and windows. Unlike Mrs. Wallace, we piled our peas outside the door. They were our snowball weapons in case we were attacked.

Our parents played along. They would judge our creations, giving us each a different award. Best House in a Blizzard, Most Likely to Be Eaten First. And just before we'd dig in and actually eat, my father would give out a final award. He'd raise his wineglass. We'd know to pick up our glasses of milk in response. "Before we conclude this evening's festivities by eating ourselves out of house and home," he'd say, pausing for a laugh, "I'd like to announce the winner of the Loveliest of the Lovely Love of My Life Perfect Wife award. And the winner is Marjorie Hurlihy, the best gosh darn wife I've had all year."

"She's the only wife you've had all year," we'd yell.

"Criminy. You've got me there."

Mrs. Wallace crossed her knife and fork like tiny swords over her plate. "Now tell me, is Laurence still in transmission?"

I wondered if she was asking about Jennifer's husband or her mechanic. "I think so," I tried.

She shook her head and adjusted her bracelets. Her hands must have been lovely once. Her fingers were still long and tapered, but bent and knotty at the joints instead of smooth and elegant. I wondered if she could still take her rings off. "You've given him more than enough time to find his itch. It's high time you told him to get a job. Trust me on that, Jennifer. A man needs to work to be a man."

"His what?"

"His itch, his raison d'être, the passion in life that helps him come face-to-face with his own morality. None of us lives forever, you know. You've given him more than enough time."

I considered her assessment of my imaginary husband while we finished our slices of pumpkin pie in a companionable silence. The Towne Taxi man walked over to the table. I thought about offering to drive Mrs. Wallace home myself. I really didn't want to see her house, though. I was lonely enough now without thinking that it might be worse someday. "We'd better get going, Mrs. Wallace," the taxi driver said. "I promised your daughter I'd have you there for dessert no later than four."

"You have a daughter nearby?" I asked. I was surprised at how betrayed I felt.

"Yes, of course. You know that. Her name is Jennifer, too."

"Why didn't you have dinner with her?"

"Cornish gay men."

"What?"

"She expects me to eat Cornish gay men. On Thanksgiving. Can you imagine, Jennifer?"

20

Even as an adult, the return ride from anywhere always seemed shorter. I flew over the Bourne Bridge and around the rotary, headed north on Route 3. Driving home when we were kids, Dad always had a beer tucked between his knees. Naragansett or Schlitz, always tall, always a can. When he finished one, he'd hand it over his shoulder to the backseat. Anything connected to Dad was just so glamorous to us that we'd fight over who got to place the empty in the brown paper bag between our feet. "Another dead soldier," we'd say.

The luckiest child got to open a fresh one. I could still feel the click of the tin ring under my finger as I lifted it away from the can, hear the effervescent release as the opening split along its keyhole lines. In those days, the ring would pull completely off the can. I would wear it proudly, and it would grace, and sometimes cut, my fingers.

None of us would ever pass up the one small sip

The Opener was entitled to before passing the can up to Dad. Even though the taste was disgusting, it was also both foreign and familiar, incredibly sophisticated. "Yum," we would say. "Just what the doctor ordered."

"Just eat around the pink parts," Dolly was saying over the whir of the electric carving knife.

"Absolutely not," Carol said. "It's an invitation to salmonella."

"Can I have another roll?" asked one of the kids. Trevor, I thought, but possibly Ian. I turned on the tap in the kitchen, filled a glass with water, drank it. Thought about whether to push open the swinging door to the dining room, or sneak back out and drive to my house. I wondered if I should at least peek in and check on Siobhan. I'd been feeling a little bit guilty that I hadn't invited her to move in with me. I'd be relieved to see she hadn't gone elsewhere, but was safe, if bored, at our dining room table.

"It's not so bad on this side," Dad's voice said optimistically. He took out his electric knife only three times a year, Thanksgiving, Christmas and Easter, and it never failed to put him in a good mood. I could hear him revving the motor now and pictured his big right hand enveloping the harvest-gold handle.

"We simply cannot eat raw meat," said Carol.

"Can't we put it in the microwave?" asked Michael.

"That'll dry it out."

"So what. We have gravy."

"I'm hungry."

"Me, too."

"Well, next time you folks can get your own turkey. Dolly will just go somewhere where she's appreciated."

"Now, now, settle down. Don't get your coconuts all in a bunch. Start sending the rest of the food around the table while I go take care of this bird."

My decision to run away took a moment too long, so my father found me when he walked into the kitchen. "Hi, Dad. Happy Thanksgiving."

"Sarry, my darlin', you're just in time. Possibly even a smidge early. Give me a hug and help me figure out how to feed my family."

Dolly was right behind him. "That's it. I have had it. Dolly wants to go home right now. And don't think you can talk me out of it, Mr. Sweet-Talking Billy Hurlihy."

"Dolly, darlin'. You march back into that dining room and sit your pretty little self down and I'll be in with the bird momentarily. Sarah, why don't you go on in with Dolly?"

Dolly was wearing shiny black slacks and a long-haired pink sweater scattered randomly with rhinestone baubles. She crossed her arms under her chest, and I noticed that two of the jewels landed on the exact points of her breasts. She stamped one tiny foot three times on the scuffed linoleum floor. "Take. Me. Home."

"Dolly, honey. We are all of us about to enjoy Thanksgiving dinner. A blessed time for any family. So you just sit tight until after dessert." My father loaded the platter of turkey into the microwave.

Squinted at the electronic panel, pushed a couple of buttons.

"Fine. If that's the way you're going to be, Dolly will walk home." Dolly picked up her coat from the back of a kitchen chair. She draped it over her bent arms, gave my father a menacing look. The rhinestones stayed in position.

My father tilted his head sideways, shook it back and forth a few times. Ran his fingers through the same clump of white hair that always strayed into his eyes. "Sarah," he said quietly. "Please drive Dolly home."

I backed my Civic out of the driveway. That was it. I had had it. It was one thing to be expected to watch my brother's Saint Bernard so his family could catch up on their sleep, or to know that my sixteen-year-old niece might show up on my doorstep at any moment. It was, however, quite another to be sucked into chauffeuring my father's disagreeable little girlfriend home so he could finish cooking her turkey. And, come to think of it, this was not the first but the second time I'd been stuck baby-sitting Dolly. I imagined myself turning the car around, marching back into my father's house and treating them all to a litany of my complaints. Even though I knew what one of them, probably Carol, would say to me when I finished: *You want a medal or a chest to pin it on?*

I was so involved in my imaginary ranting that Dolly's voice beside me was something of a surprise. "Don't think Dolly's going to let you talk her into going back. So you can just save your breath. Once Dolly makes up her mind, there's simply no changing

it. And you can tell that silver-tongued father of yours
I said so."

I pressed a little harder on the accelerator, didn't say
a word.

"And one more thing you can tell him is that he's
not the only fish in the deep blue sea. Dolly's never
had any problem attracting boyfriends from the
male population." I took a couple of deep breaths,
tried to remember how June looked when she was
meditating. Wished I'd thought to ask her for a few
tips.

"And speaking of which, you're no spring chicken
yourself," Dolly was saying when I pulled my car in
front of her trailer. "You better get busy, girlie, or all
the good ones'll be gone."

"Have a nice day," I said as she climbed out of my
car. I didn't really mean it but figured it didn't count
as a lie because it was already night. A floodlight lit
up as Dolly approached her door, and I noticed that
the turkey wreath had already been replaced. Red
and green spray-painted pinecones encircled a plastic reindeer with a shiny red nose. Rudolf, I presumed.

I had been brought up to think that if I couldn't find
something to like about a person, it was merely a reflection of the smallness of my mind, the coldness of
my heart. Even when I threatened myself with these
accusations, I still couldn't stand Dolly. The best I
could come up with was that the more my father
brought her around, the better the rest of the family
would probably get along, joined as we would be by
our mutual dislike.

I knew it was silly, but before I left, I circled twice

around the trailer park hoping to see Bob Connor. The second time, I pulled just past his trailer, put my car into park, turned off my headlights and stared into his dark, empty windows.

I felt as if I were in high school, on what my friends and I used to call a mission, scouting out a guy one of us had a crush on. We'd drive through his neighborhood, cruise past the place he worked. It was crucial not to get caught. These were fact-finding expeditions only. Parents home after school? Basketball hoop in yard? Afterschool job shift ends at seven thirty? Planning the eventual approach could take months. In retrospect, it was the most fun part.

My heart was beating as it had a couple of decades ago. I felt again the combination of the fear of getting caught and the thrill of invading the personal space of the ordinary boys we'd daydreamed into something more. Now, as then, I was propelled by boredom and loneliness and longing. And the fact that I happened to be in the neighborhood.

Headlights appeared in my rearview mirror. I scrunched down low and waited. The headlights stayed in my mirror. I heard a car door open and close, wondered why the lights were still on. I pretended to search for something on the floor of my car. A sharp knock on the driver's side window made me jump. I banged my head on the steering wheel, swore softly.

"What a nice surprise," Bob Connor mouthed outside my car.

"Hi," I said, rolling down my window. "I just dropped Dolly off as a favor to my father. I was about to drive back."

"With your lights out?"

"My lights are out? Gee, thanks, I didn't even no-tice."

"You might want to start your engine, too." Bob smiled broadly.

21

Why did I say yes? I wondered, as Bob turned the key in his lock. He pushed the door open with one hand, balanced a pile of foil-wrapped packages on the other. I could smell pumpkin pie for sure, maybe apple, too. "After you, Teach."

A small black puppy bounded into sight, barking ferociously in a high-pitched imitation of the dog it would become. It stopped a few feet away from us, hindquarters wagging along with the upturned tail. "A puppy," I said. "Aww. I didn't know you had a puppy." I knelt down to pat it and it licked my hand. Its face was a mass of wrinkles. "Wait a minute. I thought you didn't like dogs."

"I don't. But I'm crazy about puppies."

"What happens when it grows up?"

"I won't let it."

I thought for a moment. "Well, I suppose that's worked pretty well for you so far."

"Why, Ms. Hurlihy, how very witty. Any other assaults on my character before we move along?"

"No, but I do have a question about the puppy. Or, should I say, the other puppy. What *is* it?"

"Pretty much a mutt. A girl mutt named Wrinkles." Bob put his face down to hers, rubbed her ears. The top of Bob's head was inches from where I was patting. I could almost feel his curls against the backs of my fingers, the dark brown strands softer than the coarse grays. "Isn't that right, Wrinkles? And we're both going to ignore Sarah's 'other puppy' comment, aren't we?" He looked back up at me, smiled. I wasn't sure if I wanted to be that close, but I was afraid if I stood up my knees would crack. "The mother was a shar-pei. The father showed up, had his way with her and then took off. A real dog. The state is trying to track him down for child support."

I laughed, stayed where I was, kept patting. "Good, I hope they get him. She looks like a wrinkled black lab to me. That's who I'd go after first, all the good-looking labs in the neighborhood. Where did you get her?"

"She's June's."

I pulled my hand away. The puppy followed it around to my back, started licking it again. "How nice for you both," I said.

"It's payback for watching Austin. June's helped me out a few times."

"I bet." I stood up, coughing to cover the sound of my knees. Wrinkles stretched out across my feet, started sucking the toe of my shoe.

"She's been a good friend, someone to talk to. It gets a little lonely around here sometimes." He looked around the room and I followed his gaze. A solitary sofa was the only substantial piece of furniture in sight. An old green nylon sleeping bag was draped over it, worn plaid arms peeked out on either side. Strategically placed safety pins kept the sleeping bag from sliding off.

"Were you a Boy Scout?"

"Yeah, why?"

"My brothers had the exact same sleeping bags."

Two lawn chairs sat across from the couch. Woven mesh strips in brown and orange were attached to tubular metal frames. A clothesline was tied around the arm of one chair. I followed it to the other end, a dusty paddle fan with plastic blades molded to look like wicker. Socks, T-shirts and underwear were clothespinned to the line. Boxers, I noted. "I hate the Laundromat," Bob said. "Really, really hate it." He picked up Wrinkles, tipped her back in his arms like a baby. "Have a seat. I'll grab us some beer."

I sat in the chair not attached to Bob's underwear. In shorts, this type of chair might leave an imprint on the backs of my thighs. I was glad it was fall and that I was wearing a long skirt. I could see the twin of Dolly's kitchen through a doorway. "I can only stay for a couple of minutes," I said to Bob's back as he reached into the refrigerator.

Bob handed me a Sam Adams. I decided not to say anything about compatible taste in beer. I took a sip, couldn't think of a damn thing to say. Maybe I'd have to mention Sam Adams after all. I looked around the room again. Looked at Bob. Light blue shirt tucked into chinos, sleeves rolled, tie loosened. Casual prep. His aversion for Laundromats must not carry over to dry cleaners. "What exactly do you do for work?" I asked. I couldn't seem to remember from Austin's parent-teacher conference.

"I'm trying to finish my doctoral thesis."

"In what?"

"History. Civil War period. What Austin's mother affectionately calls glorified toy soldier play."

I decided not to touch that one. "What do you do for money?"

"Teach history courses at any college that will have me as an adjunct. And when I'm really broke, I work on my brother's lobster boat."

"And your wife, uh, Austin's mother, does something at a bank?"

"She divides her time equally between making more money than I do and telling me to grow up."

"Oh."

"Listen, Sarah, okay? The story about June is that there is no story about June."

I made my face neutral, reached down to pat Wrinkles. She squeezed between my ankles and watched Bob while I watched her.

"Okay, we had one date."

I put my beer on the speckled linoleum, brought Wrinkles to my lap. She stood up on her hind legs to lick my face.

"But nothing happened. June's a little bit scary, actually. From another planet or something. I couldn't talk to her. Plus, she's just a kid. She's a babe, though. God, that hair. It was the hair that did it. But we're friends now and she and Austin have this mutual love affair going." He reached over to pat Wrinkles, his hand brushing mine. "You're great to talk to, Sarah. You really are."

It was hard to think while sitting this close to Bob. I had to get away for a minute. "Excuse me," I said, handing him the puppy. "But may I please use the bathroom?"

The bathroom in Bob Connor's trailer had a cracked porcelain sink with a ring of shaving cream around the inside of the bowl. Two kinds of toothpaste balanced on top of the rim. Most likely the bubble gum flavor belonged to Austin. A crocodile mug held a big and a little toothbrush, and a pump dispenser of antibacterial soap took up the only other available space on top of the sink. I turned on the water and looked at myself in the small mirror of Bob's medicine cabinet.

There should be a rule someplace that a man who is coming on to a woman must never, ever, under any circumstances, call another woman a babe during the come-on conversation. I checked my face in the mirror for signs of babeness. I mouthed Bob's exact words, etched forever in my brain. *She's a babe, though. God, that hair.* I mean, it's not that I thought I looked like June. I just thought I had other redeeming characteristics. Like a sparkling personality and a good sense of humor. Nice brown eyes. Shiny dark hair with hardly any gray. Hairdressers always told me I had a great head of hair. Maybe not babe hair, but great hair. I had great hair. Bob Connor was an asshole and I had great hair.

That much solved, I left the bathroom. I scooped up Wrinkles for something to do, and just kind of stood there holding the puppy and scratching behind its ears.

It took Bob only two steps to reach me. He placed

his hands over mine. Wrinkles dangled between us. "Sarah, what I'm trying to say is that I made a bad choice. I was attracted to you. Then I got sort of side-tracked by June. But I'm back now."

I slid my hands out, leaving Wrinkles to Bob. "What makes you think I'm still available?" I asked. I was going for a light, flirty tone of voice, but it fell a little flat. *Practice flirting* came to me in Carol's voice, as if she were hiding over my left shoulder and coaching me on technique. Or lack thereof.

"Come on, Sarah. I'm all yours now." Bob's eye contact was intense. My heart was doing a fight-or-flight dance, an up-tempo little number with an occasional extra beat thrown in.

Fortunately, Bob chose that moment to put Wrinkles down on the floor. It was enough time for me to, if not come completely to my senses, at least take a couple of steps back. "You know, Bob," I said from a safer distance, "I don't think this is such a good idea. Austin is a student in my class . . ."

"So we'll be discreet." He closed the distance between us and put a hand under my chin. "Okay, just one little kiss, then promise me you'll think about it?"

It was slightly bigger than a little kiss, but I promised him anyway.

I kept telling myself that Lorna would know what to do. We were splitting a bottle of champagne, not that there was necessarily going to be anything to celebrate, along with an order of lobster ravioli at the Harborview. It seemed particularly festive after my odd Thanksgiving. I couldn't remember the last time I'd missed a holiday dinner with my family, though maybe meeting Mrs. Wallace would inspire me to find my own itch. I thought about Bob Connor and took a sip of champagne. Lorna and I were using one of my gift certificates and Lorna believed it was psychically important to spend gift certificates from parents wantonly and with abandon. "Or is that redundant?" she asked, taking another sip of Moët & Chandon. "Maybe I should say 'frivolously and with abandon.' My point being that it's important to just blow them. Enjoy a little bit of luxury because basically we deserve it."

I didn't tell Lorna about the three other gift certificates I'd thrown away because I wasn't so lucky on their expiration dates. It would be too embarrassing to admit that going out to a restaurant, even when it was paid for, had felt like too much work. "Thanks, Lorna, for meeting me here. Mattress Man didn't mind?"

"Not so you'd notice. He said he'd warm up some leftover turkey. Now, back to you and whatever it is that got you up off your butt and out of your house. Not," she said, wiggling back into the cushiony booth, "that I'm complaining."

"Well, I was just wondering. Do you think it's unprofessional to date someone who's, um, associated with the school?"

"Ooh, ooh, this is gonna be good. Do tell." Lorna actually rubbed her hands together in anticipation.

"Okay, but can we keep it theoretical, you know, not name any names?" I'd spent the drive over working this part out in my mind.

Lorna shook her head vigorously. "Absolutely, unequivocally not. I want the three *D*'s—dirt, dish and details. Not because of any vicarious interest on my part, believe you me, but because it's the only way I can give you accurate, state-of-the-art advice." Lorna paused for a bite of lobster ravioli, washed it down with a sip of champagne.

I took a deep breath. "All right. It's one of the parents."

"Well, that's a relief. I was afraid it might be one of the preschoolers. Come on, Sarah. Tell me."

I giggled as if I were still in junior high. Took a sip of my champagne. "Bob Connor," I whispered.

"Oh, yeah. Curly hair, sort of a flirt, kid who talks a lot?"

I giggled some more. The lobster ravioli was amazing, especially the gingery sauce. "I guess you could describe him that way."

"Is he divorced?"

"Separated."

"What's the wife like? You must have met her at the parent-teacher conference at the beginning of the school year."

"She seems nice, I guess. Pretty with auburn hair. Sort of dressed for success. She has some big job with a bank in Boston."

"Did it seem like there was still chemistry between them?"

"I don't know. It was Bob and his estranged wife and June and me all sitting in kid-sized chairs talking about Austin. It was hard to tell whose chemistry was whose. I was mostly hoping they wouldn't start fighting about who was the best parent."

"Bingo. Just one of several potential problems. Soon-to-be-divorced parents have been known to kiss up to teachers, no pun intended, with ulterior motives."

Lorna paused for a sip of champagne. "Maybe get the poor unsuspecting teacher to say something about what good parents they are, or how the other parent was late picking up their kid one day. And then before you know it, the poor unsuspecting teacher is dragged into a divorce, asked to give a deposition, the whole mess. Then, of course, there's the chance the parents could get back together, or the wife could take it upon herself to tell Kate Stone about her husband's extracurricular activities with her son's poor unsuspecting teacher, or Austin himself could . . ."

I gulped down the rest of my champagne and buried my head in my hands. "Never mind," I mumbled. "It was a stupid idea. Pretend I never said anything."

"I'm not saying forget about him. Just be careful. Maybe dabble a little, but don't put all your eggs in the Bob Connor basket."

Michael was sitting on one of my front steps when I got home from the restaurant. Mother Teresa was sprawled across the step below, her furry body draped across his feet, but he was shivering anyway. "When the fuck did you start locking your door?" he asked.

"Michael, you're the one who's always yelling at me for not locking it." I stepped around the two of them, leaned in to unlock it.

"Well, when the fuck did you start listening to me?"

"Coffee?" I asked. Michael never said "fuck" unless he was drunk.

"Got any beer?"

"Nope. Sorry." I walked straight to the coffeemaker,

put in a fresh filter and started scooping in espresso roast liberally.

Michael sat down in one of my kitchen chairs. He wasn't quite centered on it, but didn't look to be in any immediate danger. He crossed his arms over his chest. His hazel eyes glistened. "Jesus, Sarah, what the fuck am I gonna do?" he asked. A tear rolled down his cheek. Mother Teresa stood up from where she'd settled on the linoleum beside him. She lapped his face. "You big lug," he said. He buried his face in her fur.

I stood waiting for the coffee to brew. In our family, you didn't hug a person who was crying, especially one of the boys. You gave him some space until he stopped. When Michael sat up and wiped his eyes on his sleeve, I handed him a mug of coffee. "You wanna talk about it?" I asked.

"Nope. Maybe later."

"Okay." I waited to see if he'd change his mind.

"What's new with you?" Michael enunciated each word carefully.

I smiled at Michael. Whatever had happened must have been all Phoebe's fault. "Well, I actually went out tonight."

"With a guy?"

"No, with a friend from school. But she was giving me advice about a guy." It couldn't hurt to get a second opinion from Michael. With luck, he wouldn't remember the conversation tomorrow.

Michael sat up straighter. Mother Teresa nudged his hand for a pat. "Advice? Why didn't you ask me for advice? Come on, ask me anything. What the fuck do you want to know?"

"Remember the night Dolly was here? Remember Bob, the guy with the curly dark hair? His son is one of my students."

"What about him?"

"Well." Now I was wishing I'd kept my mouth shut. I mean, what a stupid thing to talk about with your brother. "Let's see, he's getting divorced from his wife, and I was sort of wondering whether I should go out on a date with him."

"Absolutely fucking not."

"Michael, you don't even know him."

"I know his type. He looks good for a while, but ya know, ya can't shine a sneaker."

"Where did you get that?" I asked. Michael was drooping in his chair now, listing a little to the left. I leaned over and grabbed his shoulders and straightened him out. I was starting to think this might be a very short conversation.

"I'm not kidding, Sarah. Stay away from him. He's fucking unreliable. Doesn't know which fucking end is fucking up. Whatever he does, he's always gonna be thinking about his kids."

"Bob Connor only has one kid. Plus, I think it's more likely that he's always going to be thinking about himself."

"No, no, it's your kids you'd never forgive yourself for hurting if you left your wife."

I was about to tell Michael that this was called projecting, but he seemed to have fallen asleep. So much for caffeine. I took away his mug, and sat there wondering if Michael's commitment to Annie and Lainie would help him find a way to fix things with Phoebe. It was the way we grew up, a world where no one

ever doubted that family was the most important
thing. I loved Michael for still thinking that way, and
knew that deep down inside somewhere I probably
did, too.

I picked up the phone and called Phoebe to tell her
he was at my house. "Great," she said. "Keep him."

22

Since neither Lorna nor Michael had exactly jumped up and down and yippeed about me dating Bob Connor, I decided I might have to pursue other options. Though I wasn't completely giving up on him. I was sipping my first coffee of the morning and planning my campaign, when the phone rang. It was George from Hanover. His wife had the kids for the weekend. He'd waited to call me back, he said, because he liked to spend as much time as possible with them when they were home. Had he mentioned that he was the custodial parent? he wondered.

I'd set up a clipboard for my new date possibilities. I found his page and brought it to the top of the pile. I drew one red flag on it, colored it in. "Yes, George, I think you mentioned that." I lifted up George's page, and scanned the list of questions I'd begun working on. "So, tell me, George, what are you looking for?"

"You mean, in terms of companionship?"

"Yes, exactly."

"Well, when I'm with my kids I don't really think about it too much, but when they're gone, it's so damn lonely around here. It'd be nice to have someone to do things with. Maybe dinner. A movie."

I made a star next to the flag. "What kind of food do you like?"

"Just about anything—Northern Italian, Asian, mom-and-pop home cooking."

I added two more stars. "How 'bout your kids? What do they like?"

"What do you mean?"

"Your kids. What kind of food do they like?"

"Why?"

"I was just thinking, if we ever all went out to dinner together, George, it might be nice to bring your kids someplace they'd enjoy." More red flags.

"My kids have been through a lot. I'd rather keep them out of this."

"So you're looking for someone to see when your kids are with your wife?"

"Yes. Exactly. You're so easy to talk to, Sarah."

"And how often are your kids with your wife?"

"One weekend a month. Extra visits on birthdays and holidays."

I started connecting the flags like the ones that flew in long strips at car dealerships and gas stations. "So, George, we're basically talking here about dinner and/or a movie and/or . . . whatever . . . one weekend a month. No strings. No commitments. Am I right, George?"

"Yes, that would be perfect. God, you're great, Sarah. So, how 'bout now? Right now. Are you busy?"

"Actually, George, I'm looking for someone with a

tad more availability. But thanks for calling. And I hope you find the part-time love of your life."

I hung up. This was good. I knew enough to stay away from George from Hanover. Maybe part of finding what you wanted was recognizing what you didn't want. Maybe there was hope for me yet.

A week's worth of newspapers lay piled on my kitchen table. Perhaps "piled" is a bit optimistic. I tended not to notice this sort of untidiness. I'd walk by the amassing stack without registering it, day after day, until suddenly it would catch my eye and I'd think, *Where did that come from?* I made a mental note to look for a guy who was laid back as opposed to fastidious. Either that or someone who liked to do housework.

I dug out the personal ad pages, spreading out the sections on the living room floor so I could see them all at once. Found my clipboard and pen, scissors, glue stick. Sat down cross-legged in the midst of it all and began my search again.

VERY ROMANTIC Southerner visits Massachusetts almost every month for a week. Seeking petite, rambunctious, attentive SWF 25–45 for unconditional fun/romance.

Hmm. Even if I added this guy's availability to George from Hanover's, I'd still come up with too much free time. Not to mention the fact that this romantic Southerner sure sounded married to me. Besides, "petite" and "rambunctious" made me think he was looking for a small terrier instead of a woman.

Maybe I'd ask John to fix him up with Clementine. If he ever called me again.

45-YEAR-OLD CARIBBEAN male, sincere, passionate, animated, fun to be with, seeks plus-sized Woman, any race, good morals.

Well, at least I could eat a lot. "Animated" made me think of Saturday-morning cartoons, though, and all I could picture was a date with the Road Runner or Daffy Duck. Then, again, my morals weren't half bad. I kind of liked that he'd capitalized "Woman," but maybe it was just a typo.

I picked up my pen, drew a plus-sized X across the Caribbean male. Stretched out on my back with my knees bent, did twenty-five crunches to make sure I'd still have abdominal muscles when I found someone it might matter to.

I wandered into the kitchen looking for some chocolate. Just a tiny piece. After all, it was a holiday weekend. The last chunk of a frozen Three Musketeers bar had somehow disappeared. I headed back to the living room, chocolateless.

MY WATERS RUN DEEP. Handsome professor, DWM, 48, brown/green, creative and passionate, fit, funny, analytical, expressive, ethical, complex, "GQ-ish," seeking woman with legs, brains and exceptional depth. Bibliophile.

Well, better than a pedophile, I supposed. Where did these guys come from? Were they trying to be funny? Had they once been ordinary husbands snoring in their armchairs while the TV droned on and on? I'd have to remember to ask Carol. She'd know. I went into the kitchen, poured myself a glass of milk that would have been better with chocolate, drank it all as I walked back to the living room.

> *HOPELESSLY ROMANTIC, old-fashioned gentleman seeks lady friend who enjoys elegant dining, dancing and the slow bloom of affection. Lonely widower of a certain age misses the good ol' days.*

Dad, I thought, *fancy running into you here.* At least he'd dropped the part about loving dogs and long meandering bicycle rides. In a lot of ways, a woman could do worse than finding my father.

Unless, of course, you were his daughter.

When the phone rang, I was so focused on perusing the personals that I almost didn't answer it. I was proud of myself for actually recognizing the irony. There I'd been, scouring the personals for that needle in a haystack, a kind, handsome, funny, charming, *normal* guy. At the very same time, like one of those split-screen scenes in an old movie, an actual man, with at least some of those qualities, had been calling me.

It was John Anderson. I was so happy to hear from him that I invited him down for dinner without stopping to worry about whether it was a date or an almost-date or even if he was still mad at me for what I'd come to think of as Dolly Night. I'd even cook, I offered, hoping I'd remember how. John said he'd stop and pick up fish and wine once he got to Marshbury. I thanked him very much and hung up. Now I only had to run around and clean the house, jump in the shower, find something to wear, and run to the grocery store to buy everything besides the fish and the wine. I looked at the kitchen clock. All in under three hours.

I opened my door to Carol and John, and the incongruity of my sister and my dinner guest standing there together, like a couple, threw me for a minute. John had one brown bag in the crook of his arm, another in the fist of his other hand. Carol carried a plate wrapped in plastic wrap. Leftover Thanksgiving dinner.

Of course, Carol spoke first. "Guess I should have called before I came, but you forgot to pick this up from Dad's fridge." She smiled at John. "Hi. I'm Carol." Still smiling, she turned back to me. "Been busy?"

I took the plate from Carol, introduced her to John. They must have just missed each other on Dolly Night. They followed me inside, and John put his bags on the kitchen counter. "Well, thanks a lot, Carol. I'll see you around," I said.

Carol wasn't budging. Her up-close-and-personal interest in my dating life was getting out of hand. "So, what are you two up to?" she asked John. She turned to me. "And where did you disappear to Thanksgiving night?" You'd think if Carol was going to hang around to watch, she could at least not ask any questions.

I blushed, remembering Bob's kiss, trying to figure out what I was doing standing here with John. Not putting all your eggs in one basket was more complicated than it sounded. "I just came home, Carol, okay? I was tired. And now I'm going to make dinner for my friend John. And if you need any more information, maybe you can fax me a list of questions."

"Like you even have a fax machine." She held out a hand to shake John's. "Well, I can certainly take a hint. Nice to meet you. However briefly."

John held her hand for a minute. "You sure you don't want to stay for a minute? I could pour you a glass of wine . . ."

"No, no, no. I wouldn't think of interrupting." Carol was checking him out as she backed toward the door, and I was happy to see how great he looked. He was wearing well-cut jeans and a nice sweater under a hunter green fleece jacket. He looked freshly shaven, and his thick hair was nicely cut and appealingly tousled. When he smiled at Carol, I could see how much he wanted her to like him.

"Thanks again for the leftovers, Carol," I said, trying to speed things up.

"If Sarah's planning to cook, you might need them as a backup," she said to John.

John and I were waiting for the water to boil to start the rice pilaf. The swordfish was almost marinated. We were sipping our wine, and I was looking into his eyes while he told me what he was like as an adolescent. John's eyes were his best feature, a slightly different tawny shade every time I saw them. I noticed we were both leaning toward each other across the kitchen table, and there was something about the way he said *Sarah* that made me almost like the name.

"I was smart and geeky and every time I tried to talk to a girl she would run screaming in the opposite direction."

"Oh, you poor thing. So when did things get better?"

"Well, once I got into the business world, I found out

that smart and geeky had huge advantages. As far as the girls running in the other direction, I guess I'm still waiting for that to change. Sometimes I feel like I'm two completely different people. At work I'm fully grown up, confident, hardworking." He reached out and rested his hand lightly on mine for a moment. "Practically charismatic." He folded his arms over his chest and we smiled at each other. "But the rest of the time I feel like I'm still sitting in a circle at an eighth-grade spin the bottle game, and all the girls are just praying that when it's their turn, the bottle doesn't point to me."

"Oh, my God, that's exactly how I feel. But I never even got invited to the parties where they played spin the bottle."

John poured a little more wine in his glass, then emptied the rest into my glass. "Maybe we should try some therapy." He rested the bottle on its side between us. "A little regression. We could start with spin the bottle, work our way up to strip poker."

We stared at each other. John Anderson was really starting to grow on me. "Can two people play spin the bottle?" I asked.

"It's called upping the odds, I think."

"Hell's bells, so this is where you've been hiding out," my father said from the doorway. He burst into my kitchen like a rescuing fireman.

"Jesus, Dad. You scared me to death. I live here. Remember." I stood the empty wine bottle up again quickly and gave John a look that I hoped said, *Sorry.*

"That you do, Sarah. Hard to believe my little girl is old enough to have her own place, but that you do.

Anyhoo, your poor old dad only wanted to be sure your turkey dinner made it over in one piece."

"Yeah, Dad, it did. Thanks. Carol just left a little while ago."

My father was sniffing the air. "Well, what's cooking, good-looking? And I mean that question literally." Oddly, he didn't seem to have noticed John sitting at my table.

"Dad, this is John Anderson and we're about to have dinner."

"Billy Hurlihy," my father said as John stood up to shake his hand. "What was that name again?"

"John." John shook vigorously. "It's nice to meet you, Mr. Hurlihy."

"What was it?" My father let go and curved his hand around his ear.

"John," he said a little louder.

"Dad . . ." I said as I turned off the heat under the pan of water.

"What?" my father asked again.

"John!"

"What?" my father yelled in the doddering voice of his father's father.

"PIERRE!" John yelled back.

My father sat down at the table. "You'll do," he said. "Now, sonny boy, how 'bout checking to see if there's another bottle of that fancy-pants wine around anywhere. I could use a wee glass."

The swordfish was completely marinated, and then some, by the time my father left. He didn't even hint around about staying for dinner, so he must have had other plans. I started boiling the water for the rice again, turned on the broiler to preheat it for the fish, took the colander of washed salad greens from the refrigerator. "Sorry about that," I said to John.

"Your father's quite the character."

I was about to tell John what an understatement that was, when we heard a knock. At least Michael didn't barge right in, but waited until I opened the door. "These are for you," he said, handing me a cellophane-wrapped bouquet. "Sorry about last night."

"This is my brother Michael," I said to John, in case the flowers were giving him the wrong idea.

"We met once before. Hi, Michael. John Anderson." John got up from the table once again and they shook hands. I noticed that Michael still looked a little rocky from last night, but he had at least shaved and lost his hangdog expression.

"Thanks for the flowers, Michael. You didn't have to do that." The arrangement looked like something that was probably called "The Harvest Bouquet" at the supermarket. Long-stemmed chrysanthemums with an orange plastic horn of plenty pick stuck in the middle.

"That's okay. I was buying some for Phoebe anyway."

"Do me a favor and go get hers, okay?" Michael ran out to the car and did as I asked him, because that's the kind of guy he is. I unwrapped both bouquets, threw away the cellophane and the picks, cut a couple of inches off the stems so they'd stay fresh longer. Then I found a piece of soft yellow satin ribbon and tied all the flowers together in one impressive bunch. I handed it to Michael. "Here, give her these. You might as well score some real points."

"Are you sure? Well, thanks. And thanks for last

night. And don't worry about Phoebe and me. Everything's going to be hunky-dory again." He said it as if he really wanted to believe it. Other people's denial was so easy to spot. I rarely knew what Michael and Phoebe's fights were about, and when I did hear details, they were trivial things like Michael letting the girls watch too much TV. And they'd make up just as fast, but from where I watched, it was hard not to see that the next fight was just around the corner, and that this had become the rhythm of their lives.

"My sister would never have done that for me," John said when Michael left. "That was sweet, giving your flowers to his wife."

"Bitch," I muttered under my breath.

"What?"

"Nothing. I just don't know what Michael's wife's problem is. It breaks my heart. Michael turns himself inside out trying to be whatever she wants him to be."

"Maybe that's the problem. The doormat syndrome. I've been there—'Just tell me what you want and I'll do it.' " He shook his head.

"Yeah, I guess I have, too, but it's painful to watch." John seemed to have taken over the dinner preparations. He had poured the rice pilaf mix into the boiling water and was now transferring the swordfish to a foil-covered cooking sheet. He seemed comfortable in my kitchen. I wasn't sure what I thought about that. Maybe I liked the idea of playing spin the bottle with him better.

I took a sip of my wine and watched him dry off my wooden salad bowl. He tossed the dish towel back over his shoulder, almost like he was about to burp a baby. It was such a thoroughly domestic gesture, one that made me think of Kevin and the thousands of hours, painful and almost palpable in retrospect, that I'd spent sitting at this very kitchen table silently watching him cook.

I didn't know how I'd missed it before. There was something entirely too familiar here. If I got involved with John, it was probably only a matter of time until I ended up back where I'd been with Kevin. It wouldn't be long before John and I were sitting at this table together night after night after night, our eyes glassy with indifference. I couldn't go back to that.

John and I took turns complimenting the meal. But the evening had gone flat for me, like when you poured yourself a glass of ginger ale from a bottle you'd opened earlier, and with one sip you can tell that the bubbles have all escaped. "Sorry," I said finally.

"For what?"

"For everything. My family. How late we're eating. The fact that it's almost winter. Global warming."

He smiled. "I had fun. Really. Your family's a lot more interesting than mine. My parents eat meals at his-and-her TV tables while they watch their favorite shows and ask each other what just happened. And I hardly ever see my sister."

I stood up and started clearing the table. John stood up, too. "Here, let me help," he said, walking over to the stove and picking up the rice pan.

"No, don't bother. It'll give me something to do later."

"Does that mean we're not going to play spin the bottle?" John asked, the remnants of his adolescent vulnerability all over his face.

I guess I hesitated too long. I made some coffee, and John got ready to leave as soon as we finished drinking it. We kissed each other a little tentatively at the door. Then we hugged for a moment or two; he broke the embrace first. I wasn't sure how that made me feel. My stomach ached but probably it was only my cooking.

23

I tossed and turned. I kneaded my pillow, trying to prod it into a shape that would lull me to sleep. I kicked off the covers, then yanked them back up. I looked over at my clock radio at least a dozen times, surprised again and again at how slowly the digital numbers were changing.

Finally, at 3:12 A.M., I climbed out of bed, unfurled the T-shirt that had worked its way up under my armpits, pulled on the flannel pajama bottoms that lay crumpled on the floor. The floor was cold, so I rooted around in my closet looking for my slippers. The closest thing I could come up with were my silver mules. I clomped my way down the hallway and turned on the light in the bedroom that used to be Kevin's and mine.

The room certainly seemed happier as an office than it had been in its last years as a master bedroom. The shelves that Kevin and I had partially filled with assorted stuff—his golf trophies, knickknacks from our vacations—were now packed with school stuff. Like most teachers, I had more books, games and materials, much of it bought with my own money, than I could ever fit into my classroom. And the bed was gone, thank God. When Kevin didn't want it either, I'd called Goodwill to come take it away. A big, cozy reading chair and a computer-topped desk were the only furniture in the room. A poster of a peace lotus, which I'd bring in soon to give the kids something new to look at, lent a primitive cheerfulness to the walls.

I tried to remember the good times with Kevin. Funny how hard it was to think of any. I know we had them, but maybe the painful memories obscured the happy ones, and they were just too heavy to move out of the way. What I remembered most was that our marriage wasn't fun. We didn't laugh, we didn't talk much, we'd gradually lost contact with our couples friends. We didn't have children, we didn't have pets, we didn't have anything for our marriage to be about. In hindsight, I thought that some of that was Kevin's fault and some of it was mine.

As for what I'd hoped for from my marriage, it was anybody's guess. I was just so relieved to have someone actually want *me*, that I didn't give it much thought. I'd mostly tried not to make any waves.

I reached for a large roll of white paper that I'd bought to make things for my classroom. Once, a few years ago, I'd cut a sheet the length of my largest bulletin board and covered it with drawings of flags from all over the world. Another time I'd cut a life-sized piece for each child. Working on the floor in the center of the classroom, I traced their bodies on the paper and let them draw their own clothes and hair and faces. I'd cut out the shapes when they were done, and taped them in rows, hands overlapping just a bit, all around the classroom. Paper dolls, we'd called it.

I unrolled the paper, cut off a sheet a few inches taller than I was. Pushed the rag rug out of the way, laid out the paper in the empty space. I opened a desk drawer, pulled out my markers. Found a nice shade of tan. I drew the outline of a man, from the back so I could give him a cute little butt. Made the shoulders broad, but not too wide. Gave him a narrow torso, added a bit of a roll just above the hips to make him human. Made his calves bulge a little, like he exercised, but wasn't obsessed with it. Found a brown marker and gave him some hair. A bit long in the back because it was thinning on top. Added some yellow and silver and black because hair color didn't matter.

I squeezed my eyes shut. When I opened them, I saw that, except for the cute butt, the paper figure looked an awful lot like Kevin. I found my scissors, cut him out carefully. Scooped him up under his paper shoulders, and pulled him close to me. His head kept flopping backward, so I creased it slightly until it rested on top of mine.

We danced around our old bedroom the way we had so many times before we made love. Old standards always, slow and romantic. Diana Krall singing "I've Got You Under My Skin" or Eva Cassidy's version of "Cheek to Cheek." My face was wet against the paper Kevin. The marker would probably run and make a big mess. But I kept us dancing anyway, and mourned a marriage that ate up years of my life and never really got off the ground.

After I finished dancing with him, I burned paper

Kevin in my fireplace. The flames licked the edges of
the thin white paper, and he was dust in minutes. I
went back to bed and slept like a newborn.

I woke up eager to start my new life. I probably should
have worn a better outfit, but I couldn't wait another
second. I jumped in the shower, threw on some jeans
that would definitely need to be washed after this
wearing. Added a turtleneck and an old green sweatshirt on top of that. Shook my head upside down while
I aimed the blow dryer in the general direction of my
hair. Left the bathroom without looking in the mirror.
Grabbed a handful of dry Cheerios and a ten-dollar bill
on my way out the door.

I started walking toward Morning Glories. It was
about two miles, and I figured I'd have a blueberry
scone and a cup of coffee, use the bathroom. Then I'd
walk back. After that, things were a little vague.

I swung my arms, picked up my pace, stretching out
my legs until I felt alive. Not many cars were on the
road in Marshbury on the Sunday after Thanksgiving.
But extra cars seemed to be clumped in the driveways
I passed, signs of grown-up children visiting their parents for the weekend. Gold and burgundy chrysanthemums were still clustered outside a few doorways and
tucked into some of the window boxes. By the end of
the week, they'd all be replaced with greenery—pine
and boxwood and spruce. And Marshbury would
twinkle with Christmas lights, most a tasteful white.

A normal-looking man of around forty was handing a
leash to a gray-haired woman holding a cup of coffee.
I noticed as I got closer that he was actually slightly

better-looking than normal. Big mustached smile and lumberjack shoulders. He held up one finger, nodded thanks. Wrinkles, June's puppy that I'd met at Bob Connor's house, was on the other end of the leash. That figured, the guy was probably June's new boyfriend. Just my luck.

I stopped anyway, smiled at the woman, bent down to give Wrinkles a pat. Realized it wasn't Wrinkles. This puppy was bigger, more lab than shar-pei. "What's its name?" I asked the woman.

"Oh, she's not mine. I'm just holding the leash for another customer. I think he said its name is Crackle. Or Crispy. Oh dear, now what was it? Something unusual." She took a sip of her coffee. The puppy stretched out and started licking a spot on the pavement where someone had dropped something. "A nice man. He said he lives down the street. He didn't want to leave the puppy all by herself while he went in because she might be lonely."

She might be lonely. Only a nice, sensitive guy would worry about a puppy being lonely. "He does sound nice. Did he happen to mention if he was married?"

The woman laughed. I blushed. "No, honey, he didn't. But I'll ask him when he comes out if you'd like me to. Are you looking for a boyfriend?"

Oh, God. What was I thinking? It occurred to me that my hair was probably sticking out all over the place. There were grease spots on my sweatshirt and green was definitely not one of my colors. I wasn't even wearing any mascara and now this sweet old woman was going to tell what could very well be the only normal man living in Marshbury that I was looking for a boyfriend.

Amazingly, a plan came to me. A real plan, just like Carol would have come up with. Maybe even better. The first part of it was to run before he saw me looking like this.

24

I circled around to the back of Morning Glories, waited until the coast was clear. I hated to miss the coffee and scone, but maybe I could come back afterward if he didn't live too far away. I followed the man and his puppy at a safe distance, hoping he hadn't been warned about a sloppy woman looking for a boyfriend.

About halfway between my house and Morning Glories, they walked into an old white Victorian that looked as if it had been divided into two apartments. Two mailboxes by the road. Driveway on each side, only one car on his side. No sign of anything feminine, no decorations on the door, no wife leaning out to kiss him while he trilled, like Ricky Ricardo to Lucy, *Honey, I'm home.*

I decided to skip Morning Glories. Too much to do. I jogged the rest of the way home, did some hamstring stretches, alternating my feet on the kitchen counter. Got out the phone book to look up a number. Picked up the phone. "Hi, June. How are you? It's me, Sarah. Just calling to see how your Thanksgiving was."

Dead silence on the other end.

"June. It's Sarah." Still nothing. "Hurlihy."

"Oh, Sarah. Is something wrong?"

"No. Nothing. I, uh, met your puppy the other night. Wrinkles. When Bob Connor was watching her. She's adorable."

"Thanks."

"You should bring her to school one day. The kids would love it."

"Oh. That's why you called. Sure. Just like tell me what day?"

I thought for a minute about how to proceed. "I'd love to take Wrinkles for a walk sometime if you want. I really like puppies."

"Okay."

"How about later today?"

June lived with her parents. Her mother opened the door when I knocked. She had to be a few years older than I was but sure didn't look it. It seemed unfair that June not only got to look like she did now, but probably had decades of good looks ahead of her, too.

"Hi. I'm Sarah Hurlihy. I'm here to see June?" I searched June's mother's face for signs that June had been complaining about me. She smiled without giving me a clue.

June came to the door wearing an old gray sweater over black tights. The sweater was stretched and shapeless and speckled with lint. She looked spectacular. Wrinkles careened into the entryway behind her, upturned tail wagging excitedly. She miscalculated

her speed and crashed into the wall. "Ooh," June and
I said at once. I bent down and let the puppy cover my
face in kisses.

"Thanks, Sarah. This is, like, such a surprise for me.
I've been thinking you didn't even like me or something."

"Oh, I'm sorry, June. I've been preoccupied lately."
My cheeks suddenly felt hot. I'd been blushing a lot
lately. I'd never really thought about hurting June's
feelings. I guess it seemed to me that if you looked like
that, how could anything touch you. "Of course I like
you, June." I mean, that was basically true. I'd just like
her better if she wasn't so gorgeous. "And I'm sorry if
I made you think otherwise."

"That's okay. Want me to come for a walk with you
and Wrinkles?"

Oh, yeah, that might work. I walk by the normal-
looking guy's house with June, and what are my
chances? "Actually, I was hoping to give you a break.
Maybe some time alone. I know how much work puppies are."

June's eyes were already starting to glaze over.
She'd be in deep meditation before I got Wrinkles into
my Civic. "Are you sure?"

"I'm sure. Next time we'll all go. Oh, and by the
way, where did you get Wrinkles?"

"At the Marshbury Animal Shelter. Why?"

"Just wondering."

"Well, will you look at that. It's like seeing double.
What's your puppy's name?"

"Wrinkles. How 'bout yours?"

"Creases." We both laughed. Our eyes met, held.

"You're kidding," he said, looking at me and not the puppies.

"What a coincidence, huh?" If he only knew that Wrinkles and I had been dawdling on the sidewalk near his house for almost an hour in order to arrange it.

"Where did you get her? Him?"

"Her. At the Marshbury Animal Shelter."

"You, too? That's where I got Creases. What an amazingly small world. Creases is a him, by the way. Oh, and my name is Ray Santia."

Ray Santia was definitely a him. Well over six feet tall, nice posture. Shiny brown eyes the same color as his long straight hair and the mustache that half-masked his smile. No beard, but he hadn't shaved the rest of his face recently, either, and the combination of nubby cheeks and scratchy flannel shirt made me want to rub my fingertips from texture to texture. I realized he was waiting for me to say something, felt my cheeks burn with at least the third blush of the day. "Hi. Sarah. Hurlihy."

He offered his hand. I shook it and liked the way it felt, kind of relaxed and amiable. I let go first so he wouldn't think I was the clingy type. I told myself that it wasn't that big a deal to be passing June's puppy off as my own. After Ray Santia and I had bonded, I would be sure to tell him that Wrinkles belonged to a friend. A friend who was overwhelmed by puppy parenthood and needed me to bail her out. Often. Quite often, in fact.

The puppies rolled around together on the lawn in front of Ray Santia's house. They were so alike in looks and style that it was hard to tell where Wrinkles ended and Creases began. I was a bit envious of their quick intimacy.

"Would you like to go get a cup of coffee, Sarah?"

"That would be nice. I'll take Wrinkles home first and meet you . . . where?"

Christmas lights twinkled at three in the afternoon in the evergreen-packed window boxes outside Morning Glories, and antique sleigh bells on a strip of cracked brown leather jingled as I pulled open the heavy door. Spicy smells met me at the threshold. The holidays were so depressingly beautiful.

Ray Santia was sitting at a table talking to my father. "Dad," I said across the button-topped tables. "Dad," I said again before I could stop myself, the word expanding to two syllables. "What are you doing here?" I sneaked a peek at Ray. He was really as handsome as I remembered him from earlier in the day. He looked like an aging Marlboro Man, dark hair and mustache, faded jeans and flannel shirt.

"Sarah, my darlin' daughter. What a delightful surprise, isn't it?" My father pushed his hair back, turned to Ray. "What have I been telling you, son? Is my little girl lovely or is my little girl lovely? Not a reason on God's green earth she hasn't been scooped up again by now." He shook his index finger sternly at Ray. "I'm warning you, though, you'd better move fast. I think you've got some competition. . . ."

"Dad!"

Ray stood up and extended his hand. "Hi, Sarah. Nice to see you again."

Not to be outdone, my father stood up, too. I gave Dad a reluctant hug, rolling my eyes over his shoulder for Ray's benefit. "Okay, Dad. Good-bye. You've done enough."

My father sat down. "I was just telling your new young fella here about the time you made it all the way to finals in your high school cheerleading competition."

"That was Christine, Dad." I looked at Ray. "Sorry, she's already married."

Ray laughed. A nice, direct laugh, right out there for the world to hear. He never would have given me the time of day in high school.

"All set, Billy Boy. One homemade chicken pie baked with extra-special loving care with my very own two hands." A waitress, not much older than me, stood too close to my father as she placed a paper bag in front of him on the table. It was a small table, already crowded. She reached down and smoothed his wandering lock of hair back. I resisted the urge to cover my face with my hands.

By the time my father left, I was ready to pack my bags and move to another state. "What a character," Ray said into the silence left in my father's wake.

"Mmm." How many hundreds of times had I heard my father described that way?

"Are you okay? Come on, he didn't tell me anything. Just that Kevin wasn't on his best day good enough for you."

"Great."

A waitress delivered our coffee. I hadn't quite forgotten the blueberry scone I'd wanted since this morning, but I certainly wasn't going to be the only one ordering food. Ray took a sip of his coffee and looked around Morning Glories, either checking out the decor or the other customers. I waited him out. "So," he said finally, turning back to me.

"So," I repeated. "Um, tell me about yourself."

"Well, I guess I'd have to say I'm your basic under-achiever. Had a lot of potential once but . . ." Ray stared wistfully into his coffee cup.

I took my cue. "What kind of potential?"

"Hockey. At one point everyone was sure I'd play professionally—"

"So what happened?"

"Well, my senior year in high school I had some of-fers from colleges. Nobody big, sort of low-end Divi-sion 1. My parents thought if I prepped for a year, I'd get bigger and better and the top colleges would come knocking. So, I went away to prep school. And, basi-cally, after a year I wasn't any better and everyone had forgotten about me. So I played on a mediocre team at a mediocre college."

"How long ago was that?" I asked gently, thinking it might really matter to this guy whether or not I had been a cheerleader over twenty years ago.

Ray stared at me with brown eyes that were framed by deep, outdoorsy wrinkles. Forgetting that I'd even asked a question, I explored his craggy features with enthusiasm. "Yeah, I know, Sarah. Get over it. Right, that's what you're thinking? But it's not just about the hockey. I think I did the same thing with everything else in my life. I was engaged twice. Well, three times, but once was only for a month. Anyway, each time, perfectly nice girls, women . . ." He slid his watch around on his wrist but kept looking at me. "Well, I couldn't go through with it. I kept thinking, *What if I meet someone better tomorrow?* You know, I'm standing on the altar and the perfect woman walks by and then what do I do?—"

"More coffee?" the waitress asked, interrupting. She poured without waiting for an answer.

"Sorry, I didn't mean to spew out my whole life story," Ray said. Immediately, I felt guilty for not listening more closely. Ray's face was so distracting. I hoped I hadn't missed anything important. "You're just so easy to talk to, Sarah."

"Thanks. And you're easy to listen to. I mean . . . I think that came out wrong."

Ray laughed. "All right. My turn to listen. Tell me about yourself."

We talked through the second cup of coffee, and then Ray walked me to my car. Standing in the mostly deserted parking lot, glittery lights everywhere, he kissed me. It was a kiss that might have meant more kisses down the road. Or it might have been just to keep in practice for when the perfect woman came along.

"I'll call you," he said, holding the door as I got into my car.

25

"Dad is seeing Marlene? She's the one from the Brennan Bake, right? In the sailor suit?"

"Right. You let her brother slip through your fingers."

"He was repulsive."

"He was rich. And single."

I tried to distract Carol from the brother. "What was up with that sailor suit, anyway? I mean, do you think she rented it at a costume shop or had it just been sitting in her closet for a couple of decades?"

"I think it's the frugal Yankee thing where you don't throw clothes out unless they have holes, even though you give catered dinner parties twice a month. She probably thought it was the perfect outfit for a quaint little Irish gathering."

I had to stop myself from bragging to Carol that I was doing just fine in the date department without Marlene's rich brother, who wasn't much of a dresser himself, as I remembered. That if things worked out and he actually called, I'd have a date with Ray Santia. And I was still considering the possibility of dating Bob Connor, though I hadn't heard from him since he asked me to think about it. Maybe he knew I was a slow thinker. And, speaking of slow thinking, then there was John. I'd tucked the details of our dinner into the back corners of my mind, hoping they'd make more sense when I took them out again. Anyway, the last thing I needed was for Carol to meddle in what might actually become a real live social life. I nudged the subject back to Dad. "So when did Marlene come back into the picture?"

"I don't think she was ever out of the picture. I think Dad's been seeing her all along." Carol must have been starting dinner. I heard pans clattering and her voice kept getting louder and softer.

"Does Dolly know?"

"Be serious. He's still alive, isn't he?"

"Do you have any idea what he sees in Dolly?"

"Absolutely. Men like Dad feel safe with a woman like Dolly keeping an eye on them. He can be the charming rogue, and know that she'll catch him before he gets himself into any real trouble."

"Wow. How about Marlene?"

"I think she might give him enough rope to hang himself. You know, all that freedom would make him nervous because he might have to stand on his own two feet for a change."

"What about Mom? Did she watch his every move?"

"Yeah, I think she did, in a quieter way, though. He didn't get away with much for long, that's for sure."

"Mom and Dad really loved each other, didn't they, Carol?"

"Yes," she said. "They did."

"Good. I'm glad—I mean, I always thought so. So, explain it again. What is this invitation we're not allowed to say no to?" Thank goodness for cordless phones. I had mine tucked in the crook of my neck so I could do biceps curls while I talked to Carol. It wouldn't hurt to be relatively buff while I was dating. I dropped to the floor, held the five-pound weights at my chest, did a few crunches. The phone worked its way loose and rolled away.

Carol was too busy talking to notice. ". . . private holiday performance of the Cambridge Symphony Orchestra," she was saying when I put the weights down on the floor and picked up the phone. "For patrons and their guests. Marlene bought out the whole first balcony. She told Dad to bring the entire family and as many friends as we want. So Dad rented a tour bus."

"A tour bus?"

"Yeah, you know Dad. Marlene wouldn't let him pay for the tickets, so he had to make some kind of grand gesture."

"Why not a limo?"

"We'd never fit in one limo, and Dad wanted us all to ride together. He looked into a trolley but decided a bus would be a more luxurious ride. Plus it has bathrooms and we can even watch movies. He also took the catering option so they'll serve beer and wine and appetizers."

It didn't seem worth pointing out that Marshbury was only about an hour's drive from Cambridge. With traffic, maybe an hour and a half. I picked up the weights again and did a few presses, working my triceps this time. I was trying to decide if a bus trip with my family to the symphony could possibly be fun. And if it was too early to invite Ray Santia to come with me. Or, if that didn't work out, to consider inviting Bob Connor.

The kids were seated happily at circle, and I was in such a good mood. I'd accomplished a lot yesterday, the actual meeting of Ray Santia all by myself, the actual drinking of coffee with him, which had led to an actual phone call from him last night inviting me to dinner. After I hung up, I even thought about calling Bob Connor, just to make sure I wasn't putting too many eggs in the Ray Santia basket. Decided I'd had enough excitement and should save something for later. I'd always been that way. When my brothers and sisters had long since finished their Easter or Halloween candy, after gorging away on it for weeks, I'd still have a small stash tucked away for a rainy day.

Now I found the United States, then held the vinyl globe up at shoulder height and moved it slowly in an arc from left to right.

"I can't see," Brittany yelled, standing up.

"You will in a minute," Max Meehan assured her. I smiled at him, turned my head to stare at Brittany until she sat down.

"Today we're going to learn a game from Australia," I said. I handed June the globe, just to prove to both of us that I really did like her. "First let's find Australia." I waited while June hunted.

"It's on the bottom, June," Austin said.

"*Shh*, don't tell her," Molly Greene whispered. Molly had come to school that day dressed for the new season in a white fur jacket with a matching muff. She'd taken off the coat but insisted on wearing the muff, which hung on a white velvet cord around her neck. She'd been filling it with assorted items all morning. A black beaded headband, a couple of crayons, her gold bangle bracelets. Right now she was sliding off her patent leathers and trying to stuff them in too. I pretended not to notice.

"Here it is!" June held the globe up in both hands, flipping her shining glory out of her face with a practiced shake of her head. Molly and Amanda McAlpine both imitated the movement, although Molly's hair flopped back into her eyes and Amanda's was too short to do much of anything.

I gave June a benevolent smile, without even a hint of *What took you so long?* in it. "Australia is a continent where many animals live. Koalas—"

Molly stuck her hand up in the air and yelled, "I have a koala bear!"

Jenny's hand went up. "Not a real koala bear."

"It is too real."

Austin jumped in. "Technically," he began, "koalas aren't bears—"

Molly was still waving her hand in the air. "*Mine* is a bear."

"Technically," Austin said firmly, "koalas are marsupials."

"Shut up, Austin. You're not the boss of knowing everything."

I made a peace sign, our classroom signal to stop talking, stop fighting. "And in Australia there are also kangaroos, kookaburras, dingoes, and emus." The children started to giggle. I picked up the pace. "But all of you have probably seen the most important animal in Australia. Sheep. Australians count on sheep for their wool."

"How do they get the wool off the sheep?"

"With sheep shears. It's just like getting a haircut," I answered.

"Does it hurt?"

"No," I assured them.

"How do you know?"

Good question, I thought. I stood up, walked to the closet, came back with two laundry baskets, two beach balls with cardboard ears glued on them, two Ping-Pong paddles. "You are the sheepdogs," I announced, "and these are the sheep." I held the beach balls up. "And these are the sheep pens," I said, pointing to the laundry baskets. "Your job is to use the paddles to get the sheep to their pens."

"We get to hit the sheep?" Jack Kaplan asked.

"No, we just pretend we're going to if they won't get in," Austin answered.

I'd have to rethink this game later, but right now I just wanted to finish it so that we could move on to snack. June and I put the kids in two lines, let them take turns whacking the sheep into their pens. I was so grateful that June didn't utter a word of reproach about the game's shortcomings that I actually invited her to the symphony with my family. I even said she could bring a date if she wanted to.

"That is just so nice, Sarah. Of course I'll come. I don't really have a boyfriend right now, but maybe I'll think of someone."

I was eating tuna from a can. Dolphin-safe, extra-fancy solid white meat tuna. I'd drained it in the kitchen sink, poured some bottled lemon juice over it, swirled it around for a while, then drained it again. I put a dollop of mayonnaise on a paper plate, grabbed a plastic fork. I found paper towels, tore off two rectangles and tucked them under the plate. I managed to get a glass of milk into the hand that was holding the can of tuna. I carried everything into the living room.

Carefully, I arranged it all on the coffee table, leaving space in the center to stretch out my feet. I turned on the TV. Perfect timing, the opening photos of the Brady Bunch were still flashing while everyone sang about the way they all became the Brady Bunch. I speared a chunk of tuna, dipped it in the mayonnaise. The lemon juice gave it just the right tang, kept it from tasting too fishy.

Jan Brady was jealous because her older sister Marcia had so many boyfriends. Well, I could certainly relate to that. Except it was worse for me when I was Jan's age because it was my *younger* sister who had all the boyfriends. Christine was as softly feminine as I was gawky and angular, as irresistible as I was resistible. She was two years behind me in school but light-years ahead of me in the date department.

I caught another lump of tuna, gave it a generous dunk in the mayo. Jan Brady couldn't take it anymore. I watched her invent an imaginary boyfriend, George Glass. Then she asked the operator to check their line so she could pretend it was a call from George. This seemed to work pretty well. I wish I'd thought of it.

I remembered that the worst part was that boys were always talking to me to get to Christine. They'd sidle up to me after math or English or out at the lockers. No matter how many times it happened, I always felt a small flutter of hope in my chest when a cute guy like Timmy Stack or Jackie Gordon approached. It could be me they wanted. Couldn't it? And then the kick, like Charlie Brown and the football, that landed a couple of inches below my rib cage, in my exact center. *Does Christine have a date for the dance? Just curious, do you think Christine would go out with me?*

Hi, George. Sure, I can talk. It's so sweet of you to call, George. Poor Jan Brady. I pierced some more tuna, felt Jan's pain, her heartbreaking attempt to invent a shred of romance that Marcia couldn't touch. My eyes teared up, so I ditched the tuna, gulped down some milk to distract myself. Oh, no. Mrs. Brady was deciding to invite George to Jan's birthday party to surprise her. The Brady kids agreed to help track him down. Jesus, why couldn't they just stay out of it, leave poor Jan alone.

When she noticed I was seriously date-delayed, Christine started trying to fix me up. She offered me her hand-me-downs, "good kids" who weren't quite up to her standards. Big sister Carol jumped right in. I'd get a phone call from a boy and I'd want to ask, okay, which one of my sisters made you call?

It's a mystery. There's no George in Jan's class.

No George in the entire school.

No George in this part of town.

And, of course, the Brady Bunch being the Brady Bunch, they got to the bottom of it by the end of the half hour. Why can't Jan find a real boyfriend? They put their heads together to problem-solve. Decided to go out and do a little investigating. Long story short, it turned out the boys all did like her, just thought she was a real *good guy. A swell guy.* And so Mrs. Brady dressed her in a light blue dropped-waist dress with a white satin bow. Put a matching satin ribbon in her long blond hair. *You make a great-looking girl*, the neighborhood boys agreed, falling in love with her at last.

I sighed, glancing down at my nubby sweatpants with the baggy knees. Before long, I'd have such a busy life that I'd almost never get to sit around by myself looking like this. I probably wouldn't even have much time for *The Brady Bunch*.

26

It was going to be an important day, so I washed my hair twice. Instead of rinsing off the conditioner immediately the way I usually did, I left it on long enough for it to accomplish something. I made good use of the extra time by shaving my legs while I waited. When I was married, I had shaved my legs on a regular basis. I didn't miss it.

I'd woken up this morning feeling great. It was more than having a date. I couldn't wait to get out in the fresh air, to see the kids at school. I turned off the water, climbed out of the shower, wrapped a towel around my hair. Dried myself with another towel while I tried to decide whether this was a permanent change in my disposition or maybe just a temporary aberration. Or if my days had a sneaky little tendency to start strong, then go quickly downhill. Hard to tell.

I applied a thick coating of moisturizer to my entire body. I looked at myself in the full-length mirror on the back of the bathroom door, while I waited for my skin to absorb it. I looked like a snowperson, my body encased in white cream. Apparently, it was not possible to make up for lost moisturizing. I rubbed the surplus off with a towel, checked myself out again. Not bad. I mean, not great, but not bad either. I still had a fairly decent waistline, unlike those of my sisters, which had mutated with repeated pregnancies. My breasts were not quite as chipper as they'd been at twenty but, again, not bad.

"You're a catch, Sarah, an absolute catch," I said to my reflection. "And if that doesn't get 'em, there's always your scintillating conversation." I congratulated myself on actually making it to a second date with Ray Santia. Whatever I wore would have to go through a Tuesday at school first, because the final afterschool jewelry-making class was today and I wouldn't have time to go home and change before I met him.

I dropped both towels on the bathroom floor, hurried to my bedroom. Found a comfy black jacket and matching pants I could bend in at school, threw them on over a black top. Boring. So I grabbed a pink chiffon scarf to dress it up, gnawed at the plastic thread that attached the tags. The scarf had been hanging in my closet, unworn, for well over a year. I reached back in and grabbed another virgin scarf, black splashed with jeweled shades of red and green, flecks of gold. I'd switch scarves for dinner with Ray. I'd seen it done on TV—outfits turned into other outfits with just the right accessory.

Austin came to circle gripping a toy mouse tightly with both hands. Before I could remind him that toys from home needed to spend the school day zipped into their owners' backpacks, Austin said, "Topo Grigio is my new friend. He's still adjusting. Can he stay with me until he doesn't feel anxious? He gets a stomachache."

"Isn't that Topo *Gigio?*" I asked, stalling so I could think. I was having a hard time focusing today. I wondered if I was up to negotiating with Austin. I could feel the other children waiting to see what I would do.

"No, Topo Gigio was in *Pinocchio.* This is Topo *Grigio.*"

"Topo Gigio wasn't in *Pinocchio,* honey. He was the little Italian mouse on *The Ed Sullivan Show.*" I remembered him vividly from those Sunday nights of my childhood. I loved Topo Gigio, attempted week after week to figure out if he was magical or mechanical. I tried to see a key sticking out of his back or strings rising above him on the snowy TV screen. I also loved Señor Wences and his talking box. "S'all right?" "S'all right!" Those were the days, curled up with both parents and my brothers and sisters and our weekly ration of Jiffy Pop and root beer Fizzies.

"Then who was in *Pinocchio?*" Austin's face was all scrunched up as if he were trying to remember back to decades before he was born.

"Geppetto?" I tried, then immediately thought Jiminy Cricket might have been the better answer.

"Are they, like, related?" June asked. She'd been speaking up more often at group since I started being nice to her.

"Who?" I asked.

"Any of them."

"No, silly." Austin hugged the mouse in to his chest. "But two of them are both mouses."

I fought for direction. Took another look at Austin's

mouse. It was crocheted, dark gray yarn edged with white. Somehow the tail curled downward in a long spiral. I wondered if there was a special crochet stitch for that or if it was done afterward. Maybe you sprayed the tail with starch and wrapped it around a pencil until it dried. My mother would have known.

"Would you like to tell us about your mouse, Austin?"

Austin smiled. "Yeah, look. Topo Grigio has stuff underneath to clean your toilet. Wanna see?" Austin pulled off the top half of the mouse, uncovering a white cylinder. He leaned over and placed it on the floor in front of me. A powdery cloud arose from the holes at the top, then settled noticeably on my black slacks. I tried to brush it off. It smudged.

Dolly, I thought.

"Dolly gave Topo *Grigio* to me because my father listened to all her boyfriend stories. Dolly said she likes to give presents to big, strong men like us. And we shouldn't worry about letting any cats out of their bags."

Austin was still talking. "Dolly said my father did her a big favor by helping her figure out how to handle that smooth operator Billy Hurlihy." He paused, took a deep breath. "Ms. Hurlihy?"

"Yes?"

"Are you, like, related?" he asked.

By the time the food arrived, I knew Ray Santia had great hands. First, there was a light touch on my forearm when we met in the parking lot of Oceana. We walked toward the restaurant and I held my pocketbook in front of the smear on my right thigh. I'd tried washing off the powder from Topo Grigio's canister, but that seemed to have only activated the bleaching agent. I'd have to call Carol to find out if there was any hope for my pants.

Next came a slight pressure on my back with one hand as he opened the restaurant door with the other. A breezy palm on my shoulder as we followed the hostess to our table. And the lightest graze of my collarbone as he helped me off with my jacket.

I was a goner.

Ray Santia was wearing another flannel shirt. Deep red plaid, probably wool. I wondered if it felt scratchy around his neck, or if it was lined with a slippery, satiny fabric. The waitress was pretty, but Ray didn't seem to notice. He kept looking into my eyes as she placed the salmon in front of me, the haddock in front of him. We smiled at each other and switched plates. "Oh, sorry," the waitress said. We ignored her.

"Nice scarf."

"Thanks." I looked down, saw pink chiffon, realized I'd forgotten to change it after school. So much for fashion versatility.

"Pink's a great color on you." Ray rubbed his hand back and forth over the stubble on his right cheek. I imagined the way it would feel under my fingertips, against one of my own cheeks.

"Thanks." I turned my attention to the way his mustache curled under at the bottom. I wasn't really crazy about mustaches, but on Ray it worked.

I held my own during our conversation, which was peppered with Ray's touches. Soft grazing of the back of my hand, firm pressure on my forearm. I actually remembered that I was a teacher, and said so, and even managed to tell a couple of cute kid stories. I added my reading and long walks to his interests in softball and basketball. I followed his one brother with my five siblings. His parents both alive and safely out of the way in the Midwest led to my father probably lurking outside the restaurant to tell Ray one more time what a catch I was.

When the conversation dwindled, I used the lag time to practice my smile. During breaks, I managed to finish my dinner without dunking a corner of my pink scarf in the tartar sauce, which I knew would make it less flattering. The firm and constant pressure of Ray's knee against mine didn't make it any easier.

I balanced my fork and knife carefully on my plate, folded my hands on the edge of the table, smiled again. Ray reached across the table, placed both hands on top of mine. "So how about let's get the sex part out of the way so we can get on with the rest of this relationship?"

"Okay," I said, or at least I think it was me.

Incongruously, I heard my mother correcting me. "I," she said. "It was I." Growing up, she always corrected us when we answered the phone.

May I please speak to Sarah? Or Christine. Or Michael.

This is her, we'd say. Or him.

She! He! Hands on her hips, my mother would await our revisions. *This is s/he,* we'd mumble into the receiver.

What was my problem? I was married and divorced and hadn't lived with my parents in years. But when my live father wasn't meddling in my life, my dead mother was correcting my grammar.

Fortunately, Ray didn't seem to notice my flashback. He scarfed down the rest of his meal, then reached across the table to hold my hand again. He ordered espresso for two without checking in with me. Great, I'd be a wide-awake consenting adult.

Now why exactly had I said yes? I wondered, as I followed Ray Santia to his house. Flecks of snow twitched in my headlights, but not enough of them for a snow cancellation. It would make a good announcement, though: *Attention, all sex has been canceled due to inclement weather.*

I tried not to think. Then I tried to think. They felt pretty much the same. Okay, maybe I was exaggerating, but it felt like I was beginning a sex spree of sorts. A mild one, but it was quite possible that was how it always started. Probably I'd end up on morning television someday, talking about how I became sex-addicted. It all started innocently enough, I'd insist.

I parked my Honda a discreet distance behind Ray's Toyota. Several compelling questions emerged from my confusion and whirled around in close proximity to my brain. First and foremost, what the hell was I doing? Several other questions, no less pressing, followed quickly. Did adults often sleep together on the first date? Was there an age limit for being a slut?

I walked toward Ray's house as slowly as I could.

"Creases!"

"Pardon me?"

I hadn't even heard the yipping behind the bathroom door. Ray's hands had been working their magic. I'd held up my end by rubbing my hands along Ray's back, around those great shoulders, down along his considerable biceps. Wool, just as I suspected, I thought as his rough shirt scratched my palms. We'd had a long kiss in the hallway, another one in the first room we came to, the kitchen. At that point, Ray lifted me up onto the edge of the kitchen counter, ostensibly to find a new kissing angle. There was a bit of a Tarzanic quality to his hoist, but since he'd refrained from beating his chest afterward, I decided it was more endearing than not.

He stopped to listen, midkiss. "Creases. I gotta get Creases. Stay right here."

I sat on the counter, pointing and flexing my feet for something to do, while Ray went to rescue the puppy. "Forgot all about you, little fellow, didn't I," he crooned, passing me without a glance. I sat, marooned on Ray's kitchen counter, while he took Creases outside to pee. Maybe they both peed, standing side by side, male bonding. I thought about jumping down, but then Ray might have to lift me up all over again. Twice might seem redundant.

Eventually, Ray and Creases walked by me again, then disappeared once more. I waited, listening to the opening and closing of doors, which escalated into the banging of a cabinet or two. "You don't have any condoms, do you?" Ray yelled from somewhere deep in the house.

I slid off the counter and tiptoed out the door.

I stared at the roughened red patch on my chin in my bathroom mirror. A beard burn, Kevin and I called it back in the days when he still bothered to kiss me but not always to shave first.

I opened the medicine cabinet. No condoms. Kevin always said they were like taking a shower wearing a raincoat. Part of my horror when I found out about Nikki was that I knew, absolutely knew, he hadn't worn one with her either. Hadn't cared enough to keep me safe. Oh, the amazing rage I felt toward Kevin while I awaited the results of my blood test. And the odd, quick flash of disappointment when it came back negative, and I didn't have a terminal disease to throw in his face along with his infidelity.

I heard a ring from wherever I'd left my cordless phone. Then two, three. The machine picked up on four. My plastic diaphragm case hadn't moved an inch on the shelf from where I'd left it last time I used it. I held it in the palm of one hand, opened it with the other. Careful as always, I held the circle of rubber up to the light to check for holes that might admit wayward sperm.

Pinpricks of light shone through, creating an entire constellation, roughly the shape of the Big Dipper.

I thought the knocking on the front door would never go away. If Siobhan hadn't moved around to my bedroom window, the one closest to my bed, and yelled Auntie Sarah, I never would have believed it could have been anyone but Ray Santia.

I turned on my bedside light. Pulling my down comforter off the bed with me, and wrapping it around my shoulders like a bad version of a superhero's cape, I met Siobhan at the kitchen door. She was shivering and hatless, her eyes seriously puffy. Tendrils of her multihued hair stuck to the sides of her face. She wore her school backpack over an old wool peacoat. The handle of her ample suitcase was extended, and after she bumped it up three steps, it rolled effortlessly into my house.

We sat on the couch, my comforter wrapped around both of us. "What happened?" I asked.

"My parents suck."

"You're sixteen. Your parents are supposed to suck." I pulled the comforter over Siobhan's legs so she'd stop shivering. "Do you want some hot chocolate?" I asked, hoping I had some.

"No, thanks."

"So what specifically happened?"

"They won't let me get my navel pierced. Can you believe it?"

I sort of could, but didn't think saying so would be constructive. "Well, you have a fair amount of holes already."

"Big deal. Everybody has their ears pierced. And, besides, this is the only thing I'm asking for for Christmas. One measly thing and they can't even give it to me. So I told them I'll get it pierced in the spring when I go to Spain with my Spanish class because you don't have to be eighteen to do it there and a whole bunch of girls did it last year." She paused for a ragged breath. "So now they say I can't go to Spain."

I was in over my head and I knew it. So I talked Siobhan into getting some sleep and said we'd figure out what to do in the morning. I got her an extra pillow from my room, found a clean set of sheets to drape over the couch and gave her my comforter. I asked if her homework was done, found out what time she had to get up for school and sent her into the bathroom with her toothbrush.

While she was brushing, I called Carol from my bedroom. She picked up on the first ring. "I just wanted you to know," I whispered, "that Siobhan is here."

"Of course she is," Carol answered. "I dropped her off. How did you think she got there?"

I tried to sleep, but I couldn't. I didn't want to wake Siobhan so I tiptoed past her to the kitchen. I'd turned off the ring of the phone so I wouldn't have to explain to Siobhan why I wasn't answering. I wondered how many times Ray had called. I wondered how long I'd have to ignore his calls for him to stop calling. I stood there, the light on my answering machine winking at me suggestively. I turned my back on it and opened the fridge. Poured some milk into my favorite Flintstones jelly glass, jumped up to sit on the kitchen counter. Blushed and jumped back down. Great, I'd never be able to sit on a kitchen counter again without thinking about making a fool of myself with Ray Santia. One more pleasure lost.

Oh, God. Okay, I would drink milk, that's what I'd do. The extra calcium would calm my nerves and lull me back into a comfortable level of denial. I glanced over my shoulder at my answering machine. If I were in an old Western I would simply shoot its nasty little light out. I took another sip of milk, walked over and pressed ERASE. There, that was better, maybe he'd go away now.

27

After I drove Siobhan to school, promising to pick her up again afterward, I called Christine. "You know what Carol's like," I said. "If I try to tell her what to do, she'll just do the opposite. But, I mean, what's the big deal, it's not like it's a tattoo or anything. When and if Siobhan outgrows the phase, she can just take it out."

"Why don't you just bring Siobhan to have it done and then we'll deal with Carol and Dennis afterward."

"I love the 'we,' Christine. I can just hear you saying that it was all my idea. And, besides, Siobhan says that if you're under eighteen, both you and a parent have to show IDs before they'll pierce anything but an ear. And if the last names don't match, you have to show a birth certificate."

"Why don't you steal Carol's license again?" Christine giggled at her reference to a famous story from the Hurlihy family archives. All these years later, I still couldn't quite find it funny. In a lifetime of fairly honest behavior, I'd strayed one night. Just home from col-

lege for winter break, I borrowed Carol's license to go
to a local club with my friends who'd already turned
twenty-one. Carol noticed it missing immediately,
thought she'd lost it, and was already making plans to
drive to the registry to get a duplicate. In the back of
my mind, the evil plan to keep the license permanently
was simmering, but I thought I would probably tuck it
back into her wallet at the end of the weekend.

I wasn't really that nervous as I stood in line to have
Carol's license checked by the bouncer at High Tide.
Carol and I looked a lot alike. Besides, I'd memorized
her Social Security number and year of birth, and practiced rattling them off quickly. The bouncer was cute,
blond and beefy with intelligent eyes that made me
think his job was an interlude rather than a dead end.

"Are you sure you're Carol Hurlihy?" he asked.

I wasn't too worried. "Yes," I answered.

He quizzed me on every bit of information contained on that little plastic rectangle, and I passed it all
with flying colors. The line was backing up behind me.
"Are you *sure* you're Carol Hurlihy?" he asked again,
peering into my face.

I was more annoyed than nervous. "Yes," I said
again.

"Funny, you look different than you did last night
on our date." The bouncer, of course, was Dennis, and
sometimes I thought he only married my sister in
order to be able to say to me, thousands of times over
the years: *Can I check your ID?*

I laughed a little to let Christine think that the
decades had eased my embarrassment. "Don't worry
about a thing," she said. "I'll call Carol and see what I
can arrange."

*   *   *

Just before Thanksgiving we'd made hula skirts. We used single horizontal strips of green construction paper for the waistbands. To make the skirt part, we stapled on evenly spaced vertical strips of the same paper. The kids each decorated an empty paper towel holder with brightly colored poster paints. Even the goopiest ones had dried over the long holiday weekend.

And now, the morning after I'd crept out of Ray Santia's house, the morning after Siobhan had shown up at my house, June and I began to staple the hula skirts around the children. We started side by side, worked in opposite directions around the circle. When it was his turn, Jack Kaplan said, "*I'm* not wearing a skirt."

"Okay," I said, turning to staple Molly Greene's hula skirt over her ankle-length black velvet jumper.

"Okay, I'll wear it," Jack said, moving to stand in line behind Molly.

The kids had to hike their waistbands up practically to their armpits in order to sit on the circle. June and I passed out the carefully labeled paper towel rolls after first cutting fringe with scissors. I explained that they would now be called puili sticks. "Can you say poo-ee-lee sticks?" I said, using my best teacher voice, which was a bit of an effort this morning, I had to admit.

"Pweelie sticks," the children said in unison.

The classroom telephone rang. I nodded to June to answer it. Turning back to the kids I said, "Hawaii is a place that is made up of many islands, which is why many Hawaiian dances are about the water."

"Sarah, it's for you," June stage-whispered from the other side of the room.

"Take a message," I stage-whispered back, not without sarcasm.

"It's a . . ." June's last word was lost to me.

"A what?"

"A guy," Austin said. "June says there's a guy on the phone."

"What's his name?" asked Amanda McAlpine.

"Handle it," I hissed at June. I unclenched my teeth enough to smile at the children, made myself keep going. "Can you say hey-ey-ee-ah?"

"Hey-ey-ee-ah," they said in a perfect imitation of my voice. I tried to ignore the annoying fact that June was still talking on the phone. "Hey-ey-ee-ah is a very, very old dance from Hawaii. It's about a canoe trip for spearing fish."

"Does it hurt the fish?" asked Jenny Browning.

June was laughing and throwing her hair around. I, however, maintained my professional demeanor. "Well, Jenny, in many cultures people have to eat the fish to keep from starving."

"Can't they just have a sandwich?" Jack Kaplan asked. "I can make a sandwich."

If June didn't get off the phone in two minutes, I was going to strangle her. I decided to ignore Jack's question, move on. I mean, why did teachers have to do all the hard stuff? Shouldn't parents have to explain some things?

"Okay, everybody. Hold your puili stick in this hand, and put your other hand like this, palm up." I showed the children shading their eyes (maka malumalu), churning the water (wili wai) and all the rest. They followed along like brightly colored little parrots. When we were ready, I put an actual record on an actual record player, a scratchy version of *Dances Around the World* that had been recorded so long ago it didn't even have a cassette version. We made it through the dance two complete times before June finally hung up the phone.

After she finished passing out snacks all by herself, which I thought was only fair, June sidled up to me. "That was Ray Santia. He is just like the nicest guy," she said, still whispering. "He's dying to see you again." She paused, watched my face. "You are just so lucky. I mean, I hardly ever meet nice guys anymore. Sarah?"

I was working up to a response when June added, "Do you know that Ray Santia has a puppy from the same litter as Wrinkles?" I looked at her, not saying a word. There was absolutely no reason to admit to a thing. "He was a little confused though. He seemed to, like, think you had one too?"

Siobhan and I sat in the waiting room at Pins and Needles, sandwiched between a mother and son combo on our right and a mother and daughter team on our left. They were surprisingly clean-cut and looked as likely to spend an afternoon shopping at The Gap as waiting for a turn at a body-piercing salon. The kids were about Siobhan's age, not quite old enough to be here alone. I was probably just about the same age as the mothers, a depressing thought.

I hadn't stolen Carol's license this time. Instead, she'd loaned it to me in a belated decision that navel-piercing wasn't a battle she and Dennis wanted to pick with Siobhan. It was, in fact, much better than either a tattoo or an older boyfriend, or even an out-of-the-country piercing experience during a school trip where who could imagine what the hygiene standards might be. Carol even decided this would be my Christmas present to Siobhan, because that way she could hang on to some vestige of parental disapproval.

Siobhan walked over to the display case to check out the navel rings, which gave me a chance to look around carefully for signs of cleanliness. PINS AND NEEDLES, said a sign over the register, CALL 1-800-STICK-ME. A larger-than-life ceramic ear, pierced within an inch of its life, hung on the wall to one side. On the other side, a long vertical file held clearly labeled information sheets: GENITAL, NIPPLE, NAVEL, TONGUE.

I shivered a little, noticed an open book lying facedown on the counter, read the upside-down title: *Essentials of Human Anatomy and Physiology.* I wondered if someone was actually reading it or if it was just a prop.

"So tell me," I said to Siobhan when she sat down again, "why exactly do you want to get this done?"

She pointed to a poster of a long-torsoed, hardbodied, bikini-clad woman, wearing a tiny, sexy ring in her perfectly formed navel. "Look," she said, "how cool is that?"

He was a bit hard to understand because of the three silver studs in his tongue, but Adrian, the owner of Pins and Needles, was really very nice. He gave Siobhan and me each a sheet of paper explaining that everything had been autoclaved and/or chemically sterilized. The misspelling of equipment—*equiptment*—made me a little uncomfortable, but that was probably just the teacher in me. While he photocopied Carol's license and Siobhan's learner's permit, I forged Carol's name on a form saying that I hereby released all agents from all manner of liabilities, actions and demands, in law or in karmic equity, by reason of complying with the undersigned's request to be pierced.

"Give me another one of those forms," I said suddenly.

"You gonna go for it?" Adrian asked.

"Oh, my God, Aunt . . . I mean, Mom. Are you really?" asked Siobhan.

"Happens all the time," Adrian assured her. "Who first?"

"Age before beauty," I said. Nobody argued.

It was cold and tickly, but not unpleasant, to have the area around my navel swabbed with Betadine solution. Siobhan and I lay side by side on orange vinyl recliners. I hoped her eyes were closed so she wouldn't chicken out when her turn came. I felt brave and brazen and deliciously wild, and more than a little sexy, and I realized that a pierced navel could symbolize all sorts of new growth for me. This might well be the first truly spontaneous decision I'd ever made. I opened my eyes just a little and lifted my head to peer at the expanse of skin below my rolled-up sweatshirt. Forty was young when you looked as good as I did. There were probably lots of women who'd trade places with me in a second.

I shut my eyes fast when Adrian attached a clamp just above my navel. The pain wasn't much, so I opened them again, just a little, thinking I shouldn't miss any of this moment or any other. Life was just too damn short not to live every bit of it. I looked over at Siobhan to see how she was holding up.

Adrian leaned over me and I felt an amazing, burning pain, truly the mother of all burning pain, immediately accompanied by nausea, and looked down to see Adrian shoving what looked like a barbecue skewer into my stomach. I opened my eyes only once more during the removal of the piercer and the endless painful threading of the hoop. I saw that my belly button had become a little wading pool of blood. *Stop,* I wanted to say. *Oh, please stop. I'm really not very brave at all.*

A half hour later, Siobhan leaned over me with a sterile cloth to put pressure on my navel. With her other hand, she angled a small mirror to get a front view of her own pierced and hooped belly button. I assumed Adrian was in the front room looking up *clotting* under *blood* in the medical book. *As we age,* I imagined it saying, *blood clots less readily.*

By the time I was ready to leave, Siobhan had called her mother to let her know we'd be a little late. She'd also finished off half of her homework. "You are just the coolest aunt in the world," she said as I lowered myself painfully into the passenger seat of my Civic and replaced my ice pack. "I can't wait to tell everybody."

28

I had just explained to June why I'd be needing a chair during circle time for the foreseeable future. I simply couldn't face the searing pain of lowering myself to the floor and maintaining a seated position. "Don't worry," June said. "It's just the first couple of days that are bad."

"That's encouraging," I said, thinking June and I might finally have something in common. "How do you know? Is yours pierced, too?"

She placed her hand over her own stomach, which I had no doubt would rival the abdominal splendor of the poster Siobhan and I had seen at Pins and Needles. "Some of my friends have had it done. I'm way too chicken, though. I would, like, never have the nerve. Wow, Sarah, you are so amazing. I always think how I wish I were more like you."

I looked at June, with her wide-set spacey eyes and her veil of long, silky hair. She looked like a doll that my sisters and I might have had as a child, one of the "good" dolls we were only allowed to take out on special occasions. "But what am I like?" I asked.

"Well, you're so strong and you're, like, such a good teacher and you know what you want and you're, um, like not afraid to go after it."

"Why, thanks, June," I said. "You're very kind." Perhaps I had been underestimating June's intelligence. I lifted the loose sweater I was wearing out of the way, and moved my ice pack around on my belly. I figured I'd keep it on for another minute or so before I put it away in the little classroom refrigerator and got ready for the kids to arrive.

"My, my, my," said Bob Connor from the doorway. "What have we here?"

"Hi, Bobby," June said, as Austin ran by us and over to the aquarium to feed the fish. "Sarah got her navel pierced. Isn't that the coolest thing?"

"Having a bit of a midlife crisis, are we, Ms. Hurlihy? Would you like to go out some night and pursue it further?" Bob Connor's shirt was the color of cranberries today. I tried to decide whether it would be worse to continue standing with my hand underneath my sweater or to casually remove the ice pack. His green eyes watched me. "After the swelling goes down, of course."

I replayed June's assessment of me in my mind. "You know, Mr. Connor," I said firmly. "You'll simply have to come up with a better offer than that."

I boiled a saucepan full of water, found a box of Annie's macaroni and cheese in the back of a cabinet. Sniffed the milk, then threw it out while my stomach lurched and I wrestled a strong impulse to gag.

Checked unsuccessfully for butter. Poured the pasta shells into the boiling water anyway, which gave me six to eight minutes to problem-solve for ingredients.

An inspired cook, I figured it out with two minutes to spare. I waited out the final boiling time, then drained the pasta, scraped it back into the saucepan, sprinkled on the packet of cheese dust that came in the box. Dug a well in the center with the spoon, poured in half a glass of white wine and stirred briskly.

On the way to the living room, I took a big bite of my new creation. Wow, a keeper. And low-fat to boot. Maybe I'd send the recipe to Annie and she'd print it on the box. I'd call it Sarah's Winey Macaroni and Cheese.

I propped my ice pack with a pillow on my lap so my hands were free to eat, and made myself as comfortable as my present condition allowed. *The Brady Bunch* was somewhere in the middle of a show. "Come on, Tiger. You're the only one around here who cares about me," Bobby Brady was saying to the family dog. "*You* still like me." I put my feet up on the coffee table, had another bite of my dinner. Bobby Brady's big blue eyes welled up with tears. "I'll show 'em," he said. "I'm not going to stay where I'm not wanted. I'll run away. That's what I'm going to do. Run away."

I considered this as a possible solution for my situation. I'd have to get a dog first. Michael would probably be thrilled to let me take Mother Teresa. I'd start a brand-new life somewhere where I didn't know a soul. Maybe I'd go to Paris after all, find an American school to teach at until I learned the language. Maybe that waiter I'd imagined before would be there, still waiting for his big break.

Nah, at my age running away would be far less dramatic. And I'd never find another teaching job midyear, especially without references. Plus, my family would find me in a minute. Damn, I hated it when an episode didn't speak directly to me. Bobby Brady was adorable though. Kids. That's another reason I couldn't run away, the kids at school were just too cute. But, then again, sometimes the cutest kids had the most horrendous parents. When Patrice Greene picked up Molly today, she eyed the hula skirts, which the other parents were certainly oohing and aahing over. Then she turned to me and said, "Really, Ms. Hurlihy, it's almost Christmas. It would provide far more consistency for the children if you linked your units thematically with the seasons." I mean, why even tell her that the kids were assaulted by the holidays everywhere they turned, and that I'd long ago toned down our classroom celebrating to compensate. Why bother to try to impress upon someone like Patrice Greene that even when I was hopelessly inadequate everywhere else in my life, I loved my job and really, truly knew what I was doing in my classroom. At least most of the time.

I heard the knock at my door while I was brushing my teeth. Carol. Probably stopping by to make sure I had enough ice. When I'd talked to her earlier, she'd thanked me again and said Siobhan was like a new person, laughing and joking. Why, she'd even set the table without being asked.

I was still brushing when I opened the door to Ray Santia. "Hi," he said while I wiped toothpaste from the corners of my mouth with the back of my hand. "Sorry to just show up like this. But I left you about ten messages first."

"That's okay," I lied. I was wearing the thick kind of gray sweatpants that nobody had worn for years. And Winnie the Pooh slippers that one of the kids had given me for Christmas last year. Most of my face was covered in a slippery moisturizer with retinol and, as if in tribute to a lingering adolescence, I had a dot of Clearasil on my right cheek and another one on my forehead. I shut my eyes to make Ray disappear.

"Can I come in?"

"Okay."

"Then you'll have to open the door a little wider."

I turned quickly, which sent a rush of pain through my abdomen, kind of pushed the door open with my heel, and made a beeline for the bathroom. "Be right back," I yelled. I grabbed a wet washcloth and scrubbed while I kicked off the slippers. Brushed on mascara with one hand while I used the other to dry my face with a damp towel. "Make yourself at home," I shouted in the hallway between the bathroom and my bedroom. I locked the bedroom door behind me in case Ray took that literally. Stepped into a pair of loose pants that had landed on the floor earlier in the week, pulled them up carefully over my navel, and grabbed a T-shirt I hoped was a step up from the one I slept in but wouldn't look like I was trying too hard.

Ray was leaning against my kitchen counter. "You didn't have to change for me."

"I didn't." It was true. I'd changed for me. So that I wouldn't have to think about how bad he thought I looked.

"Okay. Well, whatever, you look good. Now where

were we before you disappeared on me the other night?" Ray smiled. In the harsh light of my kitchen it seemed an arrogant smile, not all that far from a sneer. I noticed he'd taken off his boots, which seemed fairly presumptuous given that we barely knew each other. His hair looked funny, too, maybe a bad case of hat hair he'd tried to fluff up on the way to my door.

"I think we should go sit down in the living room," I said.

"Your wish is my command." Kevin used to say that when we were married. I'd found it an irritating phrase. I mean, it's not like he ever meant it.

Ray sat next to me on the couch, draped his arm across the top of it, inches above my shoulders. If I leaned my head back, we would touch. I stayed where I was. "So, where's your puppy?" he asked. "Asleep?"

"Well, actually," I began. He lowered his hand to my shoulder and I jumped, just a little, but enough to feel a jolt of pain from my navel. "Ouch," I said, my eyes filling with tears.

"Are you okay?" Ray slid over on the coach, as if he might catch something.

"Just a little minor surgery," I said.

"Oh, I'm sorry." Ray looked at me for more information. "Do you want me to leave?"

"Actually, Ray, there are a couple of things I need to tell you. I don't have a dog. You know June, the teacher you talked to on the phone? It's her dog. And, by the way, she liked you a lot, and you know, if you want to call her or anything, it's fine with me."

Ray considered this for a minute. "What's she like?"

"She's a babe," I said.

I heard the slamming of drawers in the kitchen, followed by the unmistakable sound of Carol's voice. "Jesus, Sarah, you're a total slob. I can't find anything here."

"Sorry to scare him away. I never would have walked in like that if I knew you had a live one here. I didn't see an extra car in your driveway. Guess I didn't factor in a street parker."

"That's okay. We'd already decided we weren't right for each other."

"Why, is he married?"

"No."

"Well, then, I don't know what your problem is." Carol had taken over Ray's place on my couch. Her feet were on my coffee table next to a bottle of Merlot she'd brought. I leaned over the bottle with a corkscrew, careful not to disrupt my ice pack, while Carol stirred a bowl of macaroni and cheese. "It's kind of runny. What'd you do to it?"

"Just try it."

"Mmm, this is good." While Carol ate, I poured the Merlot into two glasses. I wondered if I should warn her that she was about to mix red and white wine. Decided I didn't want to hear her lecture about how I lived like a transient and, if nothing else, I should at least consider making a commitment to groceries. "So, what went wrong?" she asked.

It took me a minute to realize she meant Ray and not the pasta. I sipped my wine, wondered. "I don't know. We went out the other night and one minute I was enjoying myself and the next minute he was looking for condoms and I was thinking, *I don't know anything about this guy.*"

"You mean like who he's been with?"

"No. I mean, sure. I bet you always think about that. But it was more like I didn't even know his middle name or his favorite color."

"Sarah, Sarah, Sarah."

"I know, that sounded silly even to me."

Carol put the empty bowl down and I handed her a glass of wine. She slid over to the far end of the couch, tucked a pillow behind her back, shifted around so she could put her feet on the middle cushion. Her socks smelled like wet wool. "Dennis and I couldn't find a condom once." She paused, smiled.

I waited, not particularly wanting to hear Carol's condom story but knowing there would be no stopping it.

"Wanna know what we used?"

"No, thank you."

"Saran Wrap."

I spit my wine back into my glass. "God, Carol. Thank you so much for that vivid image." I disliked Dennis enough without having to think about his plastic-wrapped penis. I decided to move the story along, just to get it over with. "So, how'd it work?"

"Not very well. Siobhan was born nine months and five days later."

I tried the wine again. "You think Saran Wrap has improved over the years? Better grip, fewer leaks?"

"Yeah, it comes in colors now, too. I imagine the rose would be the most flattering."

"You ever try it, just for old times' sake?"

"Nah, Dennis wouldn't think it was funny. He can be such an asshole."

I let that sink in. Carol actually knew that Dennis

was an asshole. I thought carefully about how to phrase my next question. "So you actually know that Dennis can be an asshole? I mean, not that he is all the time or anything."

"Sarah, Sarah, Sarah. I've only been married to him for almost two decades."

"So, what's the up side?"

"Oh, I don't know. The kids are great, even Siobhan, sometimes. He's a good dad. I love him. And he still makes me laugh."

"Kevin never made me laugh." It was probably a slight exaggeration, but it had the feel of truth. "He didn't really listen to me either. I could tell when he was pretending to. He'd repeat the last two words of everything I said."

Carol took a sip and considered this. "You mean like, if you said, 'Oh, Kevin, you have such a nice ass,' he'd say, 'Nice ass'?"

"Yeah, and if I said, 'I want to wrap you in Saran Wrap,' he'd say . . ."

"Saran Wrap," we yelled together. We laughed and laughed. Our laughter was the kind that comes in spasms, and hurts your stomach after a while, even if you didn't just get it pierced.

29

Just as I was walking Carol to the door, Mother Teresa burst in. If my life kept up, I was going to have to think about installing a revolving door.

Michael was right behind her. "Mother Teresa, sit!" he tried. Mother Teresa trotted a few laps around the kitchen, then headed down the hallway, probably looking for greener pastures.

Michael started after her. "Let her go," I said. "She's fine." Michael shrugged, stood just inside the door to let the snow melt onto the kitchen mat. "Gee, Michael, have you been trying to reach me? I haven't been answering the phone." I unwrapped the towel from the ice pack, which I put back in the freezer. Maybe I was just getting used to the pain, but my stomach didn't seem to be throbbing at all now.

"No." Michael clomped over, sat in a kitchen chair, rubbed his face with both hands.

"Did you hear I got my navel pierced?"

"No, sorry. I guess I missed the news bulletin." He

shrugged his shoulders. "Phoebe kicked us out. Both of us. I was hoping Mother Teresa and I could move in with you for a while. Just till I figure what to do?"

"Of course you can, Michael."

"No, he can't." Carol stepped back out of her boots, walked around to sit across from Michael at the table. "Don't be an idiot, Michael. It's almost Christmas. Go home, tell Phoebe you're sorry, even if you're not. Tell her you love her, love the kids, all that stuff. And leave the dog here."

Michael looked as if he was about to cry. "I'm just so sick and tired of fighting over every single little thing. If it weren't for the girls . . ."

"So don't fight," Carol said. "And if Phoebe starts something, don't fight back."

"Well, I've tried that. But then she says I'm giving her the silent treatment."

I didn't know quite how to say it. "I don't get it, Michael. You and Phoebe, what exactly *is* your problem?"

Michael put his head down by his knees and scratched his scalp with both sets of fingernails. "Good question," he said. He sat up, rubbed his hands back and forth from his knees to his thighs. "We're just so different. I like to stay home. She wants to go out more. She thinks the kids need structure. I think they should have fun like we did growing up. I don't know, it all sounds so small, but it's exhausting."

"Well," Carol said, "you're not going to solve any of it if you move in here."

As soon as I handed Michael a beer, my father arrived. In my family, when one person showed up, another was sure to follow, as if there was some natural law of synchronicity. So I wasn't even surprised to see him. If he'd given me the chance, I would have asked what took him so long.

But of course Dad had his own opening line. "I have the distinct impression that my very own family is smack-dab in the middle of a party to which I was not invited."

"Yeah," Michael said. "And we almost got away with it." He took another sip of his beer. "How's it going, Dad?"

"Can't complain, Mikey-boy. Can't complain at all. I was just headin' home, saw the cars in the driveway." He watched as Michael took a long, sad sip of beer. "Hey, what's your tale, nightingale?"

Michael stood up, poured the rest of the beer down the sink. He walked over to our father, managed to shake his hand and hug him at the same time. "Nothing, Dad. I gotta go. I just stopped by because I hadn't heard from Sarah in a while."

I slid my feet into my father's boots and followed Michael out to his car to get Mother Teresa's things. "Michael, you know you're always welcome here. We'll just have to hide you from Carol."

Michael smiled sadly. "Thanks. Carol's right, though, about staying here not helping things. I guess I've got to try talking to Phoebe. I mean, really try. God, I hate this stuff. I'm just so bad at it."

"Maybe it's genetic. But, Michael, if I have one big regret about my marriage with Kevin . . ." I took a breath, traced a squiggly line through the snow on Michael's car with my bare finger. "You know, when we just started drifting apart, it's that, well, I wish I'd tried a little harder."

Michael loaded me up with Mother Teresa's food and bowls and toys, and said he'd be back for her tomorrow. Then he kissed me on the top of my head and said thanks.

Mother Teresa had her head in my lap. We were sitting on the floor, across the coffee table from Dad and Carol. "You're a good cook, Sarah. All my girls are good cooks, thank the good Lord." He was finishing the macaroni and cheese, which had certainly been a hit. "So what were you kiddos talking about when your old dad walked in?"

I waited for Carol to answer. She was pouring the last of the Merlot for Dad, while I leaned across Mother Teresa to fill our glasses with seltzer. "Oh, you know, Dad. Life and love and why people stay together and why they don't."

My father nodded. "Well, I can't say I haven't cast an eyeball at that question a few times in my life. How a saint like your mother ever fell for a flutter bum like me . . ."

"She was crazy about you, Dad. We all know that." I looked at Carol for confirmation. She smiled vacantly, probably still reliving her condom adventures.

"Well, if I had to put it down to any one thing, I'd have to say the great magic for me was that I never once stopped wanting to know what your mother thought about something. Couldn't wait to get home to tell her some crazy thing. All day long I'd be saving up stories to razzle-dazzle her with at night. Even now, when something happens, I think about how I'm going to tell it to her." He wiped what might have been a tear from his eye, took a sip of wine. Carol sighed.

I scratched Mother Teresa behind her ears. My father continued. "I still talk to your mother every night. Tonight I'll tell her how happy I was to spend time with two of my girls. How Carol still has her eyes, and Christine has her lovely smile."

"Sarah, Dad. Sarah."

"Just making sure you're awake, Sarry girl." He raised an eyebrow at me. "And I won't breathe a word to her about this belly button nonsense. I don't want her to think I'm letting our little girls turn into a bunch of floozies."

Carol was the last to leave. We hugged carefully at the door. "Thanks, Carol. And thanks for helping out with Michael. I would have just let him move in. You're right, of course. He and Phoebe have too much going for them to let a little fight split them up."

"What are you talking about? Michael and Phoebe don't have a prayer."

"What?"

"Phoebe's spoiled and entitled and if she's not falling apart about Mother Teresa, she'll just find something else."

How was I ever going to learn to see this stuff? I wondered if there was a course I could take. I wondered how Carol and I emerged from the same gene pool. "So, why'd you send him back home, Carol? I don't get it."

"What's not to get? It's Christmas, he's got kids and a wife, and how much fun could it be for him here with you?"

"Gee, thanks."

"You know what I mean." Carol zipped up her parka, put a hand on the doorknob. "Any other questions?"

"Yeah, about Dad. Do you buy all that stuff about him still talking to Mom?"

"Yeah, I do."

"That's nice. Sad, maybe, but nice."

"But, Sarah, factor in that this is also a man who's dating at least two women. That we know of."

I waved to Carol as she backed out of the driveway. Mother Teresa joined me at the door. I held on to her collar, and we stood for a while with our faces peeking out into the cold, flaky night. I didn't know about Mother Teresa, but I was wondering why anyone ever ended up with anyone.

Bob Connor called and said he had a better offer. He picked me up early Saturday night and we drove to the highway and headed south. "Come on, tell me," I pleaded, even though I was thrilled not to have any idea where we were going. I was also a little bit relieved to be getting out of town, since I still wasn't comfortable being seen with the father of one of my students. Apparently, though, not so uncomfortable that I wasn't doing it anyway.

"Not on your life. The element of surprise is a part of my strategy. *Ms. Hurlihy.*"

I watched Bob's profile as we drove around the Cape Cod rotary, took a break to appreciate the view over the sides of the Sagamore Bridge, turned back again to Bob. "Well," I said, probably fishing for a compliment, "I hope I'm at least dressed for wherever it is we're going."

"It wouldn't have mattered. You'd be perfect anyway."

I looked down at my outfit with alarm. "Does that mean I'm dressed wrong?" I'd figured on dinner and decided on a black skirt and tights with a soft orchid sweater.

"No, Sarah, it means you'd be amazingly gorgeous no matter what you wore." He took his eyes off the road and looked me up and down. "That was the part where I butter you up. Another integral part of my strategy."

"And what strategy might that be, Mr. Connor? Or is that a secret, too?"

"No secret at all. I'm bound and determined to get you to fall for me. Hook, line and sinker."

It's probably not the type of restaurant I would have chosen, I thought, as I looked at Bob Connor in the flickering candlelight. The safari theme was a bit overdone, so many animal prints in so little space. The table appeared to have been made from an elephant foot with a round of glass placed on top of it. I was afraid to ask if it was real. Bob and I sat on big, overstuffed pillows, I assumed because the table was so short.

"Pretty exotic, huh?" Bob said. "And this is just the beginning of our little walk on the wild side." He picked up his bloodred glass of wine and clinked it against my glass of white. "To us."

"To us," I repeated, trying out the sound of it.

I was half-expecting the menu to have things like ostrich and buffalo, but instead it was an orgy of more traditional fare like pasta primavera and baked stuffed seafood casserole. I searched for something not swimming in cheese sauce, finally decided on the grilled swordfish. Bob ordered the steak-and-seafood medley. "Variety," he said, "the spice of life."

Bob was thoroughly attentive throughout the meal. He charmed me, cajoled me, sweet-talked me. I basked in the warmth of his flattery, the luxury of his focus.

While we were sipping our coffee, he reached over and held my hand. "There's more to the surprise," he said.

"I had a feeling."

"I reserved the Huggles and Bubbles Suite."

"What kind of a safari name is that?"

"Who cares?"

It is very disorienting to wake up in a round bed. It doesn't help to peer across the room through an opaque cloud of mosquito netting to a heart-shaped Jacuzzi, no longer frothing with foam, but a presence all the same. There were several possible reasons why I'd ended up here. Perhaps it was because I was dying to see what the room would look like. Not sleeping with Ray might have made me statistically and hormonally more apt to sleep with the next guy. Bob was cute and funny and I liked him. And it had been so very long since I'd slept with anyone. Besides Mother Teresa.

And once I'd ended up in this room, it wasn't like I could exactly say, *Wow, isn't this something,* and turn around and walk out. There was a bottle of champagne in a zebra-print wine bucket, a single red rose on the edge of the Jacuzzi, a packet of condoms placed casually on the pillow. Bob put his arms around me and we kissed. He sort of danced me backward over to the Jacuzzi, reached down to turn the water on full blast, then slowly removed my clothes. We kissed some more while I helped him slide out of his, and we managed to step together into the Jacuzzi without breaking our kiss.

Sex with Bob Connor was even more fun than dinner in the safari room. There were, of course, certain similarities.

Now, the morning after, curled up next to him in our round bed, tracing my fingertips lightly over his skin, I decided that whatever awkwardness might result at school was well worth it. I could get used to sleeping with Bob Connor.

He rolled over and groaned. "Jesus, what time is it?"

"A little after nine." I hooked my leg over one of his.

"Shit." He pulled his leg out from under mine. He sat up, stretched, slid off the edge of the round bed and under the mosquito netting. He walked naked to the bathroom, shut the bathroom door partway, and I heard him pee, long and loud. The jolt of the shower turning on followed.

I thought about following him into the bathroom, surprising him by joining him in the shower, but it seemed a bit pushy. Instead, I got up, lowered the lever to let the Jacuzzi drain a little, then turned the faucets on. I tiptoed over to the bathroom, peeked inside and grabbed a washcloth and towel and a paper-wrapped bar of soap from the sink. Leaning over the side of the heart-shaped Jacuzzi, I washed up, splashed some water into my mouth and spit it back out a few times. Then I dried off and put last night's clothes back on. My black tights bagged at the knees just like Molly Greene's always did at school.

Eventually Bob came out with his towel wrapped around his waist. He stretched his arms wide and yawned. "God, do I need a toothbrush," he said. "You set to go?" he said, apparently noticing I was no longer naked. Not only was I ready to go, but I wished I could fast-forward through this whole tacky morning-after scene. "Great," he continued when I didn't say anything, "just give me a sec." He turned his back, dropped the towel, and I watched him get dressed as if from a great distance.

We pulled through a drive-through for coffee and bagels on the way home. Bob talked cheerily about how built-up this area of the Cape had become, how winter was going to be here before we knew it, how he was watching the Patriots game that afternoon with a couple of buddies. When we got to my house, he walked me to the door and kissed me. "That was fun," he said. "I'll call you."

I brushed my teeth and took a long, hot shower, my tears salting the water. I put on old, baggy clothes and checked my messages. Not a one. Wouldn't you know that when I could really use the distraction of my family, they were nowhere to be found. I called Michael. "You wanna go for a walk or anything?"

"Good timing. I was just heading out with Mother Teresa. We'll pick you up."

Mother Teresa had to move to the backseat to make room for me, but I don't think she minded. She leaned forward between the bucket seats in Michael's 4Runner, and rested her head on my shoulder, nuzzling up against my neck. The tenderness of the gesture almost made me start to cry again.

"You okay, Sarah? You don't look so hot." We'd pulled into the parking lot of the golf course. Michael had one hand on the door handle. He turned and looked at me with such concern that I opened my door quickly and got out.

"I'm fine. Just a bad date. By the way, you were right, Michael." I smiled, lurched a few steps across the parking lot. "You can't shine a fucking sneaker," I slurred in a pretty fair imitation of Michael. Even drunk, Michael had seen Bob more clearly than I had.

"Cute, sis. So, Bob What's-his-name, huh?" Michael bent down to pick up two golf balls partially covered by leaves. He handed me one. "Sorry I was right about him. You want to talk about it?"

"With my *brother*? I don't think so." I threw my ball for Mother Teresa. She barreled after it.

"Well, let me know if you want me to beat him up or anything."

"Nah, he's not worth it. Come on, let's change the subject. How're you and Phoebe doing these days?"

"We're going to counseling."

"Cut it out. You talking about your feelings to a stranger?" *Or anyone, for that matter,* I didn't say.

"Yeah, well, I'm trying. Right now it's about one step forward and three-quarters of a step back. I gotta do it, though. It's not fair to Annie and Lainie for us always to be fighting. It was different for you and Kevin. You could just walk."

"I really wanted to have kids with Kevin." I couldn't believe I'd actually said that out loud. Mother Teresa had rolled onto her back in some long grass, where she was wiggling around delightedly. "What's she doing?"

"Trying to absorb some disgusting scent, probably a dead animal or something. Guess it's bathtime tonight." He bent down and clapped his hands against his thighs. "Come here, girl. Now." Mother Teresa ignored him. "You can still have kids. I mean, can't you?"

I laughed. "Yeah, at least for the next ten minutes. But, I mean, what are the chances? And I'm with kids all day long anyway." We'd caught up with Mother Teresa and Michael put the leash on her and yanked. Reluctantly, she allowed herself to be dragged away.

Michael walked Mother Teresa a safe distance away, then let her off the leash again. "Well, sometimes I think the only part I've got is the kids part. Phoebe and I are just so different. Who we are, what we want. I never knew how important that would be. I thought you just had to find someone to love, and then the rest would fall into place."

"You know," I said when John Anderson answered the phone. "I can't promise you that I'm not going to keep messing things up, and my family is never going to change—in fact, they can be even worse than you've seen—and the only thing I've ever been really good at is teaching, and I'm really sorry we didn't play spin the bottle. In fact, if we did, it might have saved me from a couple of stupid mistakes—"

"Who is this?"

"You're kidding, right?"

John laughed. Suddenly, I was glad I'd called. "Of course, I know who this is," he said. "Sarah."

"Sarah who?" I asked, just to be sure.

"Sarah Hurlihy," he answered. I liked the way he pronounced my name with such confidence, as if he could even spell it if he had to.

30

The bus was big. It was tall and long and sleek and shiny and it took up nearly half of our circular driveway. A satellite dish sprouted from its top like an upside-down mushroom. An electronic sign spanned the front and flashed HAPPY HOLIDAYS FROM THE HURLIHYS in red and green letters.

My father was greeting guests in our front hallway. He wore a Santa hat, of course, and red suspenders hooked on to black slacks over a crisp white shirt. When I kissed him, he smelled a shade too much of Old Spice. "You look great, Dad."

"And you, my dear, are a vision." My brothers and sisters were clumped around Dad. I made the rounds with hugs.

A pretty redhead in a tuxedo approached us with a silver tray and a stack of cocktail-sized napkins. "Salmon mousse?" she offered.

"Pretty fancy, Dad," I said, munching a mousse-laden cracker. "Mmm, this is fabulous."

"As I've said my entire life, when Billy Hurlihy does something, he does it up right." My brothers and sisters and I looked at each other, smiled at how many times we'd heard that one during the course of our lives. "And it all came with the bus. Catchy gimmick: they unload the whole shebang, serve at your house, load it back up, and then you eat and drink your way to wherever it is you're going."

My father took a sip of his champagne. "Make sure you find the young fellow with the risotto balls, Sarah. You wouldn't want to miss them."

I waited. It didn't take long. "Where *did* the guy with the risotto balls go?" my brother Johnny began, handing me a glass of champagne from a passing tray. "We really *must* find him for Sarah."

"Cute," I said.

"Yeah, Sarah," Christine added. "You simply haven't lived until you've found a guy with risotto balls."

"Personally, I've made them an absolute requirement," Carol said. "Risotto balls, that is."

"Come on, you guys, grow up," I said. "What does that even mean?"

"Oh, my God, it's worse than we thought," Michael said to Billy. They raised their eyebrows in identical looks of horror. "She doesn't even know. About risotto balls."

Dad was shaking his head. "All right, all right. That's enough. We'll have no trash talking under my roof. And never forget, for a single moment, that as long as your father is still alive and kicking, not one of you is too old to have your mouth washed out with soap."

*   *   *

Dozens of family photographs hung in the hallway, gallery-like, flanking the staircase. A sepia wedding photo of my parents, Dad's arm draped across Mom's shoulders like a mantle, optimistic smiles on their faces. A color portrait of all six children taken on this very staircase: the three girls seated together on one step in identical pleated skirts and round-collared white blouses, the three boys a couple of steps higher in matching jackets and ties, their knees digging into our backs.

I ran my fingers along the curved mahogany banister, the wood burnished by decades of hands guiding our everyday ascents and descents, as well as our occasional wild slides when our parents weren't looking. I studied the photographs. Six high school senior pictures in a long, staggered row. Snapshots of Christmas. Easter. Birthday parties. Summer vacations. I spent time with each photo, each face, searching the eyes for clues.

The kitchen door swung open, startling me. The pretty redhead and the guy with risotto balls emerged, managing to kiss and carry their trays at the same time. I felt like an intruder in my former house.

"Oh, hi," said the redhead, smiling, confident. Elegant flutes of champagne balanced easily on her tray.

"Mistletoe," said the other, blushing. He extended his tray to me.

"No, thanks." I joined him in his blush.

The three of us gazed at the photographs for a minute. "So, which one are you?" asked the redhead.

"Right here," I said, pointing. It was nice to know where I was for a change.

*   *   *

I sat in a seat near the back of the empty bus. Eight small television sets, framed in teal and gray to match the upholstery, hung from the ceiling in two rows. *It's a Wonderful Life* played soundlessly on all of them, while Frank Sinatra crooned "Chestnuts roasting on an open fire" from multiple suspended speakers.

I watched Siobhan climb up the stairs of the bus. She walked halfway down the aisle, then stopped to flash her navel at me from underneath a cropped purple sweater.

"Looks great," I said.

"You bring a date?" she asked.

"A couple dozen. You?"

"About the same," Siobhan said with a big smile that didn't have even a trace of an adolescent pout in it. She slid into the seat across from mine.

Ian and Trevor ran down the aisle of the bus. They ignored us and stood outside the door of the bathroom. "Liar," said Trevor.

"It does, too. Where else would it go?"

"Does not."

"Does too. Okay, you go in and pee and I'll stand outside the bus and tell you when it comes out on the driveway."

"Oh, yeah, right, Ian. If you're so stupid, why don't you try it," Trevor challenged him. Siobhan rolled her eyes at me.

Lorna came down the aisle, followed by a squat, dark-haired man with a decidedly surly expression on his face. "Lorna," I said, "I'm so glad you came. Lorna, this is my niece Siobhan. Siobhan, this is my friend Lorna, you've probably seen her at Bayberry, and this is her husband Mat—"

"Jim," Lorna said, reaching back to put her arm around him.

"Is that the bathroom?" Mattress Man said by way of greeting. He walked by us with what might have been a grunt.

We watched him disappear behind the teal and gray upholstered door. "When he comes back out," Lorna said, "you'll see that he's actually a brilliant conversationalist."

June got on the bus, followed closely by Ray Santia. I scrunched down low in my seat. The downside of living in a small town like Marshbury was that your past never went far enough away to let you forget about your mistakes. June and Ray stopped halfway down the aisle and huddled like conspirators, comparing pictures of Creases and Wrinkles. The aisle filled up behind them, and June moved into a seat. Ray followed quickly, without even glancing around for me.

Austin wiggled past the incoming traffic. "Ms. Hurlihy!" he yelled. "My father and I speeded all the way here! Is that a felony or a misdemeanor?" Austin stopped abruptly when he came to June's seat. June and Ray turned around, finally noticed me. I smiled and waved, tried to look like I hadn't been hiding.

I looked past them. The bus was almost full. My father was seated in the front seat, Santa hat still on, ready to play copilot. He was talking animatedly with Bob Connor. Apparently, my entire past was going to get on the bus. Bob Connor looked at his watch. My father said something to the waitress, who nodded. The last chrome cooler was carried aboard by the caterers. The bus driver started the engine.

                         *   *   *

Carol stood at the front of the bus, waving my good wool coat back and forth. "Where would you be without me?" she yelled down the aisle. "Oh, and here's your date."

Carol handed John Anderson my coat as he moved past her. Their movements were smooth, almost choreographed. It was probably my imagination, but it seemed as if the whole bus watched John weave his way down the aisle. He was wearing a gorgeous camel-hair coat over a black suit. White shirt, red tie. "Hi," he said when he reached me. "Is this seat saved?"

"Yeah, as a matter of fact it is." I slid over, smiling. We were both smiling.

"Sorry I'm late. There was more traffic than I expected. I probably should have left earlier but I got caught up in a *Get Smart* festival on Nickelodeon."

"You watch Nickelodeon?"

"Well, not just anything. I'm very fussy. But *Get Smart* has it all. Max is maybe a bumbler, but he gets the job done, and he and Agent Ninety-nine are such a great team. And the gadgets on the show still hold up. I've actually been wondering if Max's shoe phone design could work as a cell phone. You know how there's never a great place to carry your cell phone? Well . . . I guess I'm getting carried away. Sorry, Sarah." He reached over and held my hands with both of his. His eyes twinkled. "Don't worry," he said, "I brought the bottle."

I smiled. "I brought one, too. Just in case you forgot."

Bob Connor leaned over us. "Go ahead, Austin, I'll

wait right here," he said. He smiled and extended his hand to John. "Kids and bathrooms, what can I say. He wants to see what happens when he flushes."

"Nice to see you again," John said.

"Don't kid a kidder," Bob said.

I glanced at Bob, his tousled curls, his green green eyes and twisted front tooth. He was wearing a dark gray jacket, a light pink shirt. He didn't seem the least bit uncomfortable around me. In fact, it was as if once he'd slept with me, I no longer existed. There was simply one fewer name on the list of women he hadn't been with yet. I was surprised I wasn't more upset about it.

I looked him straight in the eyes. "One question, Bob. What are you doing here?"

"Oh, Austin and I ran into Dolly outside her trailer. She had just called your father, somebody from the caterers answered the phone and, long story short, she was on her way over here to kill that good-for-nothin' Billy Hurlihy."

"How did you stop her?"

"I didn't. I talked her into changing her outfit to something that did justice to her fine figure and milky complexion. Austin and I did a little bit of spiffing up ourselves"—Bob stopped, brushed some imaginary lint from his shoulder—"and we jumped back in the car, hightailed it over here first to warn your dad, and even managed to finagle an invitation to this shindig."

"Ms. Hurlihy!" Austin yelled as he came out of the bathroom. "Did you know we're going to ride all the way to the symphony on this bus, Ms. Hurlihy? I bet Max Meehan and Molly Greene have never even been on a fancy bus like this. But, don't worry, I won't tell anybody I got to come and they didn't. You can absolutely, positively, no crossies allowed, trust me that mummies the word."

31

Just as the bus was pulling out of the driveway, we heard the angry squeal of brakes. I pulled back the café curtain covering the window John Anderson and I shared, recognized the Ford Fiesta pulling in beside us. "Uh-oh. Dolly."

I leaned over John to look up the aisle at my father. He'd opened his curtain a crack and was peering out his window. "You want me to stop, Mr. Hurlihy?" the bus driver asked him.

"No, young man, I do not. I want you to put your pedal to the metal. The sooner the better, I might add." Dolly's horn blared repeatedly. My father stood up halfway, raised his voice. "What I mean is, let's agitate some gravel. Now." He looked back at us all, smiled reassuringly, raked his hair.

The driver grinded the gears, accelerated. We felt a thud, a mild rocking of the bus. More beeps, another jolt, this time with a slight metallic crunch. "I think Dolly really wants to come, too, Dad," Austin said.

"Stop the bus," my father said unnecessarily. All of the café curtains were open now, and the passengers who discovered they didn't have a view rushed to the opposite side. *Good thing it's not a boat*, I thought randomly. We watched Dolly back up, narrowly missing a large rhododendron with frost-curled leaves. She maneuvered back onto the driveway and parked, blocking our rear exit. She got out of her car and carefully locked all four doors.

"Why'd ya have to go and hit me, lady?" the bus driver asked over the pressurized swoosh of the opening door.

"Cool your jets, sweet stuff. That's why God invented bus insurance."

My father stood bravely. "Dolly, darlin', I made these plans long before I ever met you."

"Then I guess you had plenty of time to *un*make them, didn't you, Mr. Lying, Cheating, Good-for-Nothin' Billy Hurlihy."

Bob Connor stood up and walked bravely down the aisle. "Dolly, you made it!"

"Don't Dolly me, you little sneak. And what, might I ask, are you doing here?"

"Austin and I thought we'd better get over here just in case you needed any back up." Bob stopped a safe distance away from her. "And, by the way, those colors really bring you to your full potential." He took another step. "Don't waste your time on that old guy, Dolly. Come back and sit with us. We've been hoping another beautiful woman would show up."

Dolly put her hands on her hips, tilted her chin up at my father. "Well, I guess you had that coming." She turned to Bob Connor, grabbed his elbow. "Come on, Bobby. Dolly wants to meet your friends."

Carol leaned into the aisle from the seat in front of us. When that didn't give her enough of a view, she got up and walked back to our seat. "I knew it," she said. "I knew you two would end up together."

I covered my face with my hands. "Please make her stop," I begged. My family would not be within ten miles of us on our next date.

"Why do you say that, Carol?" John asked. He seemed to be enjoying this. I elbowed him.

"Well, I had a pretty good idea anyway, but as soon as I saw your page on the clipboard, I knew you were the odds-on favorite."

"Carol. Shut up. Now." To say I was blushing would be a major understatement.

"Okay," she said. She rested a hand on John's shoulder. "We'll talk later."

John and I looked at each other. "Do you think I'd die immediately if I jumped out that window or would it be long and painful, like this moment?" I asked.

"Relax, Sarah." John reached out, put his hand on my wrist. "It's okay. I'll pretend I never even knew there was a clipboard." He moved his hand until it was holding mine. "Just give me a quick rundown of the highlights of my page first."

Marlene greeted us at the entrance to the first balcony. She wore a black velvet jumper over a tartan plaid turtleneck. A gold tuba pin, holly sprigs poking out of its orifice, perched over her right breast. Marlene's brother Mark had his arm around a tall woman who looked suspiciously like the blonde on the poster at Pins and Needles. "Nicetaseeyaagain," he said to me.

"That's the woman from Cambridge, the singles lady," John said calmly as we stood sipping champagne.

I laughed. "Marlene? Marlene is the singles lady?"

"I'm only speaking to you long enough to tell you," I said to Carol in the marble bathroom a few minutes later, "that Marlene hosts singles soirees in Cambridge." I fixed my lipstick in the mirror and waited for Carol to acknowledge my find.

"Of course she does. Where do you think Dad went first on Thanksgiving?"

"Jeez, Carol. Can't I find out something before you? Just once? Dad went to a singles Thanksgiving soiree?"

"Um-hmm."

"And is this a singles symphony soiree?"

Carol laughed, adjusted the lace collar on her long velvet dress. "Sarah, Sarah, Sarah. Can't you for once just have a good time?"

"Hi." Phoebe walked into the ladies' room just after Carol walked out. I was leaning in toward the mirror, attending to my lipstick with the careful concentration of a child doing paint by numbers. I was in awe of women who could find their lips without a mirror. Phoebe, of course, took out her lipstick and applied it while examining a brass-and-crystal wall sconce.

"Sarah," she said, turning to look at me in the mirror. "I'm sure Michael's told you all sorts of awful things about me. But I want you to know—"

"Michael has never once said anything bad about

you." Phoebe looked at me as if wondering whether to believe it. "Really. All he's ever said is how much he loves you. I don't talk about you with Michael any more than I'd talk about Michael with you."

Phoebe put her lipstick away in a small black sequined bag. "I'm surprised. I guess I thought you all sat around joking about how terrible I am. I probably shouldn't admit this, but your whole family makes me nervous. I feel like I'm back in high school and the popular kids don't like me one little bit."

This was the most I'd ever liked Phoebe. I leaned over and gave her a hug. "I feel that way pretty much all day long," I said, "if it's any consolation."

"The First Noel" was mostly strings and it sounded like being in heaven. John Anderson reached over to hold my hand. "The Holly and the Ivy" turned into "Silent Night," which made way for "It Came Upon a Midnight Clear." In front of me, Phoebe put her head on Michael's shoulder. My father whispered something to Marlene, then wove his way back toward the bathrooms. Dolly brushed off Bob Connor's attempts at restraint and followed him.

Behind me, Carol whispered, "So, who wants to go after them?" Nobody said anything.

During the applause following "Feliz Navidad," John Anderson leaned over to whisper to me. "Maybe I'll go take a little look-see. Just make sure everything's okay."

As soon as he was out of earshot, Carol leaned forward and said, "Could be serious, he's already trying to get in good with the family. And he's got a lot of guts, heading into Dollyworld."

I drifted happily as Tchaikovsky's "Dance of the Sugar Plum Fairy" turned into a jazzy rendition of Duke Ellington's "Sugar Rum Cherry," thinking Dad would be sorry he missed this one.

Marlene sat down beside me. "Thank you so much for inviting us," I whispered, sounding like an overly polite seven-year-old. I wondered if Marlene was timing my father's absence, if I should make up an excuse for him.

Marlene smiled elegantly. "My pleasure. Billy has a lovely family. Perhaps you'll all come to dinner one night."

Even I knew whose turn it was to invite. "Or maybe you could come to Sunday dinner at our house?" I said, trying to convince us both I meant it.

"I'd love to." Marlene toyed with her brass pin. "Just let me know when the Dolly coast is clear."

"You know about Dolly?" Carol whispered from behind. She leaned her head in close.

"Of course, I know about Dolly. Although I have to admit today is my first actual sighting. Your father, by the way, is worth every bit of the commotion he causes."

"Shenanigans. Dolly calls them his shenanigans."

"I imagine she does." Marlene tucked a stray wisp of hair into her braid.

I stood behind John Anderson in the foyer outside the first balcony. He was standing in back of a bunch of cherubs and poinsettias, spying on Dolly and my father. "Anything good?" I whispered. I stretched up to my tiptoes to peer over his shoulder. Dolly had both arms clamped firmly around my father's waist, and her neck was arched back severely as she gazed into his eyes. My father's head was tilted down to her, his big shaggy eyebrows raised with some emotion I didn't want to think about.

"Well, just a minute ago, after a sizable holiday smooch, Dolly looked up at your father and said, 'Take me to heaven, big boy.' "

"Good line. I'll have to remember it."

"I hope you do." We smiled at each other. John took a step back, put his arm around me. He reached into his pocket and pulled out a small, wrapped box. "Here, this is for you. Merry Christmas, Sarah."

I opened it slowly, wiggling off the gold ribbon first, then slicing the Scotch tape with my fingernail so I wouldn't have to tear the paper. Resting on a bed of cotton was a gold navel ring, studded with a tiny, sparkly white jewel at either end. I blushed. "Thank you," I said. "It's beautiful." I kissed him on his cheek. "How did you, um, know?"

"Carol called me to make sure I'd been invited today. I guess my number was on the clipboard."

"Great."

"Anyway, we just got to talking."

"And my navel happened to come up? Is there anything you don't know about me now?"

"You mean like how Kevin wasn't good enough for you? On his best day?"

"Never mind. Let's change the subject." We both smiled. John put his arm around me and we walked back toward our balcony. "Guess what?" he asked.

"What?"

"Well, I was hoping to get your opinion before I make the final decision, but I'm pretty sure I'm getting a puppy."

"Aww, a puppy? What kind?"

"Well, there was a bit of a surprise in my building. Clementine gave birth to a litter of four last week. Turns out her rotten disposition was partly gestational. We're pretty sure they're half Yorkie, half greyhound. Long and skinny with big noses, kind of curly, scruffy fur. I was hoping you'd like to help me pick one out. Or I was even thinking two might be better, so they won't get lonely."

Despite myself, I felt hope rising somewhere in the general vicinity of my heart. John stopped walking and turned to me, and we kissed. A sweet kiss, with a promise of something more. It was as terrifyingly close to optimistic as I'd been in a long, long time. I tried not to jinx myself by wanting things too much. "You know," I said, "this probably isn't going to work out."

"The puppies?"

"No, us."

"Well, even if that's true, I think we should suspend our disbelief as long as possible."

"Okay," I said. At least I think it was I.

Must Love Dogs
Claire Cook

A CONVERSATION WITH CLAIRE COOK

Q. When did you first know you were a writer?

A. When I was three. My mother entered me in a contest to name the Fizzies whale, and I won in my age group. It's quite possible that mine was the only entry in my age group since "Cutie Fizz" was enough to win my family a six-month supply of Fizzies tablets (root beer was the best flavor) and a half dozen turquoise plastic mugs with removable handles. At six I had my first story on the Little People's Page in the Sunday paper (about Hot Dog, the family Dachshund) and at sixteen I had my first front page feature in the local weekly.

I majored in film and creative writing in college, and fully expected that the day after graduation a brilliant novel would emerge, fully formed, like giving birth. When that didn't happen, I felt like an impostor. Looking back, I can see that I had to live my life so I'd have something to write about. Twenty something years later, I have no shortage of material.

Q. What inspired you to write Must Love Dogs?

A. I've lived for most of my life in Scituate (pronounced *SIT-choo-it*), Massachusetts, which is often called the Irish Riviera. In many ways, *Must Love Dogs* is a tribute to that town. Big, rollicking and irreverent Irish-American families butting into each other's lives. Also, I'm one of eight myself, five girls and three boys. We're still close as adults, even though we're scattered all over the country. It's like a giant game of telephone. By the time something one of us says goes from Massachusetts to Georgia to Ohio to Rhode Island, it's a whole different thing. And I was a teacher for sixteen years, so the classroom scenes were very familiar to me, and lots of fun to write.

Q. Did you know all along there would be dogs in the book?

A. I had no idea there would be any dogs in *Must Love Dogs* until the novel's title emerged from a personal ad. Shortly after that, a Saint Bernard named Mother Teresa galloped into the book. Later, when I needed to link some of the characters together, Wrinkles and Creases, the shar-pei/lab puppies, were born. The puppies, by the way, were modeled after my real-life shar-pei/lab cross, Daisy Mei. Even though they were unplanned, I can't imagine *Dogs* without dogs. This is one of the great joys of writing fiction—that the surprises often turn out to be the best parts!

Q. Is Sarah Hurlihy's personal life based on your own?

A. No. In fact, I've been married for more than twenty years and have two teenage children. When I was single, I don't think personal ads had even been invented.

Q. Then why did you write Must Love Dogs *from Sarah's point of view?*

A. I thought the story would be most interesting from Sarah's point of view. One of the quirkier ways families show their love is to gang up on the most vulnerable family member under the guise of fixing that person's life. In the Hurlihy family, Sarah is the obvious candidate—she's recently divorced, has no life outside her classroom and isn't really sure she wants one, and, at forty, may or may not still have time to have children. So it's much more fun for the rest of the family to try to run Sarah's life than to deal with their own issues and problems.

As a novelist, I was also challenging myself with a point of view I could only imagine. It helped that I have friends who have found themselves in Sarah's shoes, and I've listened to lots of their stories.

Q. Since you couldn't rely on direct experience, how did you research the world of personal ads?

A. I thought I could just skim a couple of newspapers and fake it from there, but when I showed some early pages to a writing group I belonged to at the time, one of the women said that she could tell I'd never answered a personal ad. Caught red-handed, I decided to submit Sarah's ad in a Boston newspaper under a fictional name. I learned a lot about the whole process—how to work your way through the voice mail maze, the way your voice shakes and you start to giggle when you have to leave your message. Very quickly (no surprise, probably, since it contained words like "voluptuous" and "sensuous"), my faux ad received more than a dozen responses. I learned from those, too—the guys were nicer than I expected and talked a lot more than I would have guessed.

So many readers have told me that the personals in *Dogs* are very authentic, which is what I hoped for. But I have wondered a few times if some poor guy is out there, still pining away for the imaginary writer of the ad I placed. At the time I rationalized that, as long as I didn't go out on any dates, it was okay. Also, I gave the phone numbers to my single friends. I'm a big believer in recycling, and I thought the extra karma couldn't hurt.

Q. Did any of your single friends use those phone numbers?

A. My friends don't kiss and tell. Or at least they don't allow me to tell.

Q. Sarah has some unusual and very funny coping mechanisms for living alone, and although you state it indirectly, she's sometimes downright lonely. How were you able to gain such insights into, and find such humor in, this aspect of her character? Is loneliness the last taboo subject in America?

A. I think loneliness transcends marital status and the bonds of family and friendship, and I do think it's a fairly taboo subject in our culture. Personally I think we're all lonely and embarrassingly needy, and spend a good part of our day trying unsuccessfully to fill the vast, gaping emptiness. Much of the rest of the day is spent pretending to be less needy than we are. It really is absurd and darkly funny if you think about it. I don't know that single people are necessarily more lonely than coupled people, though I do think their loneliness is more apparent to the rest of the world, which probably adds a whole extra layer of stress.

Q. What kinds of comments do you hear from readers about Must Love Dogs?

A. My favorites are "I can't remember when I laughed out loud like that," "I couldn't put it down" and "Ohmigod, you're writing my life!" Also, a woman came to one of my book events to tell me that, the week before, she'd missed her subway stop because she was reading *Dogs*. That might well be the litmus test for a good read, don't you think?

Q. While promoting Must Love Dogs, *have you met some especially interesting dogs or heard some good dog stories?*

A. One of the big surprises of my book tour was just how many readers asked me to inscribe books to their dogs! I can't even count the books I've signed to Peppy and Chico and Queenie and Hunter. Several booksellers invited dogs to my events, and others partnered with local animal shelters and brought adoptable dogs or photos of them along. I love to think that my novel might have helped some dogs find good homes. And it's been so much fun to read *Dogs* to actual dogs, who are very responsive by the way, and I'll miss that with the next book.

Q. What are some of the ideas you hope to explore in future novels?

A. I don't really think about my writing that way. For me, it all starts with the characters, so I'm always surprised when I'm introduced at a book event, and I hear, "Claire Cook writes about relationships." Or transitions or suburbia or family. I thought I was writing about the Hurlihys! But I suppose I am fascinated by people and by relationships, and I'm particularly drawn to characters in transition. That's where you find the fireworks—people trying to let go of something and move on to something else are often messy and always interesting.

QUESTIONS
FOR DISCUSSION

1. What scene in *Must Love Dogs* made you laugh the hardest?

2. What gave you the biggest jolt of recognition?

3. What was your favorite "recipe" in the novel? Did you try it?

4. How would *Must Love Dogs* change if it were written from Carol's point of view? From Dolly's? From John Anderson's? Is there another character who might have narrated as effectively as Sarah?

5. Which traits of the Hurlihy family are shared by all families, and which are unique to them? Does your own family have a quirky little something that might have fit right in with the story? One that would top it?

6. Have you or any of your friends ever dated

through the personals? Would you be more or less likely to after reading *Must Love Dogs*?

7. Was it ethically/morally responsible for Claire Cook to place a phony personal ad in the name of research? Would it have been over the line to have responded to one? Should Claire have called the respondents and apologized, or was it sufficient to recycle their phone numbers to her single friends? Do you think she still has those phone numbers?

8. In the book, Sarah asks John Anderson, "What makes you think something's wrong with you?" Do you agree that people who are single often begin to think that something is wrong with them? If you've been single, was that true for you? Is there a version of this that applies to couples?

9. What are some of the ways in which people or society in general makes single people feel like second-class citizens? How has that changed for women, and men, over the last several decades?

10. Some readers find Sarah's father, Billy Hurlihy, both lovable and exasperating. Based on what we know of his marriage to Sarah's mother, and his current love life, what do you think of him, especially as a husband and father? Is he likely to remarry?

11. As a preschool teacher, Sarah spends her days surrounded by children. As a member of a large, close-knit family, she is often in the company of her nieces and nephews. Do you think this makes it harder or easier for her to come to terms with the fact that she might not have her own children?

12. Would you want your child to be in Sarah Hurlihy's classroom at Bayberry Preschool? Why or why not?

13. Claire Cook always wanted to be a novelist, yet didn't go after her dream until she was in her forties. Was she wise to wait until she'd had more life experience, or should she have had the courage to pursue her dream earlier? Do you think either path would have led her to the same place? What does that inspire you to achieve in your own life?

Please read on for an excerpt from
Claire Cook's captivating novel

Multiple Choice

Available from New American Library

Any mother who has an eighteen-year-old daughter would completely understand why I didn't mention my decision to go back to college to Olivia. *What? I can't believe it. Are you actually copying me? Don't you think you should consider getting your own life?* I could clearly hear her saying some or all of these things every time I thought about bringing it up. It wasn't that I planned never to tell her. I just figured I'd wait a bit—maybe Columbus Day weekend, maybe over Thanksgiving—until we'd had a little time to miss each other.

I chose Olde Colony Community College because its brochure promised "an accelerated program for adults interested in completing their bachelor's degrees expeditiously and affordably without sacrificing quality." I called my old college, the one I'd dropped out of well over twenty years ago, to ask them to send my transcript. I was tremendously relieved that both the college and the transcript were still in existence. I asked two of my former clients to write letters of recommendation for me. And finally, after stalling almost as long as Olivia had before she wrote hers for BU, I sat down to write my admissions essay.

In 100 words or less, what light—in the form of personal qualities, rich life experiences, and untapped potential—will you add to our already glowing, close-knit adult baccalaureate program?

As I review my life to this point and contemplate my future, I am convinced that I am at the perfect juncture for continuing my education. I have juggled work and pregnancy, toddlerhood and another pregnancy, soccer and skating practices scheduled at the same time in different towns, warring teenagers, homework and family crises, sickness and health, better and worse. Nothing can throw me. I am organized and motivated, and look to the completion of my bachelor's degree as just the first step in an integrated experience of personal growth and academic challenge.

If a more down-to-earth answer is what you are looking for, please allow me to add that I have considerable experience in teaching aerobics and exercise for all populations, as well as in planning what might broadly be called "parties," but in fact includes a wide array of functions from showers to memorial services. I bring these experiences, as well as my current work as a directionality coach, sometimes called a life coach or a career coach, with me to your program, all of which I would be happy to share with my cohorts. (I'm not sure what your policy is, but perhaps we could discuss bartering tuition for some or all of these?)

I realized that I'd gone well over the one hundred words, but didn't know what to cut, so I sent it in anyway. I received an acceptance letter a few weeks later, which seemed awfully quick to me. And here I was, practically before I knew it, sitting at Olde Colony watching the door to my *individualized academic coun-selor's* office open.

I stood up and extended my right hand. I'd planned to start off by asking why they didn't have dorm rooms for women in their forties, especially the ones who have kids at home and are still married, but one look told me she'd be way too young to get it. "Hi," I said with a smile. "I'm March Monroe."

"Right," she said. She gave my hand a rubbery little squeeze. She had baby-fine red hair and tiny square teeth that made her look about twelve years old.

It wasn't a great start, but I was sure I could bring her around. I sat down in another ugly chair across from my baby counselor's desk, and pulled out a neatly printed purple index card from my oversized black bag. "Okay, I've already registered for three classes online." I reached back into my bag and pulled out a new pair of reading glasses. "I've signed up for the English Novel Before 1800, the Dawn of Greek Civ-ilization, Quantum Physics and You."

I took off my glasses and folded them up. "So," I said, "what do I have to do to get the internship re-quirement waived so I can add a fourth class?"

"Sorry," my counselor said around the hot pink bubble gum she was chewing, "but a three-credit internship is one of the unique features of our program, and an essen-tial requirement of the degree we offer." She took a quick breath, then continued." The purpose of which is to build the confidence of our returning students and, ultimately, to enhance their value in the postacademic workplace."

"But you don't understand," I said, wondering if I should ask her for a stick of gum so we could bond, and if maybe then she might even tell me her name. "I have plenty of work experience. Did you get a chance to read my essay? It's all in there. I've done consulting work. I've owned my own businesses. Couldn't I petition out of the requirement?"

"Sorry, that's not possible. But you sound like an excellent candidate for our Business Administration major. Initiating the New Business Venture is one of our most popular courses."

I rolled my shoulders back a few times. "Let me try to explain this. I don't want to finish my degree to get a better job. I want to take classes that are brainy and ethereal and totally impractical. I want to major in something that won't get me anywhere in the real world. Something exotic and multisyllabic."

"Uh, okay, I think that would be under Language Arts. Give me a minute while I check." My child counselor worked her tongue through the bright center of her wad of gum as she flipped through an instruction manual of some sort. She stopped and shook her head. "Sorry. I just started here and I haven't had one of those yet. I'll have to ask somebody and get back to you. But, anyway, you have to do the internship for all of our majors. Check the bulletin board on the way out—and just, you know, pick one."

I managed to shake my head and check the bulletin board at the same time. I moved quickly past possibilities at an insurance agency, a bank, a market research firm, and a construction company, looking for a little glamour. WQBM RADIO a simple, computer-made flyer said in black ink. INTERNS ALWAYS WELCOME. I knew WQBM. It had lots of local news and sports and weather and traffic reports, so my husband, Jeff, usually kept it on in his car.

I had a sudden picture, crystal clear, of the whole

family taking a drive together out to the Berkshires a month or so ago while we listened to an oldies show on WQBM. I remembered cranking up the music from the front seat, and all of us singing along with the Beach Boys. Olivia reached her arm around her younger brother Jackson's shoulders, and they tilted their heads together when they sang the high parts. It was probably our last day trip as a family who lived together year-round. I felt a sharp jolt of missing Olivia.

I copied down the phone number from the flyer onto the back of my purple index card, and walked out to my car. Since I didn't seem to be late for anything, I decided to call the station from my cell phone.

"WQBM," a female voice said. "Cutting-edge news and the best in local programming."

"Hi, my name is March Monroe, and I'm wondering if you still have any openings for interns this semester. I know it's late but I just found out—"

"Three thirty in the kitchen."

"Excuse me?" I had this horrible feeling that I'd somehow identified myself as someone who'd be willing to make sandwiches.

"There's an intern meeting at three thirty. In the kitchen."

"You mean I can just show up? I haven't even filled out an application."

The woman on the other end of the phone laughed. "I don't think we even have any applications. Just bring whatever you need signed for your school. Are you in high school or college?"

It was a simple question, but it made me feel about a hundred years old. "College," I said. "The second time around."

"I've been thinking about doing that myself. Anything to get me out of this zoo."

Well, I thought, what the hell? If all the other interns were in high school, at least I could hang out with the receptionist.

I found a parking space at the far end of the WQBM parking lot. I'd been feeling a bit conflicted lately about my ten-year-old Dodge Caravan. On one hand it was paid for. And there was always plenty of room for everybody and everything, the seats were removable, and it always started. On the other hand, it absolutely screamed suburban mother, which I had to admit was technically accurate. Still, I figured the walk would distance me just a little from both the minivan and the image.

The receptionist was talking on the phone when I approached her glass cubicle. She covered the mouthpiece with one hand. She had red talonlike fingernails and must have been at least ten years younger than me. "March Monroe," I whispered. "I'm here for the intern meeting." She nodded and pointed at a door midway down a long, narrow hallway, then removed her hand to laugh into the phone. I'd pictured her older and friendlier.

I knocked softly on a door marked KITCHEN. "Sounds like another victim," a man roared from within. "*Entrez-vous*, if ya catch my drift." Against my better judgment, I turned the knob and pushed the door open.

The first person I saw was Olivia.